ANTIQUE HOUSES

ANTIQUE HOUSES
Their Construction
and
Restoration

Edward P. Friedland

DUTTON STUDIO BOOKS

NEW YORK

TO JOAN
who for over thirty years has shared with me
a love for the antique houses of New England,
and who can scrape paint and pull nails
with the best of them

DUTTON STUDIO BOOKS

Published by the Penguin Group
Penguin Books USA Inc., 375 Hudson Street,
New York, New York, U.S.A. 10014

Penguin Books Ltd, 27 Wrights Lane,
London W8 5TZ, England

Penguin Books Australia Ltd, Ringwood,
Victoria, Australia

Penguin Books Canada, 2801 John Street,
Markham, Ontario, Canada L3R 1B4

Penguin Books (N.Z.) Ltd., 182–190 Wairau Road,
Auckland 10, New Zealand

Penguin Books Ltd, Registered Offices:
Harmondsworth, Middlesex, England

First published by Dutton Studio Books, an imprint of Penguin Books USA Inc.
First printing, November, 1990
10 9 8 7 6 5 4 3 2 1

Library of Congress Catalog Card Number: 78-75292

Printed in the United States of America
Designed by Marilyn Rey

ISBN: 0-525-24229-5 (cloth): ISBN: 0-525-48111-7 (DP)

CONTENTS

Chapter 1: **ANTIQUE HOUSE STYLES AND DATING OF ANTIQUE HOUSES** / 1

Chapter 2: **TERMS AND METHODS OF CONSTRUCTION** / 20

Sills / 23
Posts / 23
Girts / 28
Plates / 28
Joists / 28
Studs / 28
Summer beam / 28
Rafters and wind braces / 28

MASONRY / 31
NAILS AND HARDWARE / 42
DOORS / 42
WINDOWS / 48
FLOORING / 56
TRIM / 58

Chapter 3: **RESTORATION PROCEDURES AND TECHNIQUES** / 66

EXAMINATION: GETTING TO KNOW THE HOUSE / 66

CHECKLIST FOR THE INTERIOR OF THE HOUSE AND ROOM-BY-ROOM EXAMINATION / 68
Flooring / 68
Timbers / 68

Summer Beams and Interior Timbers / 69
Doors and Interior Hardware / 69
Windows / 69
Interior Trim / 71
Stairs / 73
Masonry / 73

CHECKLIST FOR THE EXTERIOR OF THE HOUSE / 76
The Outside / 76
Letting Contracts / 78
Masonry Repair / 81
Repairing the Frame / 90
The Sills / 90
Posts / 92
Girts and Summer Beams / 92
Joists / 92
Flooring / 92

Insect and Dry Rot Damage / 92
Insect Infestation / 97
Dry Rot / 97

FLOORING / 101
REMOVAL OF PAINT FROM FLOORS / 103
Lye and Water / 103
Paint Remover / 103
Dry Scraping / 103
Sanding / 103
The Finish / 104

INSULATION / 104

MECHANICAL TRADES / 105
  The Electrical System / 106
    The Service / 106
    The Wiring / 106
    TV, Telephone, Fire Detection, and Burglar
    Alarm Systems / 109
    Lighting Fixtures / 109

  Heating Systems 109
    Electric Heating / 109
    Forced-Warm-Air Systems / 109
    Other Systems / 113

  Plumbing System / 113

TRIM / 113
  Paint Removal / 119
    Dry Scraping / 119
    Paint Remover / 119
    Lye Solution / 119
    Heat / 121
    Commercial Paint Dipping / 121
    Power Sanding / 121

  Window and Sash Frames / 123
  Doors, Door Trim, and Hardware / 123

LATH, PLASTER, AND SHEETROCK / 128
  Lath / 128

Plaster / 128
Sheetrock / 128

TRIM / 128
PAINTING / 132
  Antiquing New Paint /134
  Reproducing the Old Red / 134
  Painting Old / 134
  Old Milk Paint / 134

Chapter 4: THE JOHN PALMER HOUSE:
A RESTORATION LOG BOOK / 135

Chapter 5: MOVING OLD HOUSES / 157

GLOSSARY / 177
  ARCHITECTURAL PERIODS / 177
  HOUSE PLAN / 177
  THE HOUSE FRAME, ITS COVERING, AND
    CARPENTRY TOOLS / 178
  MASONRY, LATH, AND PLASTER / 180
  DOORS, WINDOWS, AND GLASS / 181
  OUTSIDE TRIM AND ROOFING / 182
  INTERIOR WOODWORK AND FLOORING / 183
  HARDWARE / 184
  STAIRS / 185

TO THE READER

The various costs for the numerous types of restoration procedures, materials, and labor specified in this book should be regarded only as approximations as these costs are constantly fluctuating. In specifying said costs, the author and the publisher make no guarantee or warranty of the availability or quality of said procedures, materials, and labor in the current marketplace.

All products recommended for use by the author must be used in strict compliance with the manufacturers' guidelines and directions, and the author and the publisher bear no responsibility for physical injury, destruction of property, or any other loss, damage, liability, or claim resulting from the use of said products whether used properly or improperly.

CHAPTER 1

ANTIQUE HOUSE STYLES
AND DATING OF
ANTIQUE HOUSES

There is hardly a house that has come down through the years without some major change having been made to it. Some of these changes amount to a complete rebuilding of both the inside and the exterior. Not infrequently one finds a 1½-story house (cape) rebuilt into a full 2½-story center-chimney structure. Even more common are the so-called saltbox houses that have had their rear walls raised to the same level as the front wall. Many hip-roofed houses on close examination reveal themselves as originally having been gambrel-roofed houses. In the early 1800s it became fashionable to change gambrel-roofed houses into hip-roofed houses. One-story ells frequently were expanded to two stories as the need for additional space became pressing.

As we have seen in the development of the house plan from a single-room dwelling into a multiroom structure with lean-tos and ells, not only the wooden parts of the houses but the masonry walls as well were altered and added on to.

How then does one recognize the date, or approximate date, of an antique house or chart the numerous changes that have taken place in it? To begin with, on rare occasions one may find documentary evidence about the building of a house or about changes that have been made. These may be in the form of a journal, inventory, letter, ledger, an early newspaper account, an account book, deeds, mortgages, etc. In assessing this kind of evidence, one must make sure that the building written about is indeed the same building that stands today, not another building constructed on an earlier foundation. If his house burned, no prudent man would have wasted a good foundation by building a new house elsewhere on his property. He would even have saved the timbers that were salvageable and used them in the basement, if nowhere else, rather than go through the effort of hewing new timbers.

Dating houses by their construction is quite possible with limited accuracy. It is most likely that the structure itself will provide the very best evidence of its age, and documentation in conjunction with this very tangible evidence can lead to a positive conclusion.

There are certain indicators that, if original to the house, point the way to a date. First, there is the general plan or style. For example, in regard to the pitch of the roof, steeper is earlier in most cases; or in the fenestration, a single line of three windows on the gable end, one over the other, is earlier than a five-window gable end. A five-window front facade is earlier than a nine-window facade. These are not proofs, just indicators, of course.

The added lean-to form is earlier than the saltbox or full 2½-story house. A chimney set well behind the ridge is earlier than one that centers on the ridge.

A forty-foot center-chimney 2½-story house with the chimney placement very obviously favoring one side (not directly over the front door) may indicate an early one-room house that has been expanded. Foundation stones on one side of a house that are longer than those on the other indicate an addition to the house. Half windows in the second story of a cape (not eyebrow

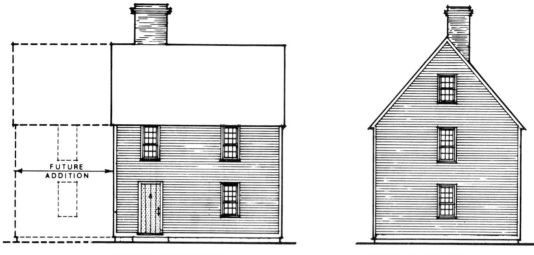

FRONT ELEVATION   SIDE ELEVATION

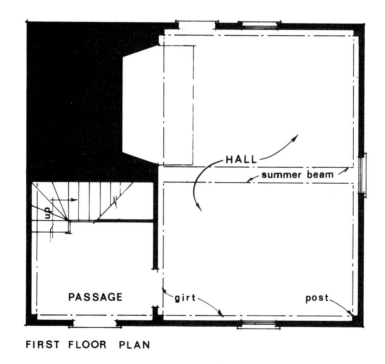

FIRST FLOOR PLAN

ONE ROOM PLAN
17th century

1. The earliest permanent houses that one can still find standing today were of the one-room plan of one story (a small Cape), or as pictured here, a full two-story, one-room-over-one plan with an attic. The stair passage, together with a massive chimney stack, occupied one entire end of the house. These dwellings had a single fireplace of great size in the hall; firebox openings from 8 to 10 feet in width are the rule. In Connecticut, dwellings like these were constructed from 1634 and continued to be built, with modifications, into the early 1700s.

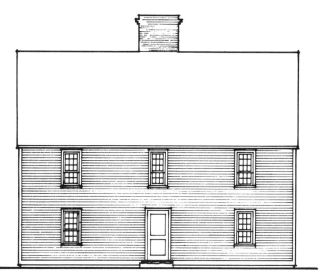

FRONT ELEVATION

SIDE ELEVATION

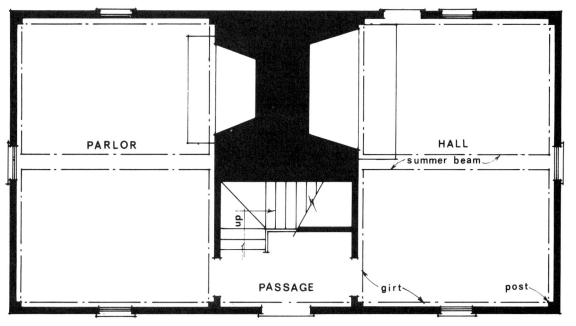

PARLOR

HALL

summer beam

up

PASSAGE

girt

post

2

FIRST FLOOR PLAN

TWO ROOM PLAN
circa 1710

2. The second stage in the development of the house plan was the two-rooms-over-two plan, a three-fireplace house, one-room deep, with two large rooms on each floor. Like the one-room plan this was essentially a 17th-century type. As families grew, many one-room plan houses were expanded into two-room plan houses by adding a parlor and parlor chamber to the opposite side of the existing chimney stack. Only close examination of a house frame will reveal whether the house is an expanded one-room plan, or was originally built as a two-room plan.

3. The Buttolph-Williams House, 1692. This restored two-room-plan house in Old Wethersfield, Connecticut, is operated as a museum by the Antiquarian and Landmarks Society, Inc. of Hartford. The casement windows with their leaded-glass panes are appropriate to the period of the structure, as are the oak clapboards, the simple boarded doors, and the chimney, longer than it is deep, set mostly behind the ridge of the roof. There are no windows in the rear wall.

4a and 4b. "The Old House," Cutchogue, New York, is another example of 17th-century house building. The chimney, which so obviously favors one side of the roof, suggests an expanded one-room plan. The typical 17th-century house is characterized by a few, small casement windows, a very steep pitched roof, and an overall plain, stark appearance. I know of no *original* casement window ever having been found in place. In the front view of this ancient house the bushes hide the front doorway.

4a

4b

windows) may indicate that the original house was a full 2½-story house cut down (Was it struck by lightning? Did a hurricane cave in the upper story?).

These are only some of the general indicators of age. A study of the styles of early houses can provide the time into which these types fall.

Again, I must emphasize that this is not an exact science, this dating of houses. Many a country builder constructed his house in a manner that the city builder of the same period would have considered old-fashioned. For example, on the island of Nantucket, Massachusetts, many of the houses that to the eye appear to be middle-eighteenth-century structures are in reality nineteenth-century buildings built in the old manner.

To get into greater detail, one must examine the following features of construction, to name the most important:

1. Size and embellishment of the structural members. Are the joists, if exposed, beaded? Are the summer beam and/or the girts chamfered? Are the chamfers stopped? Are the timbers extraordinarily massive? These are indicators of early-eighteenth-century or even seventeenth-century work. Are the large timbers hewn (early) or sawed (after 1800)?

2. Where is the old kitchen fireplace located? In one of the front rooms (seventeenth or early eighteenth century, perhaps)? Is there a wood lintel over the opening (early)? A bake oven in the rear of the fireplace (early)? Stone lintel and bake oven to the side of the fireplace (after 1740)? Look up into the throat of the fireplace. Is there a lug or bar running across the flue? This was used instead of the swinging crane up until about 1740. Are the *cheek stones* (sides) of the fireplace single stones, or are they made up of many smaller stones? Single stones came into fashion after 1800. Is the kitchen fireplace low or shallow (40 inches high by less than 48 inches wide)? This indicates an 1800 or later date or a later alteration. If the old kitchen fireplace is in the rear of the house with bake oven at the side, examine the front-room fireplaces. Does either of them have a hearthstone that is much longer on one side of the fireplace opening than on the other? Perhaps the original kitchen fireplace was located here.

3. Examine the nails, especially the flooring nails in the attic. Very few builders who were modernizing a house would renew the attic floor; consequently the nails used here are most likely original to the house and are more reliable indicators than the nails of the lower stories. Are the nails cut or are they blacksmith-wrought? Machinery that made cut nails was first used in the 1790s.

4. Is there a ridge (ridge board, ridgepole) into which the top of the rafters is framed? These appeared at the tail end of the eighteenth century and were hewn, the rafters being mortised into them and pinned with treenails. As time went on, after 1800, ridgepoles dwindled in size until today they are no more than a single 2 x 6- or 2 x 8-inch board into which modern rafters are spiked. In houses with early hewn ridges, these extend from the gable ends of the house toward the center of the house. As they encountered a chimney (or chimneys in the case of a center-hall house), they would, of necessity, terminate, only to start again on the other side of the masonry. In houses where the chimney location has been changed (and these are more numerous than one would assume), the opening in the ridge where the old chimney made its way through the roof was often left unfilled (if a mend was made at a later date, it was done in a different manner). Therefore the exact location of the original chimney and the size of that chimney can be accurately plotted. Hewn rafters of almost all houses of the eighteenth century were numbered where they joined at the top of the roof. The earliest houses are often found without numbered rafters, and later sawed rafters frequently omit the numbering. Numbers can also be found on *wind braces* (collar beams) where they are mortised into the rafters, and at that point too another number appears on the rafter. Therefore one rafter will have two similar numbers on it, one at the top and one midway, where the wind brace joins it. The wind brace itself required only one end to be numbered and the other rafter as well needed only one number. The numbers invariably start with Roman numeral I at one end of the building. This system applies in a common rafter system. Occasionally one finds a roof system of primary and secondary roof rafters. Here I have found that the primary rafters bear a separate numbering system in larger Roman numerals and that the intermediary rafters may have numbers of their own. In examining the Roman numerals of many houses, I have discovered that the early builders almost always used the figure ⊤ instead of IX on rafter number 9. I believe that the reason for this was to avoid the confusion that might occur in looking overhead and not being sure if the number is IX or XI. The numbering of the rafters can sometimes reveal a major change in the roof system of the house. I encountered a house recently that was numbered thus: I, II, III, IIII, V, VII, VI, V, IIII, III, II, I. Obviously these were the rafters from two separate houses or time periods. On further examination, it was found that indeed two separate houses had been joined. Actually one house had been moved and added onto the end of the other, and a new fireplace and flue had been added to the chimney stack as well.

FRONT ELEVATION   SIDE ELEVATION

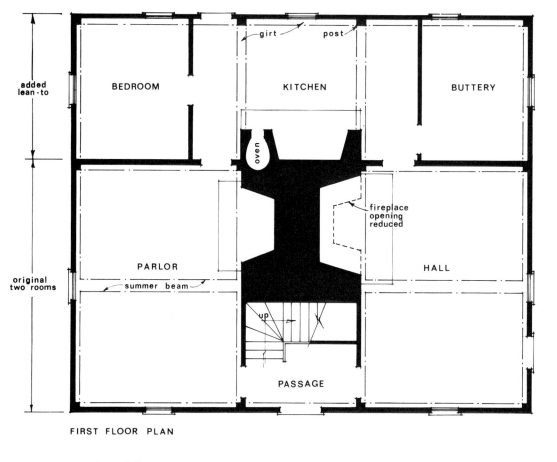

FIRST FLOOR PLAN

TWO ROOM PLAN WITH ADDED LEAN-TO
circa 1720

5. The third stage of early house development saw a lean-to added across the rear of the two-room plan (c. 1720). Although this did not provide any rooms on the second floor, it did allow space on the first floor for a new kitchen of more modern design, a buttery or pantry, and a small bedroom, all accomplished without having to add more than one new flue to the rear of the existing chimney stack. This added flue appears above the roofline as a pilaster, giving the chimney a T shape. It was usual at this period to reduce the size of the old kitchen or hall fireplace by building a smaller one within it.

6

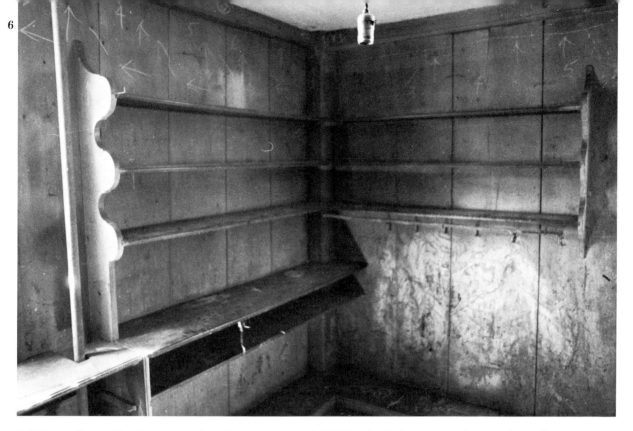

6. This is a fine original buttery, as found in an unrestored 1784 Portland, Connecticut, house. The walls are made of very wide beaded boards and the shelf brackets are beautifully scalloped.

7. The clear break in the angle of the rear roofline of the house in the foreground is proof that a lean-to was added; this break, or "kick," was made necessary to provide headroom at the rear of the first floor. Privately owned, c. 1700; Norwichtown, Connecticut. The house in the background was originally identical in plan to that in the foreground, but it was changed to a full center-chimney house in the mid-1700s.

7

7

8. This is an example of a three-stage added lean-to house. It began as a one-room plan (c. 1680) consisting of the left side including the doorway and two windows on the first story and three windows on the second story. Two rooms (parlor and parlor chamber) were added to the right side of the chimney (c. 1710). Finally, the rafters were extended to accommodate a chimney to serve the new kitchen fireplace. Privately owned; Old Wethersfield, Connecticut.

9. An "untouched" Connecticut saltbox with ell, c. 1740. Note the unbroken sweep of the rear roofline. Ells of all sizes were frequently added at a later time for storage, extra living space, "summer" kitchens, woodsheds, etc. The original house well can frequently be found in the cellar floor of an added ell.

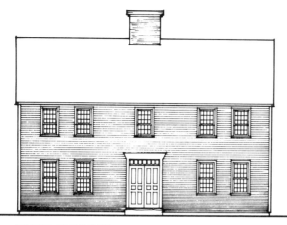

FRONT ELEVATION

SIDE ELEVATION

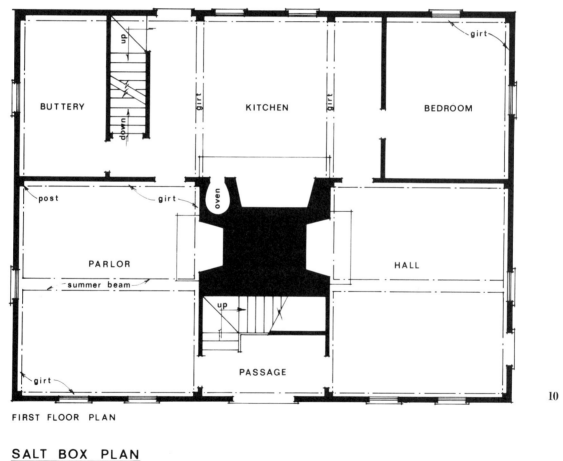

FIRST FLOOR PLAN

SALT BOX PLAN
circa 1740

10. The lean-to house (the so-called saltbox) was the fourth stage in house-plan development (c. 1740). Now the entire structure was built as a unit, with the rear rafters in one piece. These houses were built higher on their foundations to overcome the lack of headroom across the rear wall. The hall fireplace was considerably smaller than the original kitchen fireplaces of added lean-to houses. A second set of stairs made their appearance at this time.

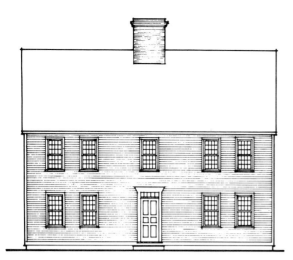

FRONT ELEVATION

SIDE ELEVATION

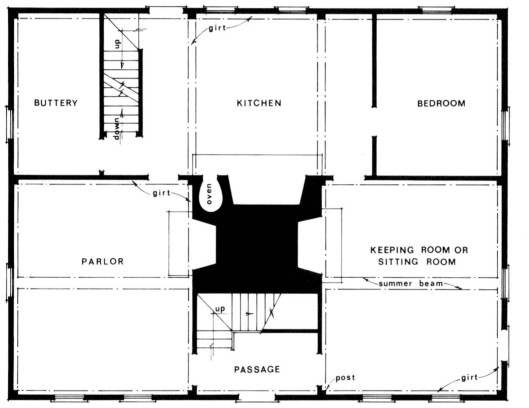

FIRST FLOOR PLAN

11

CENTER CHIMNEY PLAN
circa 1750

12

11. The center-chimney plan also allowed for expansion without the addition of another chimney (c. 1750). The rear wall now was the same height as the front wall. The second-floor layout usually duplicated that on the first floor, with the rooms taking their names from those below, for example: *sitting-room chamber, parlor chamber, kitchen chamber*, etc. The center-chimney plan became immensely popular. The earlier types had three fireplaces and a bake oven on the first floor and one in each of the two front chambers. Later examples (c. 1790) added a sixth fireplace above the kitchen in the kitchen chamber.

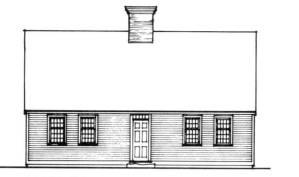

FRONT ELEVATION

SIDE ELEVATION

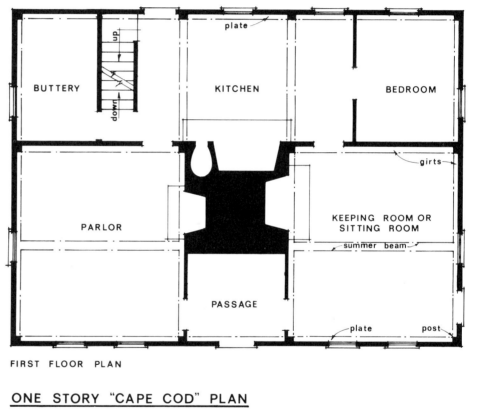

BUTTERY

up

down

KITCHEN

BEDROOM

plate

girts

PARLOR

KEEPING ROOM OR
SITTING ROOM

summer beam

PASSAGE

plate   post

13

FIRST FLOOR PLAN

ONE STORY "CAPE COD" PLAN
eighteenth century

12. The Gay Manse, home of Reverend Ebinezer Gay, built
c. 1742, Suffield, Connecticut. Here is a gambrel-roofed
center-chimney house of most pleasing proportions. The
highly decorative, broken-arch pediment door surround was
a popular embellishment used in both homes and furniture
construction. The use of decorative window frames and
elaborate doorways are more usual to the houses of important
people or wealthy families.

13. The one-and-a-half-story house (the so-called Cape or
Cape Cod) has been much neglected in the literature on early
houses, yet the Cape was probably the most frequently used
house plan in New England. Capes by the hundreds still dot
the New England landscape, and the basic form is still being
constructed today. Don't let these little houses fool you; what
they lacked in size was often made up for by a quantity of fine
interior woodwork. Almost all one-and-a-half-story houses
one finds have an ell of later date added to them.

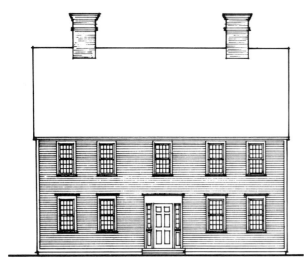

FRONT ELEVATION

SIDE ELEVATION

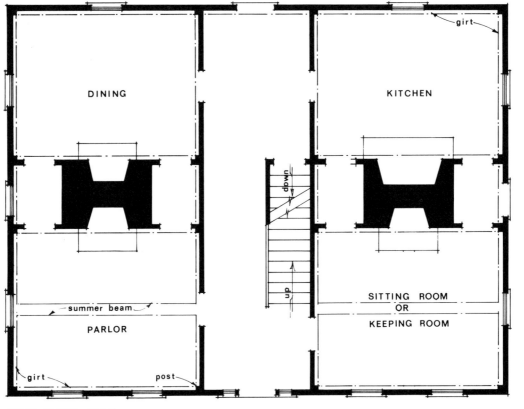

DINING

KITCHEN

girt

down

up

SITTING ROOM
OR
KEEPING ROOM

summer beam

PARLOR

girt

post

FIRST FLOOR PLAN

14

CENTER HALL PLAN
circa 1770

14. The center-hall house plan made its appearance in the mid-18th century in Connecticut but did not replace the center-chimney plan until after the turn of the 19th century. From the point of view of traffic flow it is an easier house to move around in. The passage of the center-chimney house, with it's dogleg stairs, has now been replaced by a staircase running parallel to the gable ends of the structure. The room layout of the second floor is generally the same as that on the first floor (four rooms over four rooms); however, one of the rear chambers is without a fireplace. The earliest types had simple gable roofs (c. 1760–1780); later, one finds hipped roofs (c. 1790).

15a and 15b. Here is a handsome center-hall house of the 1790s; the existence of a framed ridge pole at the peak pinpoints the date very closely. Although the exterior shutters are a 19th-century addition, there were originally sliding interior shutters. The house has eight fireplaces and fine bead-and-feather raised paneling wherever you look. The interior photograph shows a section of the raised-panel dado and a fluted corner post in the parlor. Privately owned; Coventry, Connecticut.

16. Center-hall-plan house, 1761. Almost wholly original, it was slowly restored over a fourteen-year period. Lisbon, Connecticut.

17. The Prudence Crandall House, a c. 1810 hip-roofed center-hall-plan house owned by the State of Connecticut and used as a museum. The details of both exterior and interior woodwork are outstanding. It is obvious that the sash in the first-floor windows are later than those in the second-floor windows because of the smaller panes. Canterbury, Connecticut.

18 and 19. Although most houses follow a typical plan, one encounters here and there a house that is "not in the book," such as the Samuel McClellan House (c. 1769), South Woodstock, Connecticut; or this interesting Eastford, Connecticut, structure (c. 1810).

20. Dating houses and their changes is often easier than one might expect. The Timothy Steele House, Hartford, Connecticut, pictured here, tells us many things from the outside alone. The very steep pitch of the roof angle and the line of three windows one over the other in the gable end suggest 17th-century or very early-18th-century work. The house was expanded, perhaps in the early 18th century, with the addtion of a one-story lean-to across the rear wall; it was at this time that the pilaster was added to the back of the chimney to accommodate a flue for the new kitchen fireplace. Still later, the entire rear of the house was expanded both upward and toward the rear. This old-timer was saved from its parking-lot location by being moved.

21. Neoclassic Cape, Rhode Island, c. 1835. The wide corner boards, low-set windows, and columns are typical of the American love affair with ancient Greece.

22

22. Here is another example of a "country" Greek Revival house, c. 1835. To increase the attic height of these buildings, the posts were fashioned to extend above the attic floor. The second-story windows cannot be raised above the ceiling height of their rooms; thus one finds a very wide fascia board above window height to fill in the space above the attic floor and the rafter feet.

23

23. An American adaptation in wood of a Greek temple in marble. The gable end of this Greek Revival house has become the important elevation. Privately owned; Windham County, Connecticut, c. 1840.

24. Bowen House, called Roseland Cottage, Woodstock, Connecticut, c. 1846. From the 1820s through the 19th century house styles changed at a rapid pace. Beginning with the Neoclassic or Greek Revival and followed by the Romantic Revival houses, American builders drew on European forms to copy and adapt. One finds not only Gothic but Italianate, Tuscan Villa, Carpenter Gothic, and Second Empire styles. Many of the post–Civil War houses come under the general heading of Victorian.

24

25, 26, and 27. Three post–Civil War house styles: (25) Second Empire; (26) Italianate; (27) high-style Victorian.

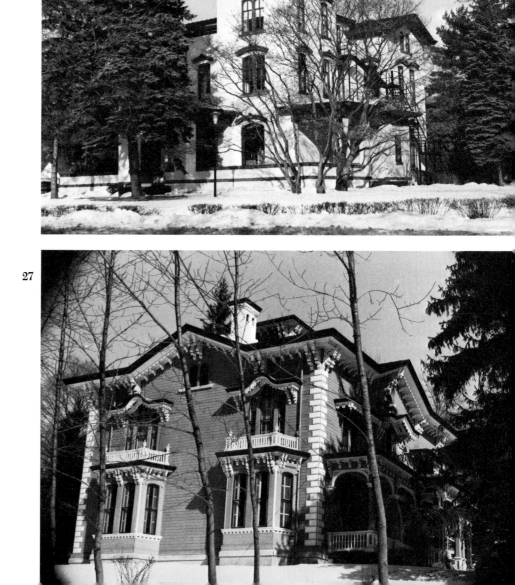

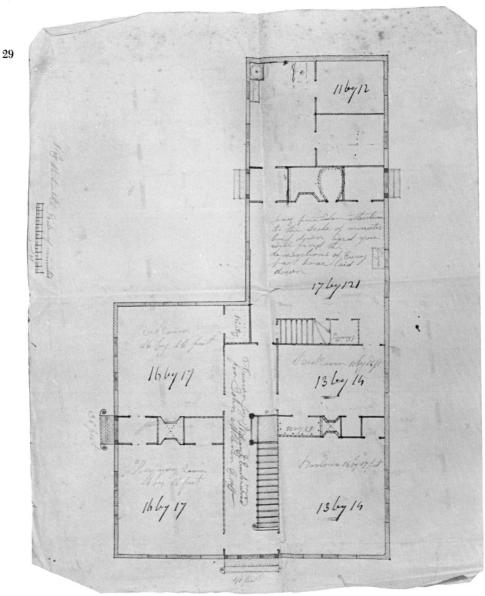

28. A contemporary drawing that helps prove that the use of the words *keeping room* as being synonymous with *kitchen* is not necessarily correct. This is a rough plan of a center-hall house that, from its dimensions, I would date as being 1760–1790. Note the use of the old "s" in the word *closet*; the modern *s* was introduced c. 1814.

29. Here is another contemporary plan showing the *keeping room* as the front left room, 16 feet by 17 feet, containing a large closet to the right of the fireplace. The kitchen, identified clearly by the outline of a bake oven, contains what appears to be a small buttery to the right of the fireplace and a "cinque" (sink) under a window on the right wall. The cross-hatching within the outlines of the wall in *modern* architectural symbols denotes brick construction. This house appears to be of early-19th-century construction. McClellan House, Woodstock, Connecticut; demolished. Courtesy Connecticut Historical Society, Hartford.

28

29

Let us see what might happen to a saltbox house that is converted into a full 2½-story center-chimney house. First, the rear posts would be lenghtened or replaced by posts of two-story height. The rear rafters, or perhaps both the front and the rear rafters, would be changed to form the new roof angle; the rear plate too must be either raised or, as happens more frequently, replaced by a new plate to catch the bearing of the new rear rafters. The floor above the kitchen, in the rear of the house, which was originally designed as storage space, will now be utilized as living quarters; consequently the joists in the old kitchen ceiling may not be strong enough to carry a live load (people moving about on them); these will be replaced with stronger joists. Since the roof ridge will be centered further to the rear of the house now that the back has been raised, one finds the chimney coming out in front of the ridge, a position which is aesthetically unacceptable. The chimney must therefore be rebuilt: it is corbeled toward the rear so that it comes out of the roof in the center of the ridge. No doubt the house is being modernized as well as enlarged; therefore lath and plaster may be added over wood walls and raised paneling may be installed. New front stairs of the box type may replace the older "winder" stairs. Certainly a rear stairs from the kitchen chamber up to the attic can now be added, and the attic stairs, which may have been in the front of the house over the stair passage, can be removed. The cellar stairs can now be relocated to the rear of the house off the kitchen. The kitchen fireplace would be brought up to date with bake oven at side, etc. All these changes and more are not rare to find in a single house, having taken place when a 1730 saltbox was modernized. Each of these changes can be seen within the building with a bit of detective work, although the precise time that the work was done cannot often be ascertained. Often a date stone has been placed in the chimney stack in the attic or exposed to the weather above the roofline to attest to the time that this work was done. Owners often attribute the original building date of a house to these later markers—a natural assumption, to be sure.

It is possible to divide the time a house was built into pre-1800 or after 1800 with some certainly. The methods of construction up to 1800 remained substantially the same for decades. In about the year 1800 things began to happen. First of all, a method was devised for splitting large stones by drilling and *feathering* (wedging). This meant that large, smooth slabs of stone were available for use in foundations and chimneys. The new knowledge must have spread like wildfire from community to community, for it is almost as though a law required all post-1800 houses to use large, drilled-and-cut stones, so sharp is the demarcation. This meant that drill holes suddenly appeared in the stonework; the stones at the top of the foundations are now long and high (4 feet long or more, by 2½ feet high), and the houses are set a bit higher to "show off" this new stonework. Also the cheek stones of the fireplaces, instead of being made up of many small building-block stones, now appear as single stone cheeks; hearth and stepstones at entrances, too, are larger and smoother drilled-and-split stone.

At almost the same time as this change in the quarrying of stone, there was a change in the ironwork of the antique house. Nail manufacture was perhaps the most important change of all. Nail-making machines were invented toward the latter part of the eighteenth century but weren't really perfected until after 1800, when they began to spit out cut nails and machine-headed nails much more cheaply and in greater quantity than the blacksmith-wrought nails of the previous century. In certain instances, wrought nails continued to be used—in batten doors, for example, or in the installation of latches and hinges, where the wrought nails could be "clinched" or bent easily. However, at this time (1800) wood screws began to be used more frequently instead of nails in hinges. These early wood screws are easily differentiated from our modern wood screws by their points, which are blunt, as though they had been snipped off.

Now too (about the year 1800) paneling began to change as well. Instead of the single quarter-round molding in the stiles and rails of doors and paneling, or even the fluted moldings found in the same place toward the very end of the eighteenth century, one begins to find first the complete absence of a molding. Then the flat panel is substituted entirely for the raised panel, and later still one finds applied molding around the panel. One can walk through an early-eighteenth-century house and spot the nineteenth-century doors and paneling that "modernized" that house a century later.

Cast latches and butt hinges were being imported from Europe soon after 1800 and were eagerly bought, for they were cheaper and were thought to be superior to black-smith-made latches and hinges. Butt hinges were applied with blunt-end screws, and cast latches were attached with nails as before, or with blunt-end screws.

CHAPTER 2

TERMS AND METHODS
OF CONSTRUCTION

It is not my intention to trace in detail the history of the early American house from its origins in "Merrie Olde England" or to give an in-depth lesson in early construction details. Other books have covered that subject rather thoroughly. However, to understand the houses you will be looking at, or the beauty you have already purchased, you will want to acquire a modest working knowledge of the methods used in the construction of these early buildings and to become familiar with the terms used in describing their sundry parts—terms, many of which are no longer employed in the building trades today outside the realm of the restorer.

First, let us try at all times to keep in mind the conditions under which these antique houses were built. By present-day standards both the tools and the methods of construction used by the seventeenth- and eighteenth-century builder were primitive. In New England certainly, and perhaps less so in the southern states, nature herself was a formidable enemy to the house builder. Clearing land for a house was a prodigious task; stones and stumps had to be coaxed from the cellar hole with hand levers and horse or ox power, while digging the cellar was accomplished a shovelful at a time. Trees were cut with felling axes and were hewn and shaped with hand tools. The foundations themselves were laboriously constructed of stones carted or dragged to the site. And then there were the heat of summer and the cold of winter to contend with. The early builder, fully aware of the effort he must exert to get a roof over his head, built with permanence in mind. If he were a farmer building for himself, he knew he couldn't afford to go through this procedure more than once in his lifetime; were he a master builder, a professional, he

knew that his client required a house to last for more than one generation. And so he compensated for the lack of sophisticated tools by developing great skill in the use of the tools he did have. (The smoothness of some hewn timbers one encounters in old buildings is remarkable; a plane could do no better!)

The seventeenth- and eighteenth-century house builder also chose his material as carefully as he could under the circumstances. If he had a choice, he always preferred a board of clear grain to one with knots.

The early house builder had a tendency to overbuild because he had no way of pretesting his materials, as far as we know, nor were the mathematical formulas for live and dead load-bearing capacities in existence. The chances are that had books on "how to build a house" been available to the average man, they would have done him little good since he may not have been able to read.

One frequently finds timbers of gigantic proportions supporting light loads or, conversely, small structural members that have been fighting for 150 years or more to sustain a weight almost too much for them. On the whole, however, the early house builder leaned heavily toward safety. The great oversized timbers are often the primary factor in giving us the feeling of strength, security, and endurance in an old structure.

Antique houses made use of the *post-and-lintel* method of construction, which is based on a series of vertical timbers supporting horizontal beams. Modern examples of this type of construction are the steel-framed buildings found frequently in large cities, where they rise to great heights.

The early carpenter created a structure with a post in

30. Clearing the building site. Today an acre of heavily timbered land (roughly 208 square feet) can be cleared in one day by two or three men with chain saws, leaving only the stumps standing. In another day the trees can be cut to fireplace length and the brush turned into woodchips by running it through a "chipper." One day more and the cellar hole can be dug, the stumps having been removed or buried. In a ledge-(rock) free area the actual digging of the cellar can be done in a matter of a few hours by a large bulldozer. If one runs into ledge, the rock can be blasted out in short order.

31. Mock-up of a 17th- or 18th-century building site as displayed in the Smithsonian Institution, Washington, D.C. In the foreground the carpenter has hewn a timber and is now in the process of mortising slots for tenons, one of which he has made and against which the broad ax leans. His primary tools would be his calipers, auger (for drilling round holes), mallet, chisel, and scribe and corner chisel (not depicted here). In the background two men are pit-sawing; the top sawyer received higher wages, as he guides the tool. The bottom sawyer often wore a large brimmed hat to protect him from falling sawdust.

32. The 20th-century restoration carpenter making replacement timbers for a house frame finds the most natural position in which to work is to sit on his work exactly as his 18th-century counterpart did. The electric drill has replaced the hand auger, but after two hundred years the mallet and chisel are still the best tools for the job.

35. Were methods such as this used to test the strength of materials?

33. Both pit-sawing by hand and water-driven up-and-down sawing were used at the same time, and their respective marks on the wood are almost the same; however, the handsaw cuts are usually more irregular and at more of an angle. Both handsawing and water-driven sawing go back in history before the settling of these shores.

36

36. Twentieth-century post-and-lintel construction. As in antique houses both interior and exterior walls are *nonbearing* (carry no structural load) and are put in after the frame has been assembled.

34

37

34. Radial (or circular) saws and continuous-band saws are used today to cut timber. Although circular saws were tried in Holland in the late 18th century, it is unlikely indeed that marks such as these pictured here could possibly have been made in this country before 1830. When I find radial saw marks on wood in an antique house, I attribute the work to the mid-19th century or later.

37. Pins were made by cutting strips of oak of appropriate size and shaping them with a spokeshave or drawknife. The one shown here was used in securing framing timbers and is 1⅛ inches in diameter at the large end. Pins used in the joining of paneling, doors, stairs, etc., can be as small as ¼ inch and are made of material such as hickory, pine, maple, or other wood.

the corner of each room of the house; above these posts and connecting one to another ran the horizontal members, the *girts* (today they would be called girders). The posts would be joined to the girts by a mortise-and-tenon joint secured from slipping apart by the use of a wood pin or treenail.

The "bones" of the house—that is, the structural members—were skillfully made up, cut, fitted, and marked by chisel on the ground. The frame was raised in sections, braced, and pinned until at last the entire skeleton stood on its foundation. Now all the builder had to do was to "flesh out" the frame by creating walls, both interior and exterior, between the posts, leaving space for windows and doors. Then as now, the floor deck was installed before the walls to give the workmen a platform on which to stand as they worked. It is important to keep in mind that the interior and exterior walls of early post-and-lintel wood-framed buildings were not built as "carrying" partitions; that is, they do not support the frame and therefore they can be removed without fear of the house collapsing.

There were two methods of creating the exterior walls of antique houses, plank or stud, and a house may be said to be of "plank construction" or "studded." In a house of *plank* construction the walls were created by the nailing or pegging of vertical boards top and bottom to the horizontal girts and sills. This boarding was cut out for the insertion of windows. The exterior clapboards were nailed directly onto it on the outside and the lath and plaster or wooden interior walls on the inside. Thus the entire "sandwich" created by these layers would be only about four inches thick.

A *studded* house is one in which smaller vertical posts (studs) were mortised into the girts and sills to act not only as additional support for the girts but to provide a structure to which the sheathing and clapboards could be attached on the outside and the lath and plaster on the inside.

Both studded and planked houses seem to have been built at the same time, and one can find two houses side by side of similar date, one being of plank construction and the other studded. One would imagine that the method chosen depended on the locality in England from which the master builder came.

From the point of view of restoration, the studded house has certain advantages over one of plank construction. The space between studs makes insulating easy. It also provides a natural channel in which to run electrical wiring. The plank house, on the other hand, is usually insulated by the addition of a protective membrane to the outside of the planks, which can be accomplished only by the removal of the clapboards. Hiding electrical wires

and convenience outlets is more difficult as well, but as will be seen, it is not an insurmountable task.

Sills: The wooden parts of the building begin at the top of the foundation walls. Laid horizontally on top of the foundation stones (or bricks) are the sills, the horizontal timbers of oak or chestnut upon which the posts stand. The sills serve to distribute the weight of the superstructure evenly across the entire foundation. Were the sills to be omitted, the weight of the house would bear only upon those points of the foundation where the posts touched, a shaky construction indeed.

Technically the sills are only those cellar timbers that have foundation walls directly under them; although they serve the identical function of carrying the weight of the building above, the timbers that span the cellar hole itself, running across open space, are called *cellar girts*, not sills.

Sills are of more concern to prospective house purchasers than any other part of the structure. Usually the purchasers have been told by well-wishing friends that the sills must be as hard as iron and free from rot of any sort. Many people carry with them knives or ice picks, which they thrust into the sills here and there as they inspect the basements. If a soft spot is encountered, they become alarmed.

Actually very few sills have survived from the eighteenth century without some rotting here or there. Entire sills of a house can usually be replaced in a matter of a few days' time at modest cost; but it is a rare house that requires such extensive surgery. Usually a short length here and there may have to be slipped out and a new piece substituted.

Posts (gunstock posts, corner posts): Rising vertically and standing upon the sills and girts of the cellar are the posts. These rise either one or two stories in height, depending upon the height of the wall of which they are a part. For example, in a typical Connecticut saltbox house frame the front wall is two stories in height and the rear wall only one story. Hence the front posts rise a full two stories, whereas the rear posts rise only to the first-floor ceiling height. In a house that has been drastically altered, such as a saltbox that has been changed into a full two-story house or a cape that has been made two stories, the changes can frequently be traced in the alteration of the posts.

The term *gunstock post* is used to describe the shape of certain posts. These posts lend great charm to a room, their slope providing a primitive look to the structure. The reason for the shape, which is that of an inverted gunstock, is a practical one. In making his frame, the builder found he had a problem wherever two large girts met at right angles over a post, where there might not be

38. I have seen this unusual method of construction (the upper story is studded and the lower story is planked) only three times in twenty-five years, but it serves as a good illustration of both methods. The tops of the planks (which are almost 2 inches thick) are set into a groove cut into the bottom of the first-floor girts to accept them. The bottoms are pinned to the sill.

38a. Close-up of the same house, c. 1784, seen in figure 38. The planks are of oak. On the second floor the studs were covered by oak sheathing 1 inch thick. The use of both systems of construction provided an overhang at the midsection of the house, which allowed the roof water to drip away from the foundation, gutters being very rare at this time.

38b. Here are two planks from the house seen in figure 38 showing how they were marked for later assembly, in this case a reverse Roman numeral VIII; these numbers were cut into the green wood with a chisel.

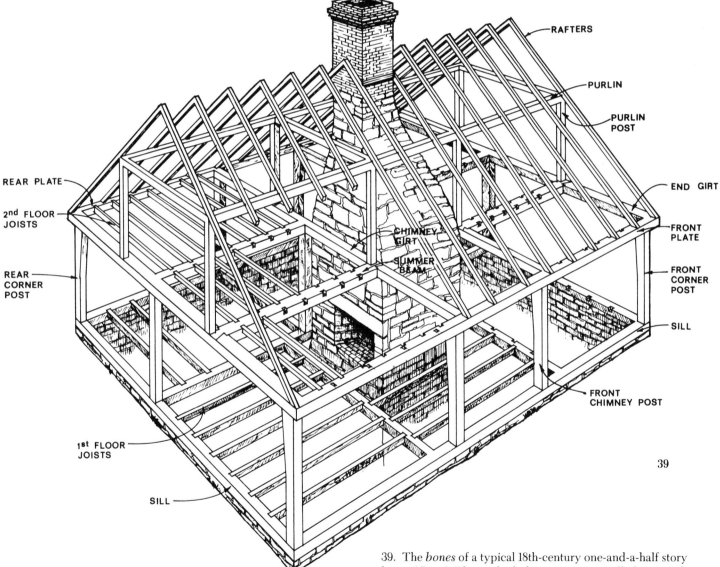

39. The *bones* of a typical 18th-century one-and-a-half story house (Cape). The method of construction is called *post-and-lintel*, as opposed to other methods such as arch, vault, truss, dome, framed, etc.

40a. Front of an early New England house frame set up in the Smithsonian Institution, Washington, D.C., to illustrate how a house was put together. The front part of the house seems to be a two-room-plan form cut in half (note a fireplace facing the outside in the left wall and the cut plates at the attic floor). Both front and rear parts are of studded frame construction with diagonal bracing in the second story; the bracing, which is frequently found, provides lateral stability. A purlin roof system was used; this requires the roof sheathing (*roofers*) to run vertically as they are top-nailed to the purlins. In a *common* rafter system there would be many more rafters to which the roof boarding would be nailed horizontally. The very heavy girt and frames and sash for leaded-glass casements in the rear wall of the back would lead one to assume that is the older portion of the building. Although the dogleg stairs, raised paneling, narrow banisters, and HL hinge on the door may conform with 1750 date, the frame suggests an earlier vintage.

40b. Rear of the house in figure 40a.

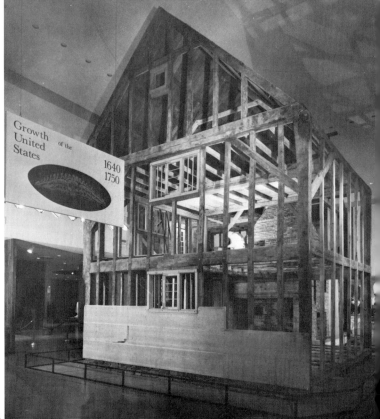

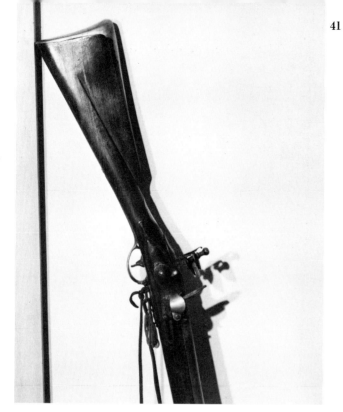

41. Gunstock of a Revolutionary War gun. It is obvious why tapered corner posts were called *gunstocks*.

42. Drawing showing a typical gunstock post in place.

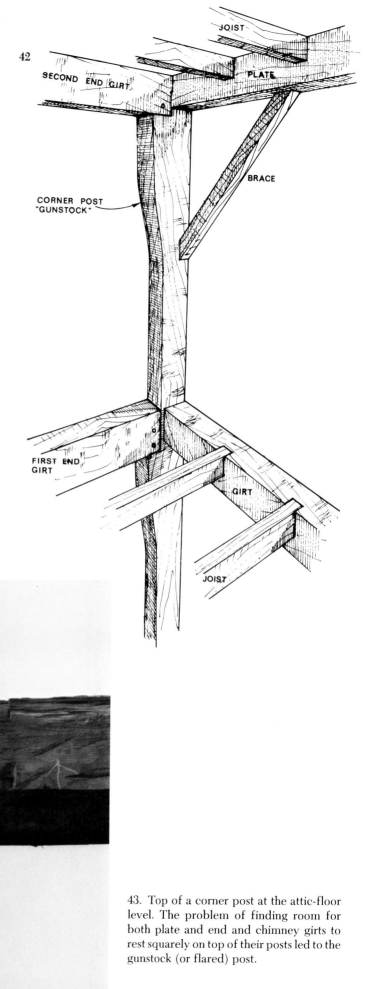

43. Top of a corner post at the attic-floor level. The problem of finding room for both plate and end and chimney girts to rest squarely on top of their posts led to the gunstock (or flared) post.

room enough to accommodate both timbers and allow sufficient bearing surface. This situation occurred especially at the second-floor ceiling, both front and rear. In a full 2½-story house, for example, the front and rear plates join the end and the chimney girts, resting for purposes of maximum strength *on top of* rather than being *let into the sides* of their respective posts. It must be remembered that these plates carry tremendous loads since they bear the downward thrust of the rafters; hence they must withstand the weight of heavy snow and ice in the winter and the pressure of 100-mile-per-hour winds during a hurricane. All this weight, including the dead weight of the rafters and the roof itself, presses down on the front and rear plates. It would not be wise to mortise these plates into the side of the posts as may have been done in the floor below; to withstand the pressure upon them, they should rest squarely on top of the posts, thus transmitting their load directly down to the foundation.

Two solutions to this space problem come to mind: either to make the posts larger or to haunch the top of the post, providing space on which both timbers can now bear. The former solution would add greatly to the size (and consequently the weight) of the posts, making it necessary to increase the size of the sills on which they rest and perhaps even the foundation wall itself to accommodate them. Therefore the second solution of a tapered or haunched post, the *gunstock* post, was created. These posts either taper from a relatively small section at floor height to a wide section at the ceiling or else rise in a straight line to within two feet of the ceiling and then flair to gain width.

The direction of slope of these posts is almost always from the front and rear of the house inward, or parallel to the gable ends of the house and at right angles to the ridge.

Girts: The girts are large horizontal carrying timbers running between posts. As with most of the larger members of the frame, the girts are almost always of oak and hewn. There are cellar girts spanning the cellar hole; front, rear, end, and chimney girts at the first-floor level; and end girts at the attic-floor level.

Plates: The plates (a term still used today in house construction) are those girts at attic-floor level employed to carry the feet of the rafters. In most houses of center-chimney design or center-hall houses the plates are one-piece timbers often forty feet or more in length. They are notched to accept the feet of the rafters, which are pegged to them through the notch.

Joists is another term still used. The floor system is formed by the use of horizontal framing members (joists) a good deal smaller in section than the girts, the ends of which are set into notches in the girts or summer beams made to receive them. Joists are not nailed or pegged in place, as after the flooring has been nailed to them, the weight is sufficient to hold them in place. As a rule joists were sawed, as were most of the smaller timbers of construction, since it is almost impossible to hold a small piece of wood steady while it is being struck by a hewing ax.

Studs: These are the small vertical posts that are the framing members of the exterior walls of an antique "studded" house. The studs are mortised into the sills and the girt above on the first floor and between the girt and the plates and the end girt on the second floor. They are set roughly 2½ feet apart, with one on each side of a window or doorframe.

Summer beam is a term no longer in use outside the restorer's vocabulary; the modern equivalent is the word *header* or *girder*. In the larger rooms (usually the front rooms), both downstairs and upstairs, of most houses of the seventeenth and eighteenth centuries the span between the girts is too wide for anything other than very large joists to be used without noticeable deflection. The most economical way to overcome the problem of a large span was to introduce an intermediate timber of massive proportions, thus breaking the span into two smaller spans. This allowed for the use of joists of much smaller section. These summer beams are the largest timbers in early houses and up to the time of the Revolution, after which time they were often concealed within the plaster ceiling, they can be seen running across the center of a room, exposed as much as four or more inches below the plaster.

Rafters and wind braces: Rafters are those members of a house frame that, in pairs (front and rear), form the roof. The rafter "feet" rest upon the plate, which has a notch cut into it to receive a complementary short tenon on the rafter. This joint is held by an oak pin (treenail). At the top end each rafter is joined to its mate with a mortise-and-tenon joint similarly pinned. In houses up to the late 1790s there was no "ridge" (or ridgepole, as it is sometimes called); after 1800 rafters are generally found to be mortised and pinned into an oak ridge running parallel to the front of the house. The ridge is made of either two or three pieces, depending on the number of chimneys that interrupt it.

There were four or five common roof shapes used in the early days, as opposed to the more than thirty-three different roof shapes we classify today. These ranged from the simple gable (or A-framed) roof to the compound angles of gambrel roofs. But in all cases the rafter feet are pinned to the sills and the top ends of each pair are pinned at the ridge.

In some houses a horizontal member was used to join each front rafter to its rear rafter. This horizontal piece, called a *wind brace* or *collar beam*, serves to create a

44. Exposed attic-floor system, Buttolph-Williams House, 1692, Old Wethersfield, Connecticut. In houses in which the timbers were meant to be exposed overhead, they were often whitewashed to lighten the room. Antiquarian and Landmarks Society, Inc., Hartford.

45a and 45b. Rafter joining at the ridge of a pre-1800 house. The oak pin secures a mortise-and-tenon joint. Note the rafter numbers—in this case Roman numeral V. Frequently the numbers will be upside down when being read from the attic floor. Center-hall-plan house, Lisbon, Connecticut, 1761.

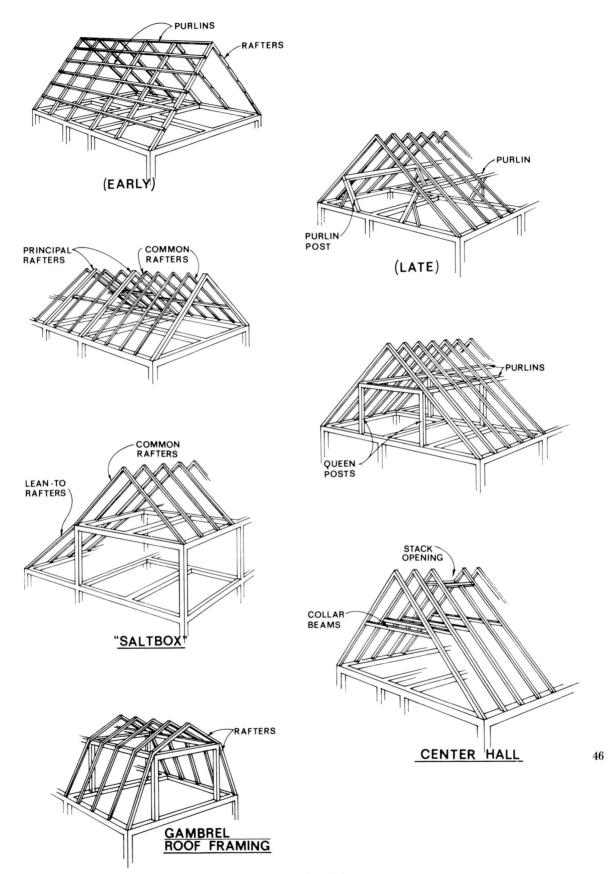

PURLINS

RAFTERS

(EARLY)

PURLIN

PURLIN POST

(LATE)

PRINCIPAL RAFTERS

COMMON RAFTERS

PURLINS

QUEEN POSTS

COMMON RAFTERS

LEAN-TO RAFTERS

"SALTBOX"

STACK OPENING

COLLAR BEAMS

CENTER HALL

46

RAFTERS

GAMBREL ROOF FRAMING

46. Drawings of roof shapes.

truss when it is mortised into the two rafters, imparting great strength to the roof in resisting wind and snow pressures. The numbering found at the top of the rafters is generally repeated on the collar beams.

In roof systems of the purlin type (see fig. 40a) the roofers (roof sheathing) run vertically from ridge down to cornice; where a common rafter system is used, such as that illustrated in figure 39, the roof boards run across the rafters, being nailed to them horizontally.

MASONRY

The masonry parts of the antique house—that is, the foundation, the chimney stack, the fireplaces, and the bake oven—vary in construction according to both time and place. One finds, for instance, in the Wethersfield and Hartford areas of Connecticut, where red clay abounds in the soil, that chimney stacks are frequently composed of brick from the cellar up through the roof and that the foundations are laid up in the red stone of the area. In the Norwich, Stonington, and New London area (only fifty miles to the east) the native stone is gray granite, a material used almost exclusively for foundations, chimney, and fireplace construction.

In the earliest times the foundations were constructed of small, flat stones taken from the site area and laid up dry with only the merest dressing so that they rested one upon the other without rocking. The foundation wall actually serves two purposes: it is first of all a retaining wall holding back the earth from the cellar hole; and second, it is a carrying wall that supports the frame above. To best serve the first purpose of retaining the outside earth, the stones had to be close-fitting. In addition, the foundation walls had to present a flat surface at the top on which to lay the sill. It was therefore usual for the builder to make the top two courses of carefully dressed stones. These would be chiseled face-square on the outside where they were visible above the ground elevation, but they were left rough inside the cellar. In the foundation walls a niche can occasionally be found about one foot wide by one foot high and one foot deep. One can only surmise the purpose of these niches; a typical cellar might have three or four of them, although I have seen cellars with only one and of course many with none at all. It is my conjecture that these niches provided a place to set a candle or lantern where it would not be extinguished by the wind, would be out of the way, and would not be subject to an inadvertent kick.

Bake ovens of the earliest fireplaces appear in the rear wall of the firebox, a location that eventually shifted in the first quarter of the eighteenth century to the more convenient location at the side of the fireplace. At first,

too, a lug, or iron bar, appeared across the throat of the kitchen fireplace from which hung a chain or trammel on which the cooking utensils might be suspended. The swinging crane came into common use as a substitute for this lug at the time the bake oven location was shifted to the side.

The earliest kitchen fireplaces were so constructed that the weight of the masonry directly above the span of the fireplace opening was carried on a great wood lintel. This timber was chamfered on the inside to lead the smoke back toward the flue rather than permitting it to pour out into the room. The chamfer itself was occasionally lathed and plastered to protect the exposed wood from direct contact with the flames or the intense heat of the fire. At a later time the wood lintel was replaced (again with the moving of the bake oven to the side of the fireplace) by a stone lintel. The fireplace opening at this time became smaller because of the bake oven's new position. Firebox openings of the earlier date—that is, those with the bake oven in the rear—are about seven to nine feet wide. Later, openings of four or five feet were most frequent.

Under the bearing surface of fireplace lintels, one will often encounter a flat board of some ⅞ inches to 1½ inches in thickness on which the lintel bears directly. The purpose of this board was no doubt to act as a cushion and leveling piece when the heavy lintel was set in place. It also provided a convenient place for a nail on which cooking utensils, pokers, etc., could be hung.

The fireplace stack itself provided an individual flue for each fireplace up to the attic floor, where all the flues join to become one large flue. In the case of stone chimneys the flues themselves are created by the placement of large flat, thin stones one over the other in the throat of the chimney, thus forming a closed channel within which the smoke from one fireplace could be kept separate from that of the others. Without individual flues the smoke of the lower fireplaces would most certainly pour into the upper rooms. Where the stack came out of the roof, a drip course of stone or brick was installed so that water running down the face and the rear of the chimney would be diverted onto the roof and would not continue into the attic. Flashing was not commonly used, although I have seen white birch bark used to plug the interstices between the roof boards and between the masonry and the wood roof. However, this did a poor job at best, and in almost every old house one encounters water damage at the roofline, where the stack emerges.

Above the roofline most chimneys present their broad face parallel to the ridge, perhaps being as much as six to eight bricks wide, 3½ to 5½ feet. There is nothing so pitiful

47. The foundation stones on the front of this Connecticut farmhouse of c. 1760 were dressed more carefully than those of the side and rear walls.

48. After 1800 the top course of foundation stones was much longer and higher than those of the 17th and 18th centuries because of improved methods of quarrying and cutting. Note the absence of a bead on the corner boards; this is another indicator of 19th- or 20th-century work.

49. The very earliest kitchen fireplaces had square, rather than splayed, sides, no bake ovens, and of course wood lintels.

49

50. A fireplace with a bake oven in the rear wall (second stage of development). Bake ovens were frequently rebuilt since constant use in the summer and winter burned out the brick.

50

51. A kitchen fireplace of 1761 with a bake oven at the right side of the firebox. One sheet-iron bake oven door covers the bake oven opening, another stands on the hearthstone. The overall width of masonry is 9 feet 2 inches with the firebox being about 5 feet wide at the front. The swinging crane supports a skillet and tea-kettle and is hinged to swing away from the oven; a standing crane stands partly inside the firebox and partly on the hearthstone at the left.

33

51

52. Wooden kitchen fireplace lintel, 9 feet 8 inches long, 1 foot high, and 16 inches deep, that once spanned a fireplace 7 feet wide. It could be as early as c. 1630 or as late as c. 1740. The house from which it came was probably a one-room- or two-room-plan structure. This oak lintel weighs over 300 pounds. As it is shown here, it rests on the side that faced into the room.

52

53. The awkwardness of working over a going fire led many people after c. 1740 to alter or modernize their "old-fashioned" kitchen fireplaces. Shown here is a fireplace that at one time had a wood lintel and a bake oven in the rear wall (it is still there); later, the external bake oven was added to the left side and the wood lintel was replaced by two stone lintels. The small opening under the new bake oven is for the storage of kindling, pots, etc.

53

54. This photograph of fireplace flues was taken at the attic-floor level of an early one-and-a-half-story house in Hampton, Connecticut.

54

55 — 3 COURSE CORBEL

DRIP COURSE

55. A simple but pleasing chimney-cap design: three courses corbeled outward and a top course setback. Modern lead flashing has been added under the drip course as protection against leaks. A typical 18th-century type. Restored by the author.

56. The variations of chimney-cap design are endless. This one has a decorative niche and two *setback* courses over a three-course corbel. Eigthteenth-century design.

56

57. A handsome "crown" of header dentils over a belt course drip caps this chimney in Preston, Connecticut. Some houses look better with chimneys of simple design; others can support an elaborate pattern. In all instances, however, a *top* of some kind is necessary to give the chimney a finished appearance.

57

58. Chimneys of the 1600s were often made of common flat fieldstone.

58

59. Although this 17th-century-type chimney is a reproduction, it was done in the old manner and includes a stone drip course just above the roofline.

59

to behold as a great center-chimney house with a skimpy chimney coming out of the roof.

Chimneys, to look their best (and to comply to modern fire laws as well), must rise above the ridge 3½ feet or more. (They were usually topped off with a simple corbeled cap of three or four courses or brick or stone, although more elaborate decorative chimneys can be seen.)

Early brick came hard-burned or in a softer, possibly sun-baked variety. The hard-burned brick is darker in color and can easily be identified by the ringing sound it emits when struck with another brick; also, when its surface is scraped, it does not powder easily. The softer brick is orange in color.

Needless to say, the antique house had no damper in its fireplaces, and by looking up the flue of any untouched old kitchen fireplace, one can see the clouds passing overhead.

Second-floor fireplaces are shallower than their brothers on the first floor; smaller fires were required in the chambers (bedrooms), where, no doubt, they were not kept going all night, but just long enough for one to take the chill out of a room and hop into bed. Perhaps one banked them for the night by covering the logs with ashes; in the morning they would spring back to life with the removal of the ashes and the addition of a few pieces of kindling. In many houses of the seventeenth and early eighteenth centuries where the timbers are exposed, the hearthstones are set on top of the flooring on the second floor; if this were not done, the bottom of the second-story hearthstones would be visible in the ceiling of the first-floor rooms.

Hearthstones for the kitchen fireplaces are about thirty inches wide and are seen as single slabs nine feet long or as two-piece hearths with a single large slab in front of the fireplace and a smaller one in front of the bake oven.

It is unusual to find a bake oven in its original condition. Almost without exception they required periodic rebuilding. The firing of a bake oven is performed in the following manner. First the bake oven door is removed and paper and kindling are set in place inside the oven itself. Once these are lit and begin to burn, small logs are added until the flames lick the dome of the oven. It is not necessary to make a very large fire. The size of the fire can be governed by the manipulation of the bake oven door. If the flames seem to be too high and are coming out past the lintel, the bake oven door can be pushed toward the oven, cutting off some of the supply of oxygen and slowing the fire. To increase the fire, the door can be moved away from the fire. In about two hours the stones or bricks of the oven will have turned dusty clean in color and will have reached

sufficient heat to provide an oven temperature of about 350° F. The fire is then removed with an iron peel and cast into the fireplace. Food can now be placed in the oven for baking, after which the oven door is pushed into place, thereby cutting off the oven from the flue and preserving the heat. I have found that my own oven will lose only fifty degrees in an eight-hour span if the oven door is tightly sealed.

In New England the great chimney stacks acted as a central core of the house, their very presence within the walls keeping some of the heat in the house. In the South, the kitchens were in separate buildings, usually behind the house proper, as it was desirable to keep the heat of the cook fire and of the bake oven out of the house.

Frequently found in the attics of New England frame houses are *smokehouses* built against the chimney. These consist of a small chamber about three feet long, two feet deep, and four feet high, made of brick except for the top, which would be a single stone. An opening in the front about one foot square has a wood door with leather hinges. Within this chamber one may find one or more wood bars running parallel to the long side. There are sometimes metal hooks on these bars on which meat was hung during the smoking period. In the rear wall of these smokehouses a small hole leads to a chimney flue. As the fires were burning in the lower rooms, smoke circulated through the hole into the smoke chamber, where it did its work.

In the base of many a chimney stack is a hole about 1½ feet square leading into a large chamber within the base itself. There is no door on this hole and no evidence of ashes at the bottom of the cavity. On close examination, it will be found that there is a small flue (about 8″ x 8″) leading from the top of the cavity and coming out in the back wall of the kitchen fireplace. Often the small hole in the rear of the fireplace has been sealed by brick or stone, but originally it had a wood or sheet-iron slip-in door that could be removed. What was the purpose of this elaborate flue system? Almost invariably I have heard people talk of their ashpit. But never an ash at the bottom can be found. Actually I stumbled on the answer one cold day. The three fireplaces of the John Palmer house had been restored and were ready to be tested for how well they drew the smoke. All the doors and windows in the house were closed when I lit all three fireplaces and the bake oven. I was astonished that in a few minutes all the fires began to throw smoke into the rooms—the chimneys were just not drawing at all. I thought that the mason had done something wrong, although he had followed to the letter the original dimensions.

In the rear of the kitchen fireplace, about halfway up to lintel height, I had noticed a small piece of charred

60. A raised hearth in a second-story chamber of a 17th-century house. The flooring runs underneath the hearth bricks to support them and conceal them from view in the exposed ceiling of the room below. A lovely wide molding gives a finished look to the hearth by providing a "stop" between brick and flooring. Buttolph-Williams House, c. 1692, Old Wethersfield, Connecticut; this is a restored museum house owned by the Antiquarian and Landmarks Society, Inc., Hartford.

61. A cellar draft hole leading to a large cavern in the base of a chimney stack is fairly common.

wood, which upon opening had led to a small flue. At the time of the discovery I had made a note of the opening and had replaced the door, thinking that surely this was an ashpit of some sort. Now, coughing and with eyes watering from the room full of smoke, I remembered the strange little door and opened it, not knowing what else to do to stop the billowing smoke. As soon as the door had been removed, the fire sprang to life and smoke stopped pouring into the room. The fires in the other rooms began to burn better almost at once.

The answer was simple. With all doors and windows shut tight and four fires going at once, there just was not enough oxygen in the house to support the fires. When the little flue was opened, the entire cellar area was added to the support of the fires.

Up to the turn of the nineteenth century hearths of fireplaces on the first floor were supported by the corbeling of the chimney stack in the basement to form a support ledge on which to rest the stones. Occasionally one runs into a trimmer arch in a brick base, that is, a curved semivault. After 1800 wood cradles began to be used, instead of masonry, for the support of hearthstones.

Within the stone chimney stack there frequently appear large and small timbers of all sorts, laid in with no apparent plan or design. These timbers are summer beams, girts, joists, etc., from earlier houses and can be identified by their notches as having come from another building. Occasionally too one finds an entire chimney built on a cradle of heavy timbers supported by two walls; in this case the builder was trying to save on material and labor and at the same time create for himself a cavernous room within the chimney base in which all kinds of produce could be stored. The random timbers are, for the most part, leveling pieces used to distribute the weight of the stone evenly over a wider surface, just as the sill spreads the weight of the house above over the entire surface of the foundation.

In some cases small timbers, such as those the size of floor joists ($4\frac{1}{2}''$ x $5''$), are built into fireplace walls near the ceiling and a little higher than mantel height. These are *nailers*, pieces of wood let into a masonry wall onto which the paneling could be nailed. Once in a while one finds stone steps leading to the cellar and almost always stone steps from the cellar hatchway out to the rear or side yard of a house.

Many houses have only partial cellars. Some of these were originally smaller houses, and the cellar portion almost always indicates the earlier part of the house. My own house has a huge rock outcropping running through the foundation wall in one corner; evidently in digging the foundation the builder found this boulder too large to remove, so he built the wall right over it and let it project into the cellar. Unfortunately it is a natural watercourse for rainwater.

Stone fireplaces carried either wood lintels (the earliest) or stone lintels; brick fireplaces have either wood or stone lintels. Very rarely one finds an iron lintel, usually of square section, perhaps two inches wide. Brick arches or curved fireplaces are also rarely discovered.

Occasionally one encounters interesting markings on old brick. There is a fireplace in Wethersfield, Connecticut, with a deer print in one of the hearth bricks; the animal made it, no doubt, by running through the brickyard at night and stepping on the wet clay in the mold. There is another fireplace with the imprint of a British coin in one of the bricks of an upstairs fireplace. Very often numbers are found on old brick; these are not generally dates but merely counting marks made by the brickmaker, who wished to keep account of how many bricks he had in a particular pile. Before 1800—and it is surprising how sharp a dividing line there is between the centuries—the cheek stones of stone fireplaces were made up of a series of stone four or five inches high in the case of the smaller fireplaces and perhaps seven or eight inches high for the kitchen fireplaces. Soon after 1800, with the improvement of stone drilling and splitting, one-piece cheek stones, some of massive size and weight, made their appearance. I have seen only one early-eighteenth-century single-cheek-stoned fireplace, and that was scored with horizontal and vertical lines to appear to be made of many smaller stones.

The angle stones or bricks from fireplaces are the important ones since they form the general angle or shape that the fireplace will take; the rear wall and rear portion of the two side (cheek) walls utilize straight stone. It is only the stone facing the room—the face stones or bricks—that have their unique angle cut in them. When a house burns or is demolished, it is worth going over the rubble, picking out the angle stones for future use.

Bake ovens have two small lintels, a front and a rear lintel. Between these two is the flue for the bake oven. In the case of fireplaces with the bake oven in the rear (the older fireplaces), there is no separate flue for the bake oven; here the smoke spills out into the main fireplace flue itself. The front lintel of a bake oven is set at a higher elevation than the rear lintel, against which the bake oven door rests when the oven is closed. A typical bake oven opening is about fourteen inches wide, allowing just enough space to feed the fire, take out the ashes, and put in the beans. Bake ovens vary in size; I have seen

62. A wooden nailer built into the masonry, in this case to attach the front-stair stringer. Notice the rear of a wood lintel in the old kitchen. This chimney is in the process of being rebuilt.

62

63. Tally brick. The number could just as well have been 1776, not 2338, as seen here. One can be fooled into thinking this was the date of the construction of the house.

63

64 and 65. Angle brick and angle stones. It is never acceptable to saw a full brick to create an angle brick, as the texture of the sawed brick will be obviously different from the real thing. The angle bricks shown here are reproductions.

64

65

66. A typical side bake oven. The first ovens of many houses were made of stone. The small oven flue joins the main kitchen fireplace flue at ceiling height.

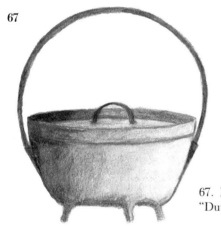

67. Drawing of a "Dutch oven" (side view).

68. View of the lid of a "Dutch oven."

69. "Cricket on the hearth." Hot coals were drawn on to the hearth and placed under a cricket on which a teakettle could be kept hot.

them as small as three feet in depth, and I have seen them five feet deep. In all cases they have the domed ceilings that have given them the name *beehive*. Frequently they are spoken of incorrectly as *Dutch ovens*; a Dutch oven is actually an iron cooking pot with a lid, the rim of which is raised to accept and hold hot coals.

NAILS AND HARDWARE

Although the main construction timbers were joined with wood joints and held together by pegs, the trim (such as base or mop boards, window and door casings, corner post, girt and summer-beam casings), flooring, lath, and clapboards were secured by the use of blacksmith-made nails, wrought at the forge by hand. Early nails are of certain general types, depending on the use for which they were intended.

One can distinguish hand-wrought nails from later machine-"cut" nails of the late eighteenth century by examining them from two views. Holding the nail horizontally and looking at it from the side, you will notice that it tapers from head to point. Now, turn it ninety degrees. Does it still taper from head to point? If it does, it is a hand-wrought nail. If it is of uniform thickness from head to point, it is a cut nail.

Nails vary in type of head and length. The rose-head nail, most often associated with antique house construction, was usually used in attic flooring and clapboarding, on the backs of cupboards, and as lath nails, and can be distinguished by the four hammer blows that give it the "rose" form.

The usual flooring nail for main rooms of houses is an L-shaped nail, the head of which is of the same thickness as the shaft. It was driven into the oak flooring until the top of the head was level with the surface of the flooring; in other words it was not countersunk. Trim nails of all sizes were made in the form of the flooring nail but with L-shaped heads of much smaller size.

Lath nails are in fact merely small rose-head nails: These were also used to install hinges and other hardware; a small piece of leather, placed under the head to provide a cushion when the nail was driven, works as a lock washer would, preventing the nail from slipping out.

The early house builder was not ashamed of his nails, for there is never an effort to disguise or hide them. In batten doors, for example, the nails are driven through the batten in the rear of the door and clinched down in the face.

Modern substitutes for old nails are readily available. The most satisfactory nail for small trim is the kind made to be fired from a gun; these come in sheets and can be easily separated by a knife for installation one at a time. Their L heads are similar to those of nails used in early window and door casings.

Flooring nails of the rose-head or L-head type can be purchased today as "reheads." These are actually factory-cut nails, the heads of which are reheated in the fire, placed in a heading tool, and struck to resemble the old head. Flooring nails can also be made in the old manner from iron rod—a process that takes more time. Since the head alone is visible to the eye, the former reheaded nail seems more practicable. Actually to purchase old nails taken from an old building is the final choice and an expensive one, because most of these nails have been bent or in some other way mutilated in being removed and must be straightened and retempered before use.

Almost every area has a blacksmith who makes reproduction nails and hardware. These craftsmen can usually be traced through antiques dealers or museums.

The basic hardware of the antique house consisted of hinges (both door and cupboard), door latches, locks, hooks, fireplace cranes, S hooks, trammels, pintles, etc.

In the seventeenth- and very early eighteenth-century house, interior doors were hung on short strap hinges hanging on pintles. Latches were occasionally made of wood but just as often of wrought iron in the form of a simple bean latch with thumb plate, staple, and keeper. Strap hinges were nailed to the door with large rose-head nails with a piece of leather under the head. At the same time, cupboard doors were attached by the use of "butterfly" hinges or small H hinges. Narrow doors often employed larger H hinges.

In the early eighteenth century the HL hinge came into fashion. These were used primarily on room doors and large closet doors and were also attached by nails with leather washers. The common sizes for HL hinges are 5 inches, 6 inches, 7 inches, 8 inches, and 9 inches, although I have seen a pair of 14-inch hinges on a very large closet door.

Toward the end of the eighteenth century the use of wood screws came into general use for attaching HL hinges to doors and cupboards. These screws were blunt ended, not pointed. If there is a question about a hinge's being original to a door, an examination of one of the screws can sometimes settle the question.

Wrought-iron door latches were used up to the late eighteenth century, when the patented English cast latches became popular.

DOORS

Exterior doors in the earliest houses are of the boarded—sometimes called *battened*—type. Actually

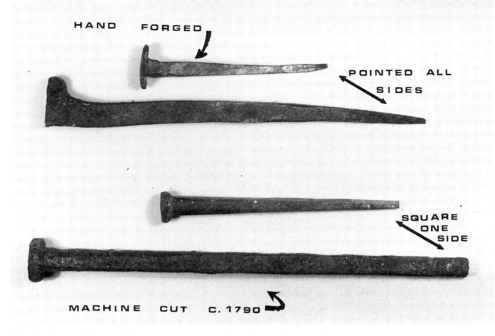

HAND FORGED

POINTED ALL SIDES

SQUARE ONE SIDE

MACHINE CUT C. 1790

70. Blacksmith-forged (wrought-iron) nails go back thousands of years.

71. Here is a sampling of early and late nails with their approximate dates; remember that there are many more variations, from tiny pins to great spikes 10 inches or more long. 1. Wrought flooring nail, 3½ inches long, before 1800. 2. Cut flooring nail, about 3 inches long, after 1800. 3. Cut trim nail, tapered view, used for nailing large boards, after 1900. 4. Cut common nail, used for nailing rough boarding, such as roofers, sheathing, etc., about 2¼ inches long, after 1800. 5. Cut trim nail, untapered view, used for casings, mop boards, chair rails, etc., after 1800. 6. Cut trim nail, tapered view, 1¼ inches long, used for more delicate work, such as moldings, where wood might split easily. 7. Power nail, modern, shot from a nail gun; these can be used as substitutes for early trim nails, about 1¾ inches long. 8. Blacksmith-forged trim nail used for crown moldings, flat window and door trim, chair rails, mantels, paneling, etc., before 1800. 9. Cut common nail (the other side is tapered to a point), used for boarding, clapboards, about 1¾ inches long, after 1800. 10. Trim nail for boarding, blacksmith-forged; used for interior trim and finished boards, before 1800. 11. Cut lath nail, about 1 inch long, after 1800. 12. Wrought lath nail, ¾ to 1 inch long; longer varieties (1¼ inches long) were used for wood shingles, before 1800.

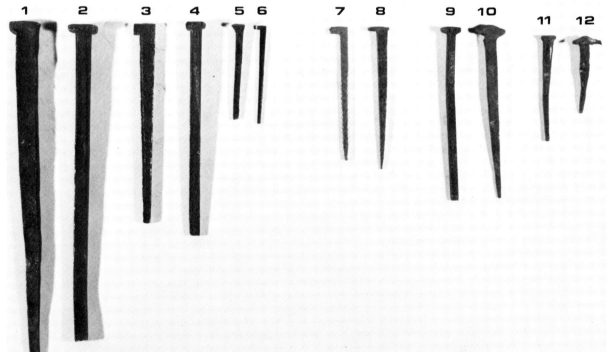

1   2   3   4   5 6   7   8   9   10   11   12

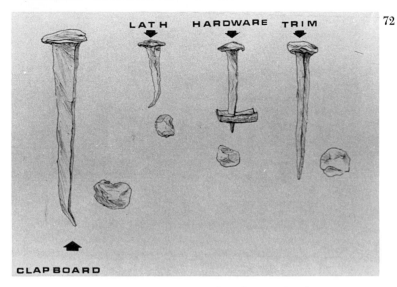

72

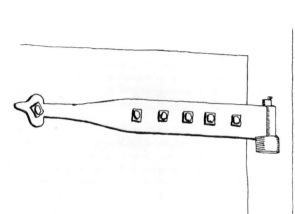

73

72. Rose-head nails came in many sizes, from large spikes down to 1-inch lath nails. Being wrought at the forge, they are tapered in both directions and are broader near the head. Almost all rose-head nails are *four*-struck, that is, the heads have been formed by four hammer blows, creating four facets to the top of the head. All forged nails are pre-1800.

73. The strap hinge is no doubt one of the earliest forms of door hardware. The nails used to hold the hinge to the door were sometimes *clinched* on the opposite side of the door so they could not work their way out. Strap hinges are still being used today to hang gates, barn doors, etc. Although straps generally went out of fashion after 1740 for interior doors, they still were used on cellar and attic doors within the house right into the 19th century.

74

74. An interesting version of a strap hinge. 18th century, Rhode Island.

75. Illustration of a 17th- and 18th-century door-latch system as seen from the inside of the door (the door swings toward you).

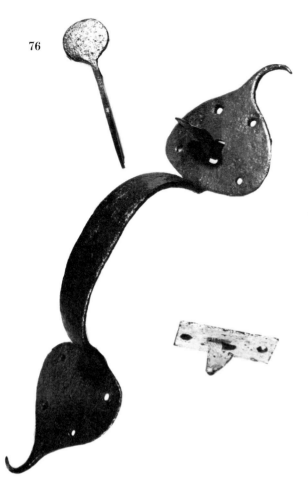

76

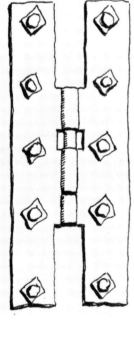

76. On the outside of the door (opposite side from fig. 75) there is the latch grip or handle with its thumbpiece. Although the latch handle and thumbpiece pictured here are of mid-18th-century vintage, the "bar keeper" (painted white) is of the 19th century because it is affixed to a nail plate.

77. Butterfly hinges were used primarily in the 17th century in America. Because they are small, they were used in most instances on cupboard doors and on furniture.

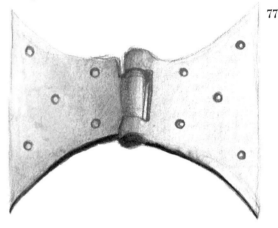

77

78

78. H hinge, a type used throughout the 18th century.

79. The HL hinge. HL hinges continued to be used on outside doors through the early 19th century. HL hinges were employed on most between-room doors whereas cupboard and other small doors were supported by H hinges, as were most narrow closet doors. These hinges were all blacksmith-forged of iron on the anvil, although one can find an occasional pair of brass H hinges on corner cupboards and furniture.

80

79

80. Typical door-hardware installation.

45

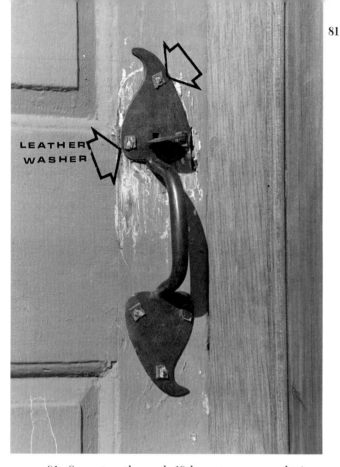

LEATHER WASHER

81

82

83

84

82. A "bean latch."

83. This shape is frequently called a "pine-tree" latch.

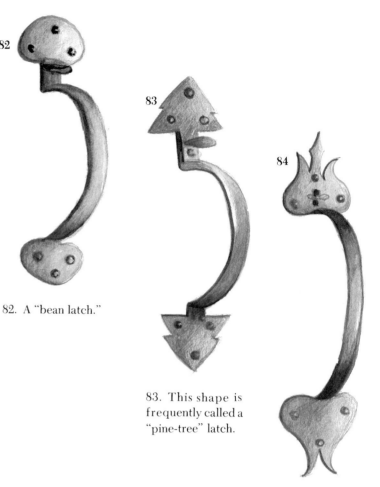

84. A "tulip" latch.

81. Seventeenth- and 18th-century wrought-iron latches came in many shapes, the names of which are taken from the nailing plate. Thus the one shown here might be called the "pear" latch. On a 1790 house restored by the author.

85

86

85. Mid-18th-century latches, called *open-box locks*, have knobs of cast brass on either side of the door, whereas the balance of the exposed mechanism is forged iron. The keeper illustrated here, like so many found in early houses, is a replacement made in the 19th century, as it has an iron plate for nailing to the doorjamb.

86. Box locks are found on the hall doors of center-hall houses of the mid- to late 18th century. In this doorway the keeper for the lock has pulled out of the wood and is missing. A 19th-century lock and keyhole were added later.

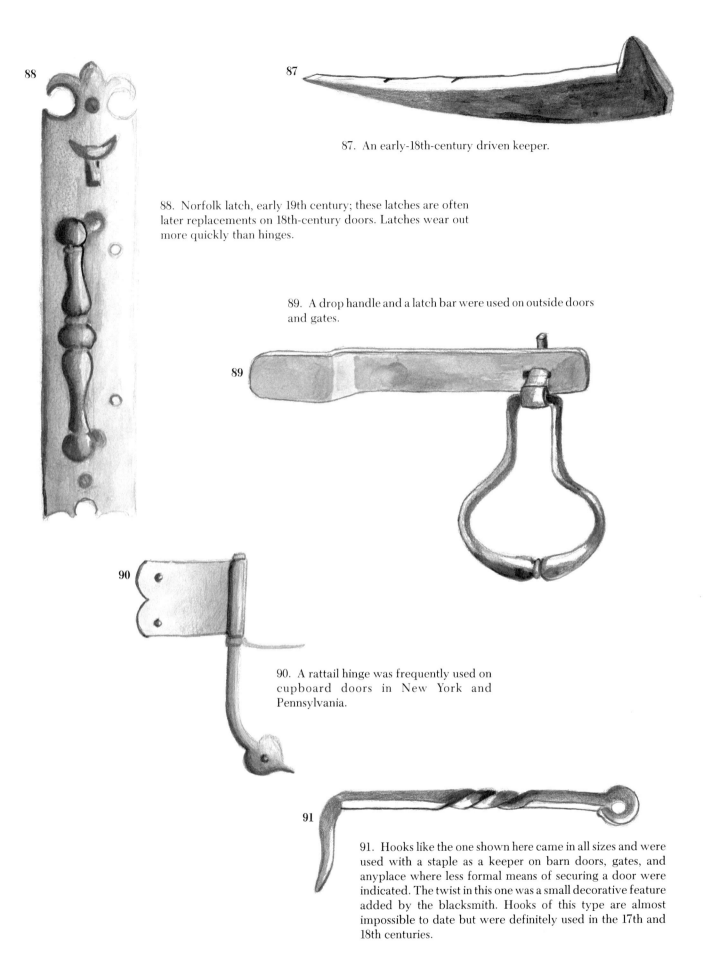

87. An early-18th-century driven keeper.

88. Norfolk latch, early 19th century; these latches are often later replacements on 18th-century doors. Latches wear out more quickly than hinges.

89. A drop handle and a latch bar were used on outside doors and gates.

90. A rattail hinge was frequently used on cupboard doors in New York and Pennsylvania.

91. Hooks like the one shown here came in all sizes and were used with a staple as a keeper on barn doors, gates, and anyplace where less formal means of securing a door were indicated. The twist in this one was a small decorative feature added by the blacksmith. Hooks of this type are almost impossible to date but were definitely used in the 17th and 18th centuries.

they consist of two separate layers of boards, the exterior layer being vertical and the interior being horizontal. These layers were nailed to each other from the exterior through both layers; the nails were then clinched over on the inside. Neither side was paneled. There was good reason to have the outside boards run vertically: water could run off the door down the grooves formed between boards, greatly extending the life of the door.

Upon occasion one finds double doors being used in the front of a house. You can ascertain if your house originally had single or double front doors by examining the underside of the front girt above the present door opening. Look for the mortises on either side of the doorway into which the door framing studs fitted. If these two holes are spaced more than three feet apart, it is probable that the house had two front doors rather than one.

The earliest exterior-paneled doors were used in the front entrance to the house, the side and rear doors still being of the boarded type. These paneled doors were made up of two separate and distinct doors, the outside one being paneled and the inside being boarded. They were attached to each other by nails clinched over. In all the exterior-paneled doors I have seen, the batten boards run vertically on the inside. The paneled portion of the door (exterior) is usually slightly smaller than the inside, thus creating a lip of about a half inch on the top and the two sides; this lip created a tight seal against the weather when it pressed against the stops of the doorjamb. Exterior doors always opened in.

In chronological order, the two-paneled door came first (1670s through 1740s), followed by three-, four-, and six-paneled doors (1750 to 1800). The panels of the earliest six-panel doors had the small panels in the center with two large panels above and two beneath. I have never seen a two-panel *exterior* door of early date. At a later time six-panel doors became fashionable with the small panels at the top; these would be dated as post-Revolution.

During the middle of the eighteenth century, when raised-panel woodwork became more sophisticated, front doors and their surrounds also became increasingly ornate, and single doors with ten or twelve panels were not unusual as front doors on the grander homes of that period. I have seen double doors with as many as twenty-two panels, eleven in each half. The inside of these doors still was of board construction in most instances. Paneled doors, both inside and exterior, like early window frames, were made of stiles and rails

joined by mortise-and-tenon joints and fixed in place by wood dowels or pegs.

If you examine an early door from either long edge, you will see the ends of the tenons, which come through the side rails. This is one test for distinguishing a made-up door from an authentic one. Interior doors are an inch in thickness.

The doors within a given room matched the other woodwork of the room. Thus, if the walls were made of beaded boards, the doors also would be of beaded board; a room with raised paneling would have doors with raised panels.

WINDOWS

Of all the parts of a house the windows are perhaps the most complicated. They can best be described by the manner in which their sash are hung and by the number of *lights* (panes of glass) their sash contain.

The simplest form of window is the fixed window, which consists of a window frame and a single sash that doesn't open. In today's house this type appears as our modern "picture window," the purpose of which is to introduce light and the view into a room without providing ventilation. The antique house occasionally had fixed-sash windows. They can be found in seventeenth-century houses, where in combination with one or more casement-sash windows, they let light into the rooms. They can also be found in the side elevation of some "capes," on the second floor, where they are used to admit light into the dead storage space under the rafters; or again over the head of a front door.

Casement windows were used in the seventeenth and early eighteenth centuries and can be described as windows that are hinged at one side and swing outward. They can be found as single casements, double casements, and casements with fixed sash.

In antique houses there are no known examples of the double-hung window of the guillotine type with which we are so familiar; instead the early house builder employed a "single"-hung sash, one opening from the bottom only, the top sash being fixed in place. The manner in which these sash were installed in their frames was most ingenious: by removing one of the window stops inside the window, one could easily remove both the movable and the fixed sash for cleaning or repair. It has been only within the last twenty-five years that modern windows have been on the market that incorporate this feature.

92. "Studded" board front door and plain-door surround on the 1692 Buttolph-Williams House in Old Wethersfield, Connecticut, owned and operated as a "museum house" by the Antiquarian and Landmarks Society, Inc., Hartford.

93. Here is a doorway of simple design with the familiar "kick" at the head; these doors have bull's-eye lights built into them at the top. More commonly one will find the lights built into a frame above the door. That the small raised panels are in the middle of the door, rather than at the top of the larger panels, indicates a date prior to c. 1776. The Newson House, 1680–1730, Wethersfield, Connecticut. Privately owned.

94. Another pre-Revolutionary door. The outward thrust at the top of the doorframe stiles (the "kick") was a decorative feature much admired in the 18th century.

95. Here is a pair of handsome front-entrance doors with "crossbuck" panels at the bottom and lights within the doors themselves rather than in a fixed transom in the frame. This door surround with its fluted columns, Connecticut rose, keystone (in wood, of course) and pediment, as well as the pedimented window-frame heads, is of very pleasing proportions. Note the graduated widths of the clapboards. From a house in northern Connecticut, privately owned.

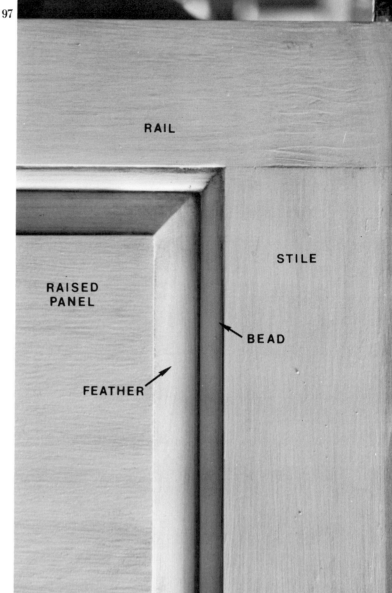

96. Detail of Ionic capital, fluted pilaster, and Connecticut "rose," from the entrance of the Whitman House, East Hartford, Connecticut.

98. Flat-panel door, c. 1800.

97. The feathered, raised panel of this door floats free in a groove mortised into stiles and rails; no glue has been used. This photograph occasionally presents an optical illusion wherein the *raised* panel appears to be a *sunken* panel: by concentrating on the upper feather and bead, it will appear as it truly is after a time. The panel is from a mid-18th-century door.

99. End view of the top of a typical raised-panel interior door showing the tip of the rail tenon as it appears coming through the stile. There was no attempt to "blind-tenon" doors.

99

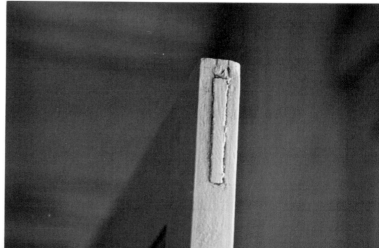

100. Exterior view of a 17th-century diamond-pane casement window hung on small strap hinges (left) with two fixed sash (right). The vertical wooden piece separating the two fixed sash is called a *mullion* today but was referred to as a *munnion* in early days.

101. Inside view of a casement window, Buttolph-Williams House, Old Wethersfield, Connecticut, 1692, owned by the Antiquarian and Landmarks Society, Inc., Hartford.

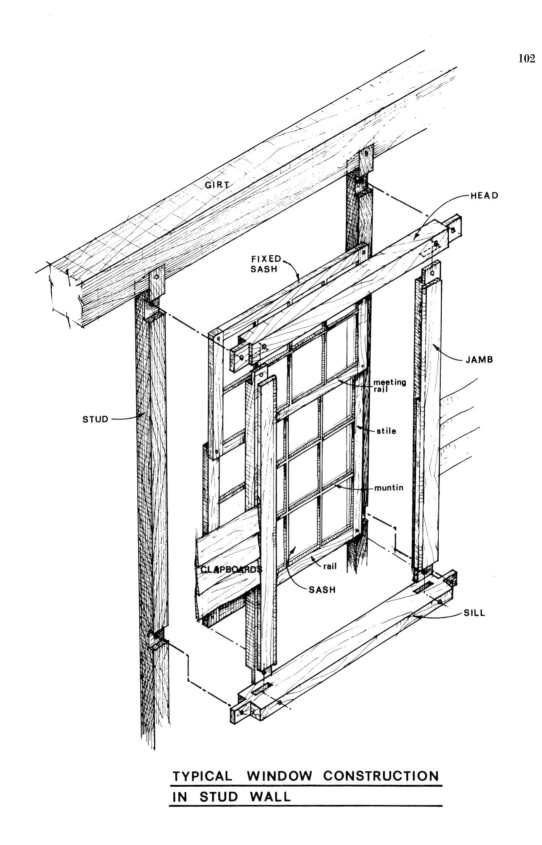

GIRT

HEAD

FIXED
SASH

JAMB

STUD

meeting
rail

stile

muntin

CLAPBOARDS

rail

SASH

SILL

TYPICAL WINDOW CONSTRUCTION
IN STUD WALL

102. Isometric drawing of window parts.

A window is also described by the number of lights in its sash. Thus, if the upper sash has six panes and the lower has nine, the window is said to be a six over nine (6/9). The number of lights of glass in the sash was often governed by the size and type of house. For example, a 1½-story (cape) might have nine-over-six sash or six over nine; a 1720 added lean-to house might have twelve over eight (or vice versa) upstairs, where the ceiling height was lower, and twelve over twelve downstairs. Most houses of the middle to late eighteenth century, both center-chimney and center-hall types, have the twelve-over-twelve arrangement, except for the attic windows, which are smaller.

It is interesting to note that the amount of window opening—that is, the amount of ventilation—is the same in a nine over six and a six over nine or in a twelve over eight and an eight over twelve. There seems to be no rule covering when each was used.

The early casement window had diamond panes held in lead channels. These are rare indeed, and in twenty-five years I have not found an original one in place. Reproductions can be found in restorations of seventeenth-century structures, and originals are found within museum showcases.

One encounters six primary combinations of sash: 9/6, 6/9; 12/8, 8/12; 6/6; 12/12. Occasionally a special form may be found, such as four-light or two-light fixed; these were used to bring light into attics, to light rear stairwells, or as sidelights at either side of a front door.

Throughout most of the eighteenth century glass panes six inches wide by eight inches long were used. The best-quality glass—that is, that with the fewest imperfections of color or texture—was reserved for other uses; old window glass has swirls and bubbles of air in it. It may even have a slight bluish, rose, or purple tint. The more deformed the glass, the more it is sought after today because it lends a primitive quality to a house glazed with it.

Toward the end of the eighteenth century larger panes of glass became available, and soon builders were installing panes seven inches wide by nine inches long.

In the very earliest of the single-hung windows the *muntins*—that is, the wood bars that hold the glass in place—were quite flat in section and at least one inch in width. As time progressed, these muntins became narrower and deeper, so that by the time of the Revolution and thereafter, when 7- x 9-inch glass was used, the windows had lost their heavy appearance. Old sash with its imperfect glass can sometimes be found in country chicken houses or barns, where it was relegated when the original sash was replaced by large two-over-two or even one-over-one lights in the 1870s and 1880s. Prices

vary considerably; I have been given old sash from a chicken coop that was about to be demolished, and again I have paid as much as $1.50 per window pane for a sash in good condition, containing all its original old glass. A price of $1.00 per pane, counting only the glass with imperfections and including the window sash, seems fair at this writing.

The fenestration of antique houses is a most interesting study. In the very earliest houses the fight against the cold of winter and heat of summer was real indeed. I think it would be a fair assumption to say that windows were used less for looking out than for admitting light. This might account as well for the poorest-quality glass being used for windows. If they were opened at all in winter, it would have been for the purpose of letting smoke out or for gaining more oxygen for the fires. In summer they would be opened to cool the old kitchen when cooking or baking was going on. One must remember that the kitchen fireplace had, of necessity, to be going in the summer as well. The old houses seem to have a natural insulating capacity to keep themselves cool in summer; it was keeping warm in winter that was the more serious problem. Hence one finds the Buttolph–Williams house in Old Wethersfield, Connecticut (1692), with no windows at all in the rear wall of the house and only five small casements across the entire front facade.

Window fenestration for each type of house was standard in the seventeenth and eighteenth centuries. In the plan of the one-room house one finds five windows in the front elevation, that is, three on the second floor and two on the first. Looking at these houses from the side, one discovers a line of three windows, one above the other: in the first floor, second floor, and attic. In the two-room plan there was some variation in the front elevation, as either a five- or a nine-window front elevation appears. The fewer the windows, the more primitive the house seems. Where the house has five windows facing the front, three are in the second story and two are in the first, one on either side of the front door; where nine windows appear, five are in the second story and four on the first floor, two on either side of the front door. This nine-window arrangement became established as the most desirable, and from the 1730s on into the nineteenth century it was used in almost every house built, center-chimney or center-hall.

The side elevation fenestration, with the introduction of the added lean-to house, departed from the three-window setup because it now became desirable to allow light into the buttery (or the pantry, as it was sometimes called) on one side of the old kitchen and into the small bedroom on the other side of the kitchen. Again, on the

103. Drawing of an exterior 8-over-12 sash and frame with "ears," early- to mid-18th century.

104. Twelve-over-twelve (12/12) sash, c. 1760, with 6-inch-wide by 8-inch-high lights. The two wider horizontal parts of the sash (the bottom of the top sash and the top of the bottom sash) are called *meeting rails*. The bars separating the glass ("lights") are called *muntins*. Notice the beautiful window-head cornice and the fine molded and doweled sill; the clapboarding is also original.

105. A simpler yet pleasant frame and sash from The Gay Manse, Suffield, Connecticut, c. 1742. The "keystone" in the frame is unique to my knowledge.

106. It is more the rule than the exception to find the windows on the second floor of a lean-to-plan house or added lean-to (saltbox) shorter than those on the first floor. Here, in this nine-window-front house we have 12-over-8 sash on the second floor but there are 12-over-12 sash in front on the first floor. Over the front door is a fixed sash of six panes to admit light to the "passage." The small attic and lean-to windows are 6-over-6; the side elevation sash are again 12-over-8.

107. View of the exterior of a window sash of c. 1750. The face of the glass is almost at the same plane as the face of the muntins that hold it. This window needs reputtying badly.

108. An early-18th-century window frame showing a dowel holding the right stile to the sill by pinning the mortise-and-tenon joint. The absorption of water has caused the dowel to protrude from its hole.

108

109. The Palladian window appears in late-18th-century Georgian houses. These were placed on the second floor over the front door. Mullions separate the 12-over-12 center sash from a two-light wide 6-over-6 on each side. Only the bottom sash opens. Above is a delicate fixed fanlight. Everything is underneath an interesting molding with dentil.

109

second floor the extension of the rafters of the original house toward the ground created a small storage area behind each of the two upstairs rooms, this area being barely enough space to allow one to stand erect but being an ideal place to keep spinning wheels, yarn winders, and other necessary but cumbersome equipment. A bit of light in this area could be obtained through a fixed window a little above floor height at each end of the house. Thus the side elevation now had five windows overall, one of which was usually a small, fixed, four-light sash toward the rear of the house on the second floor.

When the true saltbox house replaced the added lean-to, this configuration still held true because the only basic change was that rear rafters of one piece from the ridge down to the back plate replaced rafters that were made in two sections.

With the coming of the full 2½-story center-chimney house, a five-window side elevation appeared with two full-size windows on each of the first two floors and a smaller window in the attic. Occasionally one runs into a house deeper than usual, and here one can find seven windows in the side elevation. In this instance the front rooms of the house on each full story have two windows facing the side; the buttery and the small bedroom off the kitchen have one apiece; and the attic has one.

As for the rear elevation of antique houses, their arrangement was dictated largely by the ell or lean-to and its placement. Almost without exception there was at least one window in the rear wall of the old kitchen and a similar one in the kitchen chamber above. Only an examination of the stud spacing in a studded house or of the way that the planks were cut in a plank house can make one positive of the rear-wall window layout. The early houses were oriented on their property so that the front almost always faced south, and it was of advantage to the owner to have as few windows facing the cold north exposure as possible. It is an interesting footnote that the small bedroom (sometimes erroneously titled the *borning room*) was on the warmer side of the house, whereas the buttery more than likely would be placed toward the colder side.

Up to the 1800s, windows were set with the top of the frame tight against the first-floor girts or against the plate on the second floor. From the outside, therefore, only a narrow fascia board shows, running horizontally above the windows in the front and the rear of the house. After 1800, windows began to appear lower in the rooms, and wide fascia boards became the rule. Speeding by in a car, one can often date a house as being before or after 1800 by the position of the upper windows.

FLOORING

Oak, chestnut, and pine flooring was used in antique houses. It is interesting that pine floors were considered dressier than their oak and chestnut counterparts. Thus one finds that in the work areas of the house—those rooms most traveled, such as the kitchen, buttery, passage, kitchen chamber, etc.—oak is the most frequently used material. The front rooms—that is, the parlor, the sitting room, and their respective chambers—of a center-chimney house, for example, would be of pine in most cases. But again, it must be emphasized that availability of material and local custom frequently make the exception that proves the rule.

Timber of great proportions was available in the forests, and since sawing boards was arduous work (and expensive, as well), the carpenter would chose the widest and longest boards for his floors; these he would saw a full inch thick. Almost without exception flooring ran in single length from wall to wall across each room. Both underflooring, if it was used, and the finished floor above ran in the same direction, one over the other, across the joists. The floorboards were of great width, occasionally being eighteen inches or more wide, in which case three nails were used to hold the board tight to the joist; twelve inches is about the narrowest width of boards used before 1800, two nails being used to hold them at each joist. The spacing of the lines of nails is from eighteen to twenty-four inches apart. Flooring was top-nailed, as opposed to the modern method of *toenailing*; in other words the nailheads were exposed to view. I have never seen a "pegged" seventeenth- or eighteenth-century floor.

In rooms such as the kitchen, the kitchen chamber, the hall (in center-hall houses), and the attics, single floorboards long enough to span the entire distance from wall to wall were impossible to produce. In these places the floorboards were laid down in panels or sections, with all the boards in that section of uniform length. The next panel began at the end of the first. The joints where the panels met were staggered. Flooring sometimes was splined, sometimes shiplapped, and sometimes fitted with a butt joint.

The best flooring was used in the lower rooms of the houses, and flooring of inferior quality was laid down in the attic. Occasionally this attic flooring is good enough to be used to fill in downstairs where flooring must be replaced or has been removed.

Once in a while a floorboard is found with a Roman numeral cut into it, and perhaps an initial as well. I believe that the house owner would bring his logs to the

110. Here is a view looking upwards from the old kitchen of the author's former house toward the kitchen chamber above. No attempt was made to "square" the edges of the underflooring or even to take the bark off some of the boards. The bottom of the finished flooring of the kitchen chamber is visible between the slitwork, which is up-and-down sawed chestnut half the thickness of the finished flooring. The finished (top) flooring is nailed through the underflooring, which is laid down without nails. In this room the joists (from which hangs a sprig of herbs) are also of chestnut. At one time this ceiling was lathed and plastered but since documentation was found that the house stood for forty years without plaster, we chose to expose the "raw" wood in this room again.

111. These floorboards have been laid down in panels of even length. As a new panel of boards was added to the first, the joints were "staggered" as shown so that the seams between the boards of one group would not line up with those of the next.

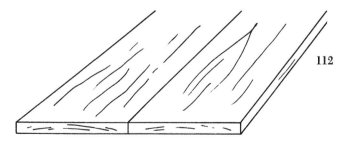

112

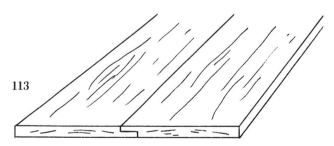

113

112. In almost every instance where boards are "butt-joint" laid, underflooring, called *slitwork*, was used under them. The space between abutting boards opens and closes with the seasons, with separations of ⅜ inch or more occurring during the heating season or other times of low humidity. Were it not for the underflooring one could look through to the upper stories from a room with exposed ceilings, or a pencil or other object might fall through from story to story.

113. *Shiplap* flooring would always be found where underflooring is not used and often even if underflooring was installed. It is, of course, a "tighter" joint made by rabbeting the upper edge of one board and the lower edge of the adjoining one. The boards would more properly be described as being "half-lapped" along their long edge. Where two boards join end-to-end, they are not *ship-lapped* at their ends.

sawyer, who, after cutting them into boards, would mark the number of square feet and the owner's initials on the topmost board for identification. Each piece of wood being precious to the owner, the marked boards were installed, marked side up, just as they came from the sawyer. There is hardly an attic without one such marked board visible in its flooring, and many a downstairs room bears such a mark as well.

Flooring was installed as a platform to stand upon before the inside walls were erected. Thus the floorboards run *under* the partitions in an antique house.

TRIM

The exterior trim, or finish woodwork, of an early house basically consists of the water table (the horizontal board running like a skirt around the bottom of the clapboards); the corner boards (which run vertically and form the corners of the house, acting as a "stop" against which the clapboards can butt); the rake or vergeboards (which one can see by looking at the house from the gable end and which run diagonally from the peak downward in both directions just below the roof shingles); and the cornice (which is made up of at least two boards: the fascia board running horizontally across the face of the house just beneath the roof shingles, and the soffit, which meets the fascia but forms the underside of the overhang of the cornice). Door surrounds, window cornices, etc., also fall into this category. The variations of these trim members are infinite, and the elaborateness of their construction depended on the ingenuity, patience, and artistry of the builder. Exterior trim serves two purposes: the first is to act as a shield against the weather; the second is decorative. It is entirely possible for the clapboards of the front of the house to meet those of the side and be nailed at their point of intersection; however, the slightest warping or opening up of a joint would allow the rain and wind easy access to the inner structure. The two vertical corner boards at this critical point greatly diminish the danger of water and wind entering, for now, instead of fifty separate clapboards joining each other, there are only two vertical seams.

The clapboards of the earliest houses were made of split oak, a material that has a marked tendency to twist and warp. It was later replaced by the use of pine clapboarding. Today the use of red or white cedar has taken over, as these materials last for years even without being painted or treated.

It is of interest to examine the method of installing clapboarding in the seventeenth and eighteenth centuries. In many localities the houses had no sheathing on the outside of the studs (in the case of a studded house), and the clapboards were nailed directly to the studs. In both the studded and the plank house it was desirable to make as "tight" a job of putting the skin on the house as possible. Therefore wherever the ends of two clapboards met, they were chamfered and spliced or overlapped, not butt-jointed as is done today. Of course, today we have the advantage of being able to keep out the weather with plywood, building paper, and insulation, but in the early days these lapped joints did much to seal the house. This lapping gives to the outside covering of the house a waviness that lends a great deal of charm to the appearance.

In the middle of the eighteenth century, builders began installing graduated clapboards on many houses, sometimes on the front wall only and at other times completely around the house. Starting at the top of the water table, the first few courses of clapboards were placed with very little surface to the weather; as they rise, course upon course, the lap, or exposure to the weather, becomes wider and wider, generally reaching about four inches at the head of the first-floor windows, where the lap might remain or keep spreading until it reaches the cornice, where I have seen the exposure reach as much as six inches. The purpose of this variation of the clapboards was both aesthetic and practical. Many laps of clapboarding close to the ground, where the snow piled high against the house, gave added protection. There is something very pleasant about graduated clapboards on a well-proportioned house.

The interior trim of antique houses ranges from the very simple woodwork of the earliest and most primitive structures to the very elaborate rooms of paneling of the Georgian and Federal periods. In the first true houses, the interior walls were entirely of wood with no plaster applied. Generally the earliest of these walls were made of feather-edged boards applied horizontally to the exterior walls and vertically to the interior walls. The boards themselves were of random widths and were nailed directly to the girts and the studs. They were often stained red, painted blue or green, or left natural. One must remember that most of the wood used in early houses was "green" lumber when it was installed, and it took many years for the deep brown patina to cover the surface. It was natural for the house builder to wish to dress his walls with paint or stain. Feather-edged boards are very rare today and often bring a price of $7.00 or more a square foot, if they can be found.

There was very little pretense in what they were, these feather-edged walls: they served to separate the space

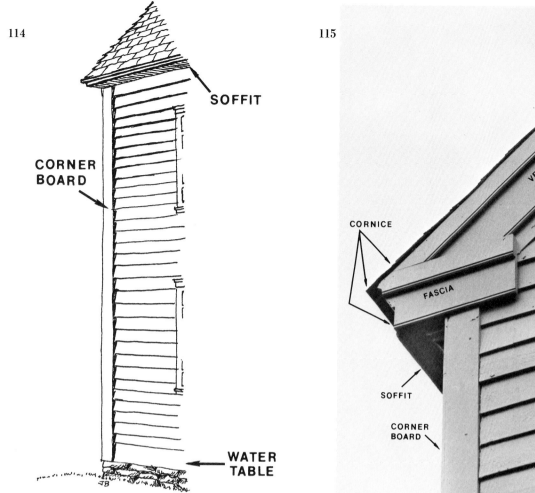

SOFFIT

CORNER BOARD

WATER TABLE

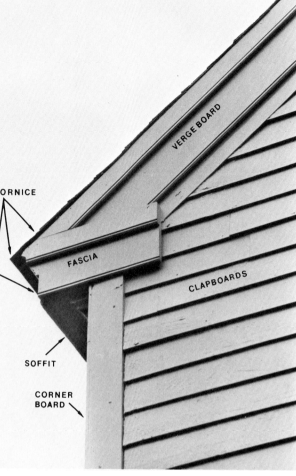

CORNICE

VERGE BOARD

FASCIA

CLAPBOARDS

SOFFIT

CORNER BOARD

114. Parts of the exterior trim at the corner of a house as seen from the front elevation.

115. A view of mid-18th-century house trim as seen from the gable end.

116. A poor way to join clapboards at the corner of a house. I have never encountered an *original* clapboarding job like this one.

116

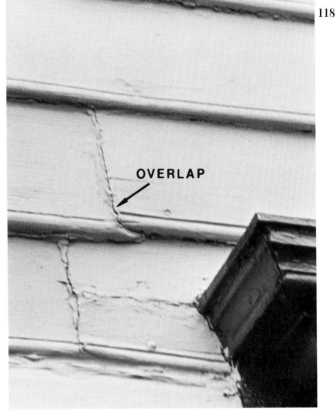

117. Oak clapboards of 17th-century type. These are reproductions but have been installed, lapped, and chamfered in the old manner.

118. Original beaded clapboards from the front of an 18th-century Connecticut house. The clapboards are of random length and are chamfered and lapped where they meet.

119. A slick is a broad chisellike tool used to chamfer clapboards. It can measure as long as 3 feet, with a cutting edge as wide as 4 inches; it was pushed by hand, not struck with a mallet.

120. The clapboards on the front of this Eastford, Connecticut, house are graduated from a mere 2 inches "to the weather" at the water table to over 4 inches of exposure at the head of the first-floor windows. The builder felt it unnecessary to dress up the other walls by graduating the clapboards. The front clapboards are beaded as well (right wall in the picture); this would suggest that these procedures were primarily decorative and only secondarily protective.

121. The interior walls of the earliest houses boarded with either feather-edged (bead and feather) boards, as pictured here, or beaded boards (without the feather) with a heavy bead. Shown in the photograph is an original c. 1740 wall in its original Spanish brown paint. It is safe to assume that at first the ceiling timbers of this room were exposed to view, as was the underflooring of the room above. This would be an interior wall between rooms (vertical). Doors were made in the same manner as the walls themselves. Wainscoting was the exception, running horizontally on *all* walls from window sill to floor.

122. Feather-edged boarded room in Old Wethersfield, Connecticut, restored by the author. You are looking at original boards here, for the most part; a few had to be replaced with new ones made in the old manner. Boards were cut to follow the taper of the tree (note small arrow, left of stairs). Although it is generally assumed that feather-edged boarded walls are of earlier date than beaded-board walls, this is not always the case; however, 17th- and early-18th-century beaded lumber had a larger radius bead than late-18th-century work. One must also keep in mind that there was a strong overlapping of methods of constuction. Many a feather-edged boarded wall was built after the Revolutionary War by builders whose apprenticeship had been served many years before.

within the house into rooms. At the time I do not believe they were thought of as being decorative in themselves. In a house with feather-edged walls it was usual to find the ceiling timbers and the underflooring of both the second floor and the attic floor exposed in the rooms below.

Toward the middle of the eighteenth century, feather-edged boards were replaced by beaded boards in the creation of certain wood walls, such as rear stairwells, attic stairwells, kitchen walls, the interior walls of closets and butteries, "hired men's" rooms in the attic, etc. At the same time these beaded walls were being installed, the builders were using lath and plaster on top of rough-sawed plank walls to create interior partitions. Beaded walls were utilized in the less important places within the house, places that did not warrant the effort of lath and plaster.

Contrary to the manner in which a modern house is "trimmed out," the antique house had its trim installed not on top of the plaster but before the plaster was put on. Therefore the trim acted as a "ground" for the plasterer, a board to which he could screed his work to get a uniform thickness and an even surface to his plaster wall. And so before the plasterer could begin, all door and window casings, all corner-post and girt casings, mop boards, and paneling were securely nailed in place and the lath installed.

The feature of early trim (up to 1800) that is most constant and sets it apart from later work is the bead. No early builder worth his salt would feel "right" butting one board against another without a bead to give it a finished, closed, and decorative look. The beading plane must have been a much-worked instrument in the hands of the woodworker, as beading appears not only in house construction but also in furniture construction. Mop boards were beaded, corner posts were beaded, summer beam and chimney girt casings were beaded. Window frames on the exterior of the house, corner boards to which the clapboards were butted, and rake boards on the gable ends all were beaded. As we have seen before, entire wood walls were made up of beaded boards. Even clapboards were occasionally beaded. Why am I emphasizing this little idiosyncrasy of the early house builder? Simply because the bead is an almost foolproof way to distinguish changes of trim within the house. Doors added at a later date frequently omit the bead from the casing. Mop boards unbeaded on one wall but beaded on the three other walls of the room indicate that changes have been made in that wall. An unbeaded corner-post casing in one corner of a room with beaded casings in the other corners is a signal of later alteration or of the location of a missing corner cupboard.

Although, technically speaking, wooden or boarded walls (both feather-edged and beaded) and wainscoting are classified as paneling, one thinks particularly of raised panels held in stiles and rails when using the term. The wainscot walls gave way to raised paneling during the first quarter of the eighteenth century, after which time almost all fireplace walls were paneled from floor to ceiling, and corner posts, girts, and summer beams were sure to be cased. The patterns in which these walls were laid out is infinite: they ranged from simple rectangular panels with modest bolection molding around the fireplace opening to intricate designs incorporating dentil crown moldings, fluted pilasters, and bolection moldings surrounding each panel.

Volumes can be written on paneling and its variations. Let it suffice for our purposes to point out that the stile and rails into which the panels are set are joined with the typical mortise-and-tenon joint, the pegs holding these being clearly visible on the surface of the wall. The panels float free within the grooves of the stiles and rails made to receive them, so that they may expand and contract with changes of humidity. Raised panels were almost always made of clear, well-seasoned white pine and were intended to be painted. It is usual for the two first-floor front rooms of center-chimney houses to have fireplace walls completely paneled, one of these rooms being more elaborate than the other and often having a raised-panel wainscot running completely around the three other walls of the room; this was the parlor, a room used for special occasions such as weddings. There appears as well a chair rail, which was set at the height of the windowsill. This chair-rail height gives the exact height of the original windows and tells us the construction of those windows without our having ever to see them. In certain areas interior sliding, or folding, shutters were placed in the colder rooms of the house; these were composed of panels matching those of the fireplace walls and still serve well the purpose for which they were originally intended.

123. Shown here is "split lath," second half of the 18th century. Wide boards of oak or chestnut were struck with a hatchet and then expanded (like an accordian) on the wall. The two arrows in the photograph outline the width of one expanded board. On large surfaces, where single boards were not long enough to span the entire distance, lath was installed in the manner of flooring—in panels.

124. Illustrated is a beading plane with its "iron." These tools came in a variety of radii and when razor sharp were capable of turning out beaded boards quickly. Modern combination planes with an assortment of blades can be bought today.

124

125. Here is a horizontal (outside) beaded-board wall with small-radius beads (about ¼") from a house of c. 1775.

125

126. A rare arched fireplace with simple raised-panel chimney breast in a sitting room chamber (bedroom). The author found this fireplace buried behind plaster in a c. 1770 house he restored in Old Wethersfield, Connecticut.

127. A lovely early chimney breast. The entire woodwork from floor to ceiling is called the mantel (it "mantled" or hid the masonry behind it); the shelf, if it has one, is the mantel-shelf. A well-defined roll-bolection molding frames both the firebox and the overmantel panel. Square hearth bricks form a narrow hearth. The shape of the firebox (tall and rather narrow) points to the 17th or very early 18th century; the paneling is of later date.

128. Simple tombstone paneling as found in a "raw" (unrestored) house. Privately owned; Preston, Connecticut.

TOMBSTONE
PANEL

129. Sophisticated double-arched tombstone paneling like this is infrequently found in Connecticut but is more commonplace in Rhode Island houses. Compare this to the simple paneling of the Preston house (fig. 128); here we find paneling not only on the wall but also on the summer-beam soffit. There are fluted keystones between panels, double dentil moldings above the panels and an ogee "crown" molding as a plaster "stop." The fireplace has been rebuilt, at which time a Greek Revival (c. 1840) mantel shelf was superimposed over the paneling, and the fireplace lintel, which was probably stone, was replaced by a "soldier" course of brick supported by iron. Originally the HL hinges on the lovely three-panel door would have been painted the same color as the rest of the woodwork, which I believe to have been mustard.

Fig. 129a. Detail of the summer-beam casing, keystones, and dentil moldings seen in figure 129. After 1760.

129a

DENTIL MOLDING

130. Paneling came in a multitude of patterns, giving the builder an opportunity to express his creativeness. Here is an interesting arrangement in a full fireplace wall of a c. 1740 Connecticut saltbox. It was the custom to paint the mop board a dark color in the earlier houses. The corner post casings at the floor and lower door rail would also be dark painted.

CHAPTER 3

RESTORATION PROCEDURES
AND TECHNIQUES

Beginning the restoration of an antique house—especially one that has been damaged by fire, been neglected, or has changed a great deal—is similar to the procedure employed by a dentist in preparing a tooth for an inlay or filling. The very first step is to remove all late work, or debris, and to "open up" the house so that it can be thoroughly inspected. This usually takes three or four days for four men to accomplish. If closets have been added where there were none before, they must be ripped out; the same with partitions. Almost without exception new flooring has been put on top of the old, especially on the first floor, where dampness from a dirt cellar plus heavier traffic has made the replacement necessary.

Before removing new flooring on the first floor, it is wise to go into the cellar and check the cellar ceiling (which is the underflooring of the first-floor flooring); it can often be determined from here if the original flooring remains under the new on the first floor or if it was completely replaced. If it has been replaced, the new floor should not be removed until a later time, as it serves as a strong platform on which to work. On the second floor a small section of new flooring can be removed in any room to reveal the old.

Before it is discarded, all debris should be examined for evidence of old work. Pieces of old trim or paneling were sometimes used to fill out walls and ceilings, or as backing material or bracing. Any wood, however small, with a bead or feathered edge should be set aside with a notation made to label its original location. This piece may be a clue to the color or construction of a wall in another part of the house. Old nails should be saved, especially lath nails if they are blacksmith-forged, as

these will have a practical use later in the installation of hardware.

Windows of a date much later than the house should be left in place, of course, to protect the inside of the structure from the elements until replacements have been procured. Interior walls that are obviously new should be removed unless they form the partitions of rooms that are to be part of the finished structure, such as a new bath or kitchen. The entire interior should be swept clean.

Attics and cellars should be cleaned out as well as the main living areas. Here quite frequently one will find parts of the house that were removed. Doors, windows, and trim of all kinds frequently find their way to the attic. I have noticed that batten doors are often used in the basement to make a walkway in the dirt floor and that raised-panel doors also find their way to the attic, where they become shelves. Fireplace cranes and bake oven doors were sometimes saved, perhaps for sentimental reasons, and are stored in either the attic or the cellar.

EXAMINATION: GETTING TO KNOW THE HOUSE

Once the house has been "opened up," a methodical examination, both interior and exterior, is made. Most houses will tell you what they were originally no matter how much change may appear on the surface.

The following checklist, which is by no means complete, may serve to point out the places to examine for clues to the age and condition of the house. By making a detailed examination of the house, one can ascertain the

131. Step number 1: remove the debris and "new work."

132. Examine all materials removed for evidence of age.

extent of the alterations made to it over the years, the amount of original house still remaining, etc. A list of old material to replace missing parts can then be compiled, and the search for these materials can begin at once so they will be on hand when required.

There are two areas that must be covered by this examination: what the house was originally—its original type (it may have been changed), age, and features; and the condition of the component parts.

A single examination will not be enough. It will be necessary to go over the house time after time, analyzing and searching for clues to the early construction, but this quest for answers and the discoveries that are made can be the most exciting phase of restoration. I do not think there is a thrill in house restoration comparable to the one experienced in discovering a hidden wall of paneling behind new plaster or finding a huge wood lintel and early fireplace behind a much later one. Examine the rooms one at a time, slowly and carefully. Carry a flashlight, a pad and pencil, and a rule.

CHECKLIST FOR THE INTERIOR OF THE HOUSE AND ROOM-BY-ROOM EXAMINATION

Give the rooms of the house names: old kitchen, buttery, parlor, parlor chamber, etc.

Flooring

Of what wood is the floor made? Flooring in old houses was of oak, chestnut, or pine. Generally the working areas of the house—that is, the old kitchen, stair passage, and buttery—would almost certainly have been floored originally in oak or oak and chestnut. The dressier rooms—especially the front rooms, such as the parlor or sitting room and the best chamber—were sometimes done in pine.

What is the width of the flooring? Generally speaking, the older the house the wider the original flooring boards. Up to 1800 most flooring was a minimum of ten inches in width, with an average width of twelve to sixteen inches. Some early flooring reached a width of twenty inches or better. After 1800 eight-inch floors are found.

How long are the floorboards? It was customary to floor a room with boards that ran in one piece from wall to wall across the room. However, in areas such as long rooms or long halls it was necessary to piece the flooring, or rather to floor the room in sections. The flooring of each room should be examined with particular attention paid to any areas that seem to have been replaced. Do the floors go under the mop board? Are there any sections of shorter boards (about three feet wide by about eight feet long) that might have been installed to cover a former stairwell? If such a place is found, check the flooring in the area directly above and below. Does the same replaced flooring appear in the cellar ceiling and in the attic floor? To conserve space, stairs always ran one above the other.

What kind of nails hold the flooring in place? The attic flooring was the least likely to have been changed over the years; therefore the nails in the attic floors may be a good clue to the age of the house. Are these square-head cut nails? Rose-head forged? L-shaped forged? Remove one or two so that they can be examined for their taper and construction. Have any of the floors been completely renailed with modern nails? Is there a double set of nails of different types?

What is the condition of the floor? Are any of the boards buckled across their width? This would indicate that at some time they were wet. Are the spaces between boards excessive? Some owners insist on their floors being tight; others don't object to wide spaces between boards.

Examine the attic flooring. Do some of the attic floors appear to be good enough to be used as replacements on the lower floors?

Is the color of the floor right, or has it been sanded too much? Does it have a high polish, or has it been painted? The finish of old flooring is another one of those features that is one of preference. A highly polished floor is easier to maintain and if the color is pleasing may be just what you want. On the other hand, a painted floor that has been taken down to bare wood and then waxed may have the "look" you would expect of a floor two hundred years old.

Are the floors of adjacent rooms the same height? Very often new flooring has been nailed over the old. If this has been done in any of the first-floor rooms, a trip to the cellar can tell you if the old floors are still under the new flooring. On the second floor you will have to remove a strip of the new flooring to discover the old floor, if it is there.

Timbers

Examine the cellar timbers. In going down the cellar stairs look at the sill or girt falling within the width of the stairs. Is there an empty notch? If there is, it indicates that the cellar stairs were not originally in this location, since there would have been a floor joist in that notch. This situation occurs frequently. If such an empty notch is found, check the attic stairs as well for a notch on the plate. Is the attic stair directly above the cellar stair? The plan may have been altered, necessitating the moving of the stairs. If one of these stairs has the empty notch and the other doesn't and one is not in line with the other, the one with the empty notch may have been moved from a location in line with the other.

Examine sills, girts, and joists for soundness. Jump up and down in the center of the rooms on the first floor. Do the floors "bounce"? If so, the underpinnings will require reinforcement, a relatively easy task, as all the timbers are exposed to view. Are there wooden posts in direct contact with the dirt floor? Are the bottoms eaten out? Can you find termite channels? Is there bark on any of the cellar timbers? Is there evidence of powder-post beetles under the bark?

Examination of the attic structure. Aside from age cracks (shrinkage) running parallel to the grain, are there cracks running across the grain in the rafters? Is the wood soft at these cracks (dry rot)? Do the rafters sag in the middle or are they bowed? At the deepest part of the bow, is there a space of an inch or more between the top of the rafter and the roof boards? Some bracing may be required if this condition exists. Are there water stains on the rafters? This would indicate a roof leak at some time.

Check the rafters where they meet at the ridge. Are they pegged together? Are they numbered with Roman numerals? Check the numbers of each rafter starting at one end of the house. Are they consecutive? If, for example, they read I, II, III, IIII, V, II, I, the part of the house under rafters II and I may have been added either as new "old" construction, or a piece of another old house may have been added. In any case it would lead one to suspect a change in the size of the house. Is there evidence of a change in construction? Further investigation may reveal double sills in the basement and double plates under the attic floor at the point of the suspected addition.

Are there collar beams (wind braces) between rafters? Are they numbered on one end to correspond with the rafter numbers? Have any been removed, as evidenced by empty notches halfway up on the rafters? These would show the possible location of a loom that was used in the attic. Or perhaps the brace was removed to make headroom for a new attic stair location.

Check the rafters around the chimney stack. Are they charred or smoke-darkened? Are there any other darkened rafters not near the chimney smoke? Perhaps the chimney was rebuilt in a new location.

Summer Beams and Interior Timbers

The interior timbers of the house—that is, those not in either attic or cellar—are more difficult to examine because in most instances they have been cased. However,

there are certain signs that may lead to suspicion of internal rot that may need correcting.

If timbers of any rooms are exposed, check them for dry rot, termite and beetle damage. Do the ends of the summer beams or girts sag? Perhaps they have slipped out of their notches. If cased, do the summer beams or girts bow in the middle? Has the casing split open?

Most of these conditions are minor, and unless the condition is a progressive one and not just one of normal settlement, it requires no action to correct. A pulling away of the end of a summer beam from an end girt may point to a water leak through the clapboards over a nearby window. This condition would require remedial action in the form of angle irons lagged to summer beam and girt.

Doors and Interior Hardware

Are the doors original? Doors were sometimes shifted from room to room within a house as alterations were made. The first step within each room is to examine the doors in that room for type. Are they all the same? Do they all have the same kind of hardware? Have any of the edges of the doors been cut down (compare the size of top and bottom rails and stiles); or has a piece been added to make the door wider or longer? If the door being examined is of the batten type, look closely at the nailheads on the battens. Are they rose-headed?

What kind of latches are on the door? Latches gave out more frequently than hinges, and doors are often found with early hinges and late latches. If a door is butt-hinged, remove one of the screws. Is the tip blunt or pointed?

Scratch a small patch of paint from each side of the door. What color is it? Remove a patch of paint from the doorjamb or trim. Does the first coat of paint on the door match that on its jamb? If not, the door may have come from somewhere else in the house. The first coat of paint may tell you the room from which it came.

Where bean latches, HL hinges, or small strap hinges are found, are there leather patches under the nailheads? If the leather is still there, is it on both the door and the trim? Or is it just on the door? If it is on both parts of the hinge, it is likely that the door has always hung in this place.

Windows

Are the windows correct for the house? Windows, like doors, were changed as time went on. Without the advantage of storm windows, the early window—which, after all, is a moving part of the house—suffered from use as well as exposure to the weather. The desire

133. A section of sill and sheathing eaten through by termites. This repair was a simple and inexpensive one.

134. One must play Sherlock Holmes. What does this picture tell us? As we know that the windowsill height was always the same as chair-rail height, neither of these windows was lengthened; however, noting the larger panes in the sash, it becomes obvious that the window on the left has been made wider. The heaviness of the gunstock post in the corner shows this to be a second-story room. The summer beam and front and end girts being exposed below the plaster of the ceiling suggest a date no later than c. 1760.

135

136

135. Compare this to the previous photograph. One can see at a glance that this window in the same house has been lenghtened by cutting into the raised-panel dado. What is not quite so obvious is that the window was widened as well. This was ascertained by an examination of the other windows.

136. Here the chair rail was added to the original feather-edged boarded wall (this is the same house we saw in figure 134). As things come to light, the date gets earlier (no later than c. 1740). The chair rail was added at the time the raised-panel dado was installed (1760-1780); the window was enlarged still later; and the light fixture is from the 1930s.

for more light led to a change of window types. Sometimes only new sash were installed, but frequently both the sash and their frames were updated.

Check the windows for type. Are they 12/12, 8/12/, etc.? Next measure the size of the panes. Are they six inches wide by eight inches high? Seven by nine inches? Larger? Are the muntins one inch or better in width? Wider is generally older. Is the glass set almost on the same plane as the outside of the muntins, or are the muntins deep, with the glass recessed? Again, the flatter, the older is the rule. Is the form of molding of both muntin and rail and stiles a simple arched molding, or is it fluted (striated)? Is any of the glass wavy? Is it slightly tinted rose or bluish or purple? Are there swirls?

Now examine the window frame on the inside and the trim surrounding it. Does only the bottom sash move? If both move, there is little doubt that the windows and frames are not eighteenth century. Is the top sash held in place by a rabbet in the frame? Is the trim beaded on the edges?

Is the sill at the same height as the chair rail? In antique houses the chair rail is made in one piece with the window sills and is always at the same height above the floor.

Are the window *stops*—the thin pieces that hold the sash from falling into the room—beaded on their inside corner? Is it possible to remove one of these stops (usually the left one) by pulling sideways?

Are the windows the same type as those in the attic, that is, in the conformation of the moldings, the size of glass, etc.? Attic windows were usually left alone when all the other windows in the house were changed. They are usually smaller in size—nine over six, for example—than the lower floor windows.

And lastly, are the windows tight up against the ceiling of the upstairs rooms in the front of the house?

Interior Trim

Does the chair rail go completely around the room? In those rooms where there is a chair rail, it usually runs along at least three walls of the room, assuming that the fireplace wall was fully paneled. If it is missing on any wall, examine the corner-post casing carefully, at chair rail height, for telltale marks of a previous chair rail. Does the plaster on a wall indicate a patch where a chair rail might have been? Most formal rooms had chair rails on the first floor.

At and near the windows, is there evidence on top of the chair rail of there having once been sliding shutters? Sometimes there is a small half-round molding on top of the chair rail; at other times grooves were rabbeted into the chair rail to take the shutters. These shutters appear mostly in the north and east rooms of the house and are erroneously called *Indian shutters*. Check at the same time the molding, if any, at the ceiling over the windows for evidence of a top shutter track.

Are the trim members beaded? As described in the chapter on construction, the bead was a major embellishment of early trim. Almost without exception all casings within a room had beaded corners. Thus, if three corner posts, for example, are beaded and one is not, it is possible the odd corner post was recased at a later time. If the summer-beam casing is created of three plain boards without beads, it was almost surely changed at some time. The reason for the change may be more difficult to ascertain. Was the room replastered? Was the summer beam repaired, necessitating the removal of the original casing? Were the windows replaced and the new windows recased in the manner of later times, without beading?

Are there places on any of the walls where the mop board shows a short section (about three feet in length) with vertical cuts on either side, as though there may once have been a doorway here? Standing back from the wall, examine the plaster. Does there seem to be the outline of a doorway in the plaster? Check the mop board in the room on the other side, if there is one. Is there a similar pair of cuts in the mop board in the same spot? Removal of a small piece of the plaster may reveal a door buried in the wall.

In the old kitchen one would expect to find wooden walls, or at least wood wainscot from the windowsills down to the floor. As a rule of thumb, in the case of full walls of sheathing, the direction of the boards is horizontal on the outside walls of the house and vertical on the inside walls. In the case of wainscot, these boards run horizontally around the room. In the earliest houses wooden walls might be made up of beaded and feathered boards (although some houses as late as the Revolution reveal the use of feather-edged boarding); in later houses beaded boards (without the feather) were used. Occasionally, in buttery, woodshed, milk and flour rooms, etc., the exterior walls were made of square-edged boards set horizontally. In order to determine the existence or nonexistence of boarded walls behind the plaster of a wall—for example, in the old kitchen—you must remove a bit of plaster as well as at least one piece of lath. This should be done below windowsill height, in the area of any wainscot that may be hiding behind the plaster.

In all rooms with fireplaces, examine the walls directly above the fireplace if there is no paneling showing. Work carefully, as the paneling, if it exists, may be just below

137. The beaded corner-post casing boards are probably original.

138. This old kitchen fireplace and bake oven (behind the door) were completely out of sight, buried behind a plaster wall. The two raised panels were once badly damaged by fire. This fireplace was later restored by the author to its original condition. Lisbon, Connecticut; built by John Palmer, 1790.

139. Frequently, paneling was covered by wallpaper as shown here, or by lath and plaster or by beaverboard or sheetrock. In probing one must work carefully. Note the stovepipe hole underneath the panel stile.

140. Marble mantelshelf installed over 18th-century raised-field paneling. Changes like this were frequently made in the 19th century. Sometimes the entire early wall would be demolished; at other times the change was minimal. Butler-McCook house, Hartford, Connecticut. Owned by the Antiquarian and Landmarks Society, Inc., Hartford.

the surface of the plaster and thin lath. No need to gouge it with a sharp tool. If paneling is found, examine it for type. Is it plain boarding, feathered, or beaded? Is it raised-field paneling? If so, what kind of bead does it have? Is it simple single-arch (early) or fluted (later) beading? Does the paneling match the panels on the doors in the room? Get down to the first coat of paint on a small patch and compare it with the color of the doors. Again, this will tell something about the doors rather than about the paneling, since the chances are greater that the doors were moved than that the paneling was moved.

Look at the mantel shelves. Are they of the period of the house? Do any of the mantel shelves go over the bottom edge of a raised panel, covering the feathered edge? This is a clear sign that the top shelf board or perhaps the entire mantel was added later. Do the insides of the two legs of the mantel line up with the outside edges of the hearth? Within three or four inches? Many, many houses have had their fireplaces made smaller. It is not uncommon to find two and sometimes even three fireplaces, one within the other. When the earliest fireplace was made smaller, the wood surrounding it—that is, the mantelpiece—was replaced or, more often, filled in to fit the proportions of the firebox opening. At the same time a mantel shelf was added to those fireplaces not having them. A close examination of the wood surround may give clues to the existence of earlier fireplaces.

Are there any panels in the room of a different type from the rest in the same room? For example, are one or more panels flat in a wall of raised panels? If so, they were at one time replaced. Check the raised-panel dado at the windows. Are the windowsills below the top of the dado chair-rail molding? This indicates an elongation of the windows. The top of the dado would establish the height of the windowsills at the time the dado was installed.

Look in the corners of the room (especially the corners of the wall opposite the fireplace wall) for the telltale line made by a corner cupboard (removed) on the chair rail, the crown molding, the flooring, and the plaster walls and ceiling. Unless the area was carefully sanded and repainted, there will be some sign, however slight, of the outline of the former corner cupboard.

Stairs

Are the stairs original and in their original position? Stairs in antique houses were frequently shifted and added as the need arose. Many 1½-story houses, the so-called cape houses, had only one stair, and that was in the rear of the house off the old kitchen. Later on, with the addition of a dormer in the front of the house, front stairs were added between the chimney stack and the front door.

Often, too, the stairs to the cellar in early one-room-deep houses were later shifted to the rear, and a closet was installed underneath the front stairs leading from the first floor to the second. Because stairwells take up considerable space within a house (a space about four feet wide by thirteen feet long), the most economical way to build them is to place them one over the other.

Examine the undersides of the treads and risers (this can be done in a closet). Are the risers and treads nailed together with square-cut nails or rose-head blacksmith-forged nails? Are the strings nailed to the wall with old or new nails? Still examining from the underside, do you find that the wood of the treads appears to be new wood? Of the risers?

Now, looking at the stairs from the finished side, are the balusters, newel-post, and handrail of the period of the house? Are the stairs located where you would naturally expect to find them in a house of this type? Is the handrail doweled into the newel-post? Are the balusters turned or square-sawed? Is the turning strong and bold, or is it slim and graceful? Are there no balusters at all, with no evidence of their ever having existed? Is there raised paneling on the face of the stairs? Check the form of the bead. Are there half balusters against the newel-post? Is there a closet under the stairs? Is the door paneled? Does its paneling match the rest of the stair paneling? Is the exterior of the open string scrolled or scalloped or decoratively treated? Is this decoration a half inch thick or better (early), or is it thin (later eighteenth or nineteenth century)?

Masonry

The cellar walls, both exterior and interior, should be examined under good light. Look for straight seams in the stonework, that is, crude places that appear to have been added where the stones of one part of the wall don't bond with the stone wall next to them. Is water entering the cellar through the walls? The most common place for such a condition to exist is where an ell has been added to a house at a later date and a new foundation extended from the existing one.

Check the walls for evidence of water running between the stone, and examine the dirt floor for erosion created by running water. Check the walls for niches and for severe leaning. Check the cellar floor for hearthstones that may have been removed from fireplaces (especially the large hearthstone of the old kitchen) and dropped into the cellar. Have the spaces between stones ever been pointed up with mortar? This would have been done to prevent water or air seepage.

141

142

141. A handsome staircase with bold paneling and strong, gracefully turned balusters (c. 1700–1720). "Winders" are outlawed by most building codes today but were the rule in front stairs of the 17th and early 18th centuries (through the added-lean-to-plan house). One must keep a sharp eye for heating ducts such as the one cut into the mop board and panel at the floor. Early house, Milford, Connecticut (since moved).

142. Delicate scrollwork with "whale's tail" on the stringpiece of this 1761 center-hall-plan farmhouse. Note the dowel protruding where the handrail meets the newel-post. The balusters are turned cherry wood; the stringer, a structural board not visible from this side, is made of chestnut. All but the balusters, treads, and risers were painted green; those were left natural.

143. The heavy handrail and turned balusters of an early stair with its original green paint still on it. The photograph was taken at the second-story front "passage," the correct location for the stair in a house of this period, c. 1700–1720.

143

144. What a story this tells! The small section of wall showing on the left dates no later than 1740. Over this has been added a chair rail, c. 1776. The hearthstone is much longer than the firebox itself, which can only mean that the fireplace was made smaller (perhaps at the same time the raised-panel dado, chair rail, and chimney breast were added, c. 1776). The fireplace lintel was cut and two slots made in the hearthstone to accept a Franklin stove at a still later date. The door bears a "Bennington" knob but is hung on 18th-century HL hinges. A 20th-century light fixture hangs from the summer beam. The flooring is original, although at some time the owner painted around a carpet.

144a. Detail of figure 144 showing the obvious narrowing of the firebox opening, a very frequent occurrence when wood, coal, or kerosine stoves replaced fireplaces for heating. No one would carry a stone larger than he required to a second-story room, when a stone such as this could be cut on the ground in twenty minutes.

Fireplaces often tell us a great deal about the house and perhaps even about the former owners. For example, if there are two sets of crane pintles, one on the right side and the other on the left of the kitchen fireplace, they would indicate that at one time a lady of the house was left-handed, since a crane swung from the right makes stirring or lifting a pot easier with the left hand.

First, examine the hearth. Is it brick or stone? Does it extend beyond the face of the fireplace itself (not the opening, but the reveal of brick or stone that form the sides of the opening)? Is the firebox of the same material as the hearth?

If there is wood covering the lintel so that it is not visible from the front, examine it carefully from inside. Is it made of wood, stone, or iron? Or is it a brick arch? Are the sides of the fireplace of the same material as the back? Are the side walls of the firebox of one piece, or are they made up of many smaller cut stones. Are the bricks at the corners of the firebox ("corner brick") made at the angle formed by the face and the side, or are they rectangular brick set at an angle?

Is there a damper in the fireplace? If not, look up the chimney. Can you see light of day? Do the sides appear to be in good condition? Can you stand up inside the large kitchen fireplace? Using your flashlight, can you see any other flues behind the present one? Is there an iron bar running across the throat of the flue? Are there any terra-cotta flues running from rear to front across the throat of the flue, indicating former stovepipes that exhausted into the main flue?

Is the bake oven in the old kitchen on the side or in the rear of the fireplace? An oven in the rear will often, although not always, indicate a date prior to 1750. Is the bake oven flue open or closed (in fireplaces with the bake oven in the front only, as rear bake ovens utilize the main flue and have no flues of their own)? Is the bake oven door in place? Is it of iron? Wood?

In the rear of the old kitchen fireplace is there a small hole about four inches high by eight inches wide? If not, is there a stone or are there two or three bricks that appear to be about the size to have been used to fill in such a hole? This is a draft hole leading to a large air chamber in the stack in the basement.

In the attic, is there a smoke chamber built against the chimney stack? Has it pulled away from the stack at all? Is the door to it wood or metal? Are the hinges leather? Metal? Is the hole entering the chimney open, or has it been sealed (for safety)?

Is the chimney top of stone? Brick? Has it been narrowed as it goes out the roof? Are the joints between the stone, brick, clay? Lime mortar? Cement mortar?

Look at the chimney from within the attic. Does most of the stack come out of the roof in front of (toward the front of the house) or behind the ridge? Is there evidence of a drip course at some point in the front of the stack *within* the attic? Look at the stack from both sides. Is there a diagonal line or a pair of diagonal lines indicating a former roofline? Does the stack curve as it rises from the attic floor? Does the back gradually slope toward the front? Is the front straight? Does the front slope toward the rear?

Near the exit of the chimney, or chimneys, through the roof is there any indication of water entering? Are some of the bricks shaled away? Are there signs of pitch seeping between stones or brick? If there is a hatchway through the roof, you can examine the outside of the stack by standing on the stairs or on a ladder inside the attic. Is there flashing? Of lead? Is there a drip course? Has the chimney been added onto or capped?

It is possible to look down the chimney itself with a flashlight. I cannot emphasize caution enough: if you are squeamish about heights, it would be better to send someone up who is not squeamish, or not to examine the chimney from above. It is helpful, but not necessary. The main purpose of this examination is to check the number and types of flues. If the fireplaces are of brick, the flues within the stack will be divided into brick flues. If the stack is of stone, the flues will be formed by stones set vertically within the throat of the stack. These flues can be counted from above. One or more fireplace flues will sometimes join and continue as a single flue from the attic floor or higher. If your house has three fireplaces, for example, and you count five flues, you no doubt have two concealed fireplaces—a most exciting discovery.

Are any of your first-floor fireplaces very shallow? In the old kitchen fireplace, are the pintles for a crane set very close to the rear wall of the firebox? This would indicate a false back with an earlier, deeper back hidden behind it.

CHECKLIST FOR THE EXTERIOR OF THE HOUSE

The checklist has so far covered the inside examination of the house only. The exterior of the house deserves as thorough a search for clues to its originality and its condition.

The Outside

What material covers the house? Modern asbestos shingles? Wood shingles or clapboards? Most early houses were clapboarded, although wood shingles were sometimes preferred in areas near salt water. If the house

145. This chimney was rebuilt using some "soft" brick originally intended for inside work. After the first winter's exposure to freezing rain, it looked like this. After the second winter, it required surgery.

145

146

146. During the stripping of this house, no less than four exterior layers were found with the original clapboards still in place.

147. The outline of a former window is evident here (see arrows). One quickly develops an eye for changes made over the years. The prerestoration inspection not only tells you what requires doing but can be most interesting, as surprise after surprise comes to light.

147

is clapboarded, these clapboards will, for the most part, not be the original ones. However, very often a few of the original clapboards are still in place. They can be identified both by the nails used to fasten them to the house and by the way in which they are spliced where they butt each other on a long run.

Are the clapboards graduated in the front wall of the house? If so, these are likely to be original. Look particularly at the covering on the side away from the prevailing wind. One side of a house, the side facing the prevailing winds, takes more abuse from the weather than do the others. It is on this side that the paint fades and wears off most quickly.

Look at the clapboards under porches and especially in the attic of any lean-to that may have been added to the house, if it is possible to gain access to this area. Scrape a little paint from the clapboards on the sheltered side of the house. It is often possible to arrive at the original color of the house.

Is there a wide water table at the bottom of the clapboards? Are the corner boards beaded? How about the verge-(rake) boards? Is the crown molding under the cornice of the early type? Is it very wide? Narrow? Are the windows set up tight against the soffit, or is there a wide (over eight inches) fascia or bargeboard running across the face of the house?

Look at the window frames. Are there dowels in the sill and head where the stiles are mortised into them? Do the frames extend out from the clapboarding (are they heavy) or are they even with the face of the boarding?

Are there any places around the outside of the house where the clapboards seem to have covered a doorway or a window? Good indications of such a cover are a panel of clapboards in the shape of a door or window or in a difference in nails.

Check the stones of the foundation. Are they granite, brownstone? Are they over two feet long? Are they evenly cut and dressed? Are they the same all around the house? Only in front? Are there any places that seem to have been repaired or changed? Perhaps there was a former doorstep or a cellarway there.

Are there any stones, such as stepstones outside the house, that may have been fireplace lintels or hearthstones? Is there a well stone lying around (this is a huge stone with a large round hole in it) or a leaching stone (a stone with a groove cut in its surface describing a complete circle, with a small connecting groove leading to the edge)? Although these are not parts of the house, they are of interest and are often overlooked when they are used as steps or stepping-stones. Examine the stone walls, if any, near the house for more stones from the house.

Is the chimney capped? It wasn't originally. Look at the size of the chimney in the front elevation. If it is of brick, count the number of bricks across the front. Are there fewer than five? Perhaps the chimney has been rebuilt from the roof up. Is there a drip course? Is there modern lead flashing? What is the material of the roof? Wood shingles? Is the roof in good condition? Examine the cornices. At the corners of the house, have they been eaten away by squirrels or rot? If so, they must be repaired.

Do the front door and entrance appear to be of the period of the house? The side or rear doors? Is the front door paneled? How many panels? When viewed edgewise, are the exterior doors made up of two doors nailed together in the eighteenth-century manner? Are they reproductions? Is the hardware original to the exterior doors? Are there strap hinges? HL hinges? Butt hinges? Are the doors weather-stripped? If so, they have been rehung, of course, and may not be original. What kind of locks and fasteners are on the exterior doors?

Are the window frames beaded on their inner edges? Is the upper sash permanently fixed in a rabbet in the frame? Does only the lower sash open? Examine the placement of the glass in the muntins. Is the plane of the glass very close to the outside surface of the muntins, or are they deep-set? How is the putty? Do some of the panes require reputtying? Are any of the frames rotted? You can best examine the glass from the inside against the light to see if it is old.

Does the land directly around the house slope away from the foundation, or does it lead water toward the house?

The location of a well (covered over) in the basement of part of the house shows that that part was a later addition, as most wells were located to the rear of the house, close to the kitchen.

Letting Contracts

Having familiarized yourself with your house from the cellar floor to the top of the roof, noting as many details of construction and condition as possible, you are ready to begin the operation of restoration. The authenticity of your restoration will be a matter of your choice: whether you want an "exact" duplicate of the original or just a "feeling" of the old place, the procedure will be the same.

It is important to set stages of work for yourself. Some jobs can be done only in the warm-weather months and must take priority if winter is approaching. You will no doubt have for your first plateau getting the house to a point where it is livable. This means structural

148. A completely untouched gem shown before restoration. It never had plumbing, heat, or electricity. Hampton, Connecticut, c. 1740.

149. The same house after the outside has been stabilized. Originially the house was painted another color, probably red; the white coat is a first or preservation coat.

soundness, a kitchen, a bath, electric service and wiring, and heat. Some aspects of the work, such as rebuilding fireplaces, ripping out new floors, and lathing and plastering, can disrupt the entire house and may be worth doing before you move in. It is possible, however, to isolate rooms in which work is going on from the rest of the house by closing off the doors with a polyethylene barrier; this will keep the dust and dirt from the other rooms.

In restoring their house, most people will contract for at least some of the work to be done by others. Building codes generally require a licensed contractor to make the mechanical installations. Most buildings are constructed under the supervision of a job superintendent who, in home construction, is the carpenter contractor or restorer. Without an overseer to coordinate the trades, seeing the job in its entirety, confusion would reign, as each contractor is concerned only with his own aspect of the work. Plumbers, for example, are noted for cutting into structural members to make room for their pipes, and electricians not familiar with restoration, may not hesitate to cut into a fine wall of paneling to install their convenience outlets. Someone must prevent this kind of thing from happening. Once they get into it, most contractors, enjoy the "old" work and will ask before they cut.

A preliminary discussion in which the importance of respecting the old features of the house is emphasized can often make the difference between a good restoration and a butchered job. In each area there are contractors and workmen who have done this kind of work before; one can find their names by inquiring at local museums and historical societies or from owners of other restored houses.

I cannot stress strongly enough the importance of dealing with reputable, honest contractors. The very nature of this work lends itself to misunderstandings. References should be asked for and checked on. Anyone who objects to giving a reference should be looked on with suspicion.

There are two kinds of work performed in the restoration of antique houses: that which can be done under a written contract at a set price, and that which must be on a *cost-plus* basis. For example, the mechanical work— that is, the heat, electric, plumbing, etc.—can be accurately estimated beforehand and firm prices can be given. The installation of a wood roof, clapboarding the exterior walls, or plastering a room can also be contracted for at a price. The cost of the replacement of sills, the rebuilding of a fireplace, or the installation of paneling, on the other hand, cannot be ascertained accurately beforehand, since one cannot know the

extent of the work until the hidden areas are opened up. The best one can do is to make an "educated" guess. Were the contractor to give a "firm" price on this work, he would, for his own protection, be obliged to include a sizable safety margin.

One can estimate beforehand the cost of new work, such as the addition of a new kitchen lean-to or an ell to a house, by multiplying the floor area by the cost factor for new construction. Thus an addition 15 feet wide by 15 feet long and one story high would be 225 square feet. At a cost factor of $50 per square foot, the rough cost estimate would be $11,250 for the work. This estimate would be modified either upward or downward as the work departed from standard new house construction. If there is to be no basement, an allowance downward must be made; if old paneling is to be put in the ell, then the estimate will go up. The actual true figure will not be arrived at until a solid bid for the work is obtained based on a plan or sketch and specifications.

The surest way of knowing that a price is "right" for contract work is to get three or more bids on it. The yellow pages of your telephone book can supply you with names. You must supply the specifications for your bidders. Do you want sheetrock walls or plaster? Do you want circulating warm-air heat or electric heat, etc.? Each bidder must be given the same specifications if the bids are to mean anything. Each bid should be accompanied with a detailed list of what the contractor intends to do. Is he supplying both material and labor?

When all the bids are in for each trade, they are compared. If you find that one heating contractor, for example, will supply a boiler with an output BTU capacity of 100,000, this must be measured against the capacities of the other boilers. Your bidders can make excellent suggestions about saving money or getting a better job; these suggestions are worth considering. As the bids come in, a new, revised estimate of costs will take shape.

No contractor should be allowed to begin work on your house until he has supplied you with certificates showing that he carries both public liability and workmen's compensation insurance. If he does not carry workmen's compensation insurance, then you must, since anyone injured while working on your job will no doubt sue both you and the contractor. In most states the law requires this insurance to be carried by each employer, but some of the smaller employers take a chance and ignore this requirement in order to save money; thus they may be able to underbid their insurance-carrying competitors. If you carry workmen's compensation insurance yourself, you will be given credit by your own company for each certificate you get from your contractors. This is the safest procedure, and you may only have a small minimum premium to pay.

You will be adding to the value of your house as work progresses day by day. Do not forget, therefore, to increase periodically the amount for which you have your house insured against fire and extended perils.

Before work begins, too, it will be necessary to get a building permit; this can be obtained in your name by your restorer. Your building inspector will visit the job from time to time to see that the work conforms to the building code and that safety standards are being maintained. The building inspector can be your best assurance that you are getting sound work from your contractors. Most building inspectors will bend over backward to help you in your restoration. Building codes give the building inspector leeway in the interpretation of the code. If you approach him in the spirit of enlisting his aid, almost any building inspector will cooperate in overcoming some of the problems that crop up only in the restoration of antique houses.

If you have had no previous experience in construction, the man on whom you will lean most heavily will be your restorer, or carpenter. He will be as concerned as you are that the work turns out well, for like the pitcher in baseball, he will be credited with a good job, and he will also be blamed for a poor one even though his own aspect of the work was excellent.

It is usual to open an account in your name at a local lumberyard if your carpenter is supplying labor only. It is important that this merchant be told who may charge to your account. A limit should be set; charging beyond this limit must be done only with your authorization. This will keep you in control, and you will know where you are going financially.

Having this account is necessary unless you are going to be on the job all the time. It is most costly to have work stop for want of a few nails or pieces of wood.

Finally, the local and state police should be notified that work is going on at your house. Their patrols will check the site both day and night and may keep vandalism and theft to a minimum.

Masonry Repair

The first step in restoring a house, just as in building a new house, begins with the foundation. You have examined the cellar walls both inside and out. Those places in the foundation that are in imminent danger of caving in (if indeed, such places exist) must be rebuilt first. (If you are going to do other masonry restoration in the house, such as installing dampers in fireplaces, rebuilding a missing chimney stack, opening up fireplaces, or rebuilding the chimney in the attic or through the roof, it is best and most economical to have all the masonry repair done by the same mason.)

A small section of stone wall is removed at a time. The sill over the portion removed (if rotted) may require support until the wall underneath it can be reconstructed. In the seventeenth and eighteenth centuries, concrete footings underneath walls were unknown. In rebuilding the fallen or defective wall, it is wise to dig down and pour a concrete footing to support the rebuilt wall for all time. Most antique foundations were built *dry-wall*, that is, without mortar between the stones. You will want your mason to rebuild using mortar. He can rake the joints between stones so that to the eye the wall will appear just as it did before: dry or with stones set in clay. Rebuilding the cellar walls gives you the opportunity to add a cellar window or two for added light and ventilation.

In a situation where there is air or water seepage through the cellar's stone foundation, all that is required is "pointing up" with mortar between the stones. If you are doing the job yourself, it is easier to purchase a ready-mixed mortar from your local lumberyard. All you need is to add water, mix, and go to work.

First, remove as much of the old clay or dirt from between the stones as possible. Do a small section at a time. Then, using a small trowel and a jointing tool or stick, force the mortar between the joints until you are satisfied that you have filled up the space between the stones. All but those stones above the level of the ground on the outside of the house will be done from the inside alone. The one or two courses of stone showing above the ground on the outside of the house must be done both from the inside and from the outside. Only in a most extreme case will you find it necessary to dig down along the outside of the foundation wall to point up between stones from the outside. A proper sloping of the soil away from the foundation wall on the outside with a minimum pitch of one-quarter inch to each foot will, in most cases, prevent water seepage.

Occasionally a basement is found in which water comes up from below or seeps in in such quantity that a mere pointing will not suffice. Houses built on ledges frequently have this problem. A dry well dug in the cellar floor with a sump pump is the least costly remedy. Your local plumber will be well acquainted with this problem and can install the pump for you, at a firm price. Again, it is wise to get two or three estimates before proceeding.

Many an antique house has had its chimney entirely removed sometime during its long life. Although the replacement of an entire stack is costly, it affords certain advantages. There is no question, of course, that a new stack will be completely firesafe. There will be terra-

150. Rebuilding a section of cellar wall. The rough stones will all be below ground level after backfilling.

150

151. The finished wall partially backfilled. The two window frames on the left are new additions, the one on the right is original.

151

152. This drawing illustrates in exaggerated form a minimum ground slope of ¼ inch for each foot from the wall of the house. The steeper the pitch and the farther away from the house one maintains it, the less the chance of water seepage.

12 ft.

3 inches

152

153. A rule of thumb for the total flue area for a fireplace is ¹/₁₀th the square-foot area of the firebox opening: thus, if your fireplace at the front is 3 feet wide by 2 feet high, you have 6 square feet of opening; converted to square inches (multiply: 6′ x 12″ x 12″) you arrive at 864 inches; divide by ¹/₁₀ and you get 86.4 inches for the flue area. Most lumberyards carry flue linings 8 inches square (64″ sq.), 8 inches by 12 inches (96″ sq.), and 12 inches by 12 inches (144″ sq.); you would therefore install a flue lining of 8 inches by 12 inches. In kitchen fireplaces it is often necessary to use double or triple flue linings. Too small a channel for the smoke is worse than too large; you can always partially close the damper. In this illustration the firebox has been brought up to bake-oven height. Note the pintle for the crane has already been set in place on the right cheek.

153a. The bake oven has been formed. The mortar was tinted to look like clay. This fireplace was constructed entirely of reproduction "sand-struck" brick, as original material was unavailable at the time; after a few fires blackened the inside face, it looked quite authentic. The protruding brick face (reveal) of about one-fourth of a brick at both sides of the opening to the bake oven is necessary because together with the inner lintel it gives the bake-oven door a backing to press against.

154. A rebuilt kitchen fireplace, finished with its paneling and crane.

155. Reproduction corner brick. These custom-made angle bricks are not as good in texture as the original bricks.

155

156. An original angle stone.

156

cotta flue linings, dampers, smoke shelves above the fireboxes, etc. Provision can also be made with a new chimney for a flue for the heating system and *chases*, that is, channels within the masonry stack for heating and air-conditioning ductwork, plumbing pipes, and electrical wiring.

A new chimney can be so built that all the visible stone or brick will be exactly as it would have been originally, with new material hidden from view. As the chimney and its fireplaces are the very heart of the old house, it is imperative that the substitute stack be planned carefully before work begins. First, one must consider the age and type of house. A 1720 Connecticut saltbox would require a huge kitchen fireplace, with wood lintel and bake oven in the rear of the firebox, and perhaps three additional fireplaces. The examination of the house should have revealed the number and even the sizes of the original fireplaces. The attic floor and the ridge should pretty well define the size of the stack as it comes through the floor and goes out the roof. Sometimes the original chimney has been taken down only as far as the cellar ceiling, in which case a new concrete "pad" can be poured within the old chimney base to support the new stack.

A decision must be made about how much "new" work can be open to view. What about the masonry within the attic area? Achieving the original look is more expensive than exposing new material. Is it important that the chimney within the attic look original? How about the basement, where a new base must be built? Stone or concrete block? One way of getting past the "newness" of modern block construction is to stucco the blocks where they are objectionable, that is, cement-plaster them. This is a decision that is up to you, the owner, and will be governed by the degree of "authenticity" of your restoration and the condition of your pocketbook. If money is no object, the choice is a simple one; however, if the budget is a strict one, a choice may have to be made between exposed block in the attic and a fine wall of paneling for the parlor.

A typical chimney with five fireplaces and a flue for the oil burner, with a new concrete block base in the cellar and only the fireplaces themselves made of old material, will cost about $14,000 complete for labor and material.

Special attention should be paid to the design of the chimney on the outside of the house as it rises above the roof. There are many picture books of old houses and an appropriate design can be chosen, whether in stone or in brick. Make sure the size is adequate to the house. Most masons will tend to skimp in the interest of saving money. The full width of the old chimney, as revealed in the attic, should be maintained.

Before the fireplaces can be built, old material must be gathered. There are many ways of obtaining old material, the most obvious being to look around the building itself. Are there fireplace stones in the stone walls of the garden? Are the doorsteps old hearthstones? How about the stone paths? Is the kitchen hearthstone in the cellar floor (where it was frequently dropped when the stack was removed)? Are any of the outside stones lintels? Fireplace stones can be identified by traces of fire charring.

If no stones can be found about the property, a good source is the local newspaper where an ad asking for old fireplace stones or old brick will frequently bring results. Demolition contractors are a good source, not only for masonry materials but also for old window glass, timbers, etc. Asking at the firehouse if there are any old chimneys standing in town where an old house has burned to the ground can sometimes bring results; the firemen are acquainted with all the structures, both sound and decayed, in the town. Of course, if time is of the essence, the "antique material" dealers will probably have what you require; it is sometimes worth paying the retail price to get what you want when you need it and to have it delivered to you on the jobsite.

In rebuilding new fireplaces on walls in which there will be old paneling, the mason must measure the height and width of the paneled fireplace opening. He must take into consideration the stone reveal, that is, the amount of stone showing at the lintel and also at each side.

When the entire chimney stack is not being rebuilt and repairs are being made, we have a different situation. Many old chimneys were only one brick thick from the attic floor up. Over the years, the resins in the wood have seeped through the clay mortar joints, creating a fire hazard. Often too, the movement of the house, both expanding and contracting, and the pressure of high winds have had a tendency to "rock" the chimney, and it is not unusual to find joints between bricks in the attic that have opened up. Again, we have an aesthetic choice to make. The simplest solution would be to chip off the tarlike resin deposits and then stucco the entire chimney within the attic area. Some masons prefer to surround the exposed brick with wire lath and then plaster it. In either case, the chimney will be completely covered with cement mortar and will be both stronger and safer. If, on the other hand, the choice is to make the chimney within the attic area appear original, then the painstaking job of raking out the joints between the bricks (or the stones, in some cases) and repointing the joints with cement mortar must be begun.

As for the chimney above the roofline (that is, the part exposed to the weather), if it has never been worked on

157a. This fireplace had been made narrower to accommodate the later stair case at right (c. 1870). Note the hearthstone extending beyond the right wall of the firebox (arrow). To restore its original 1790 appearance the entire fireplace required rebuilding.

157a

157b. The stairs have been removed and the fireplace and flue have been taken apart preparatory to reconstructing it to its original dimensions.

157b

157c. The fireplace has now been rebuilt. The flue is firesafe and a modern damper has been installed. Once the paneling has been put on, only "old" work will be visible.

157c

157d. The rear wall of the firebox shows the extent of the increase in width. Now the hearthstone fits the corrected opening exactly. A few fires will make it uniformly black.

157d

before, it will not be flashed and will have leaked over the years. If this part of the chimney is in reasonably good condition, the mason can install new flashing by cutting a raglet (groove) into the mortar joints horizontally, slipping in lead flashing, bending it down, and tucking the other end under the top course of shingles. If a new wood roof is to be installed on the house, the mason will let the flashing hang down, and the roofer will take care of weaving it into his shingles.

If the chimney above the roofline is in poor condition, with obvious cracks in the joints or bricks out of line because of frost heaving, it is time to rebuild the chimney from the ridge up. Don't forget the drip course when rebuilding and don't, in the interest of "purity," omit the flashing. Almost without exception old houses have constant water leakage around the chimney at the ridge, with the consequent rotting of roof boards, timbers, and attic flooring in that vicinity. It is possible to paint the flashing if the sight of it is objectionable. If the flashing is installed under the drip course (not over it), the amount of flashing visible can be kept to a minimum. At a height of twenty-six feet or more from the ground, it will hardly be noticeable. As a matter of fact, the only one who will notice its presence will be a mason (who will approve) or a purist of the purest kind, who no doubt will have a house with rotted timbers at the ridge. The cost to rebuild the chimney above the ridge is about $1800.

One can inspect the interior of most seventeenth- and eighteenth-century house chimneys by looking up from each fireplace with a strong spotlight. Most stacks are in pretty good shape structurally, although the walls of the flues may be coated with black clinkers of resin. The mason can clean these flues from the top by inserting either a long chain or a bag of rocks on a rope, allowing these to scrape against the sides of the flues. The debris will fall down into the fireplaces.

Most fireplaces can be fitted with a modern damper purchased from a lumberyard. The idea is to install the largest possible damper that can be fitted into the throat above the lintel. If the opening is cut down too much, a smoky fireplace will result. Most cast-iron dampers are constructed with a shelf at the bottom that is built into the wall and on which they rest. It may be necessary for the mason to cut or chip off part of this bottom flange to get a tighter fit. The door of the damper is removed and the damper is inserted as high as it can go. It will be held in place by nails driven under it into the joints between stone or brick. Once it is firmly held in place, the mason mortars it in place by carrying the mortar through the opening and filling in around the perimeter between the damper and the wall on all four sides. When the cement sets, the damper can be cleaned of debris, and the door

can be reinstalled. If all has gone according to plan, you will now have a fireplace with a damper set sufficiently high so that the handle will not be visible even if you sit on the floor in front of the firebox.

Sometimes, especially in the upstairs rooms, fireplaces were built so shallow as to prohibit the installation of a "store-bought" damper. In this case a special damper can be made by a good welder. The mason can take the measurements of the opening on a piece of cardboard inserted where the damper is to go. These dampers must be made to afford the greatest possible opening through which the smoke may pass. It is possible to get a 100 percent opening by making the damper in the form of a flat plate that pivots on two points at either end. When it is open, the only obstruction to the smoke will be the thickness of the metal. Another method of constructing a damper for a very small fireplace is to make one in the form of a removable plate. In a very small fireplace the damper will be either open or closed. There will be no in-between.

Fireplace cranes came into general use when bake ovens were being brought to one side or the other of the firebox, rather than extending from the back wall of a larger fireplace. A good date for this transition in the construction of "kitchen stoves" would be 1740. The crane was a pretty handy gadget and consequently was installed in almost every pre-1740 kitchen fireplace at a later date. The crane is installed so that as it swings out, the far end passes under the lintel with about one-half-inch clearance. The crane must be set sufficiently far forward in the firebox to permit a sizable round kettle or pot to hang on it when it is straight across the fireplace. It would not do to have the pots hitting the rear wall of the fireplace each time they are pushed over the fire. Old cranes can be bought, together with their pintles for hanging, for about $125 for a good-sized kitchen crane. The crane should extend at least three-fourths of the way across the kitchen fireplace.

Other fireplaces in old houses had cranes also, as it was not uncommon to take tea or cook meals in bedrooms and parlors as well as in the kitchen. If you plan to construct a brick hearth, it would be wise to consult a good book on eighteenth-century house construction. Most brick hearths had a pattern. Try to use stone of the same type as the lintel when choosing a replacement hearthstone. (Nine-inch-thick old kitchen hearthstones are very difficult to obtain, and if one is found, $500 or more is not too much to pay. You will buy the stone only once.)

If you want a single, long kitchen hearthstone, and it will be necessary to have one quarried, place your order early in the restoration. It may be months before a

158a. This 17th-century fireplace was filled in to make a mere three or four footer when a lean-to with a new kitchen and a bake oven on the side was added to the back of the house in the 18th century. This fireplace, some 9 feet or more wide, was found buried. Note the original stone bake oven in the rear wall of the firebox (left side). To restore it, it was thought best to remove all the second-floor joists and flooring. The kitchen-chamber fireplace is visible upstairs as is the 18th-century paneling added to it. House in Durham, Connecticut, c. 1690–1720.

158b. It was necessary to set a replacement wood lintel as the existing one found in the wall was badly axed.

158b

158c. The rear wall of this room (right) was originally the rear wall of the house. Joists were never nailed; it is a matter of a few minutes work to remove them from their notches after the flooring is taken up.

158c

158d. To the left is the underside of the front stairs rising to the second floor, under which are the cellar stairs. Although this may appear to be a gigantic job, for the skilled mason it was perhaps easier than building a brand-new fireplace. There was the inconvenience of not being able to use two rooms for the short time the work was going on, but result was worth it!

159. A new damper being built into a reconstructed chimney.

160. Resetting the front steps.

suitable slab will be available from which your stone can be cut. An old worn stone is preferable to a new-quarried one. However, if old stones are not available, a new one will have to suffice. It will begin to look older once it has been dirtied with soot and the drippings of fireplace cooking.

In rebuilding brick fireplaces that are to have corner bricks forming the sides of the openings, it is always better to obtain old corner bricks than to try to cut whole bricks to make corner bricks. If the bricks are sawed with a brick saw, the faces cut will be too smooth and will stand out obviously. If the bricks are cut with a brick hammer or a trowel, they will appear too rough in texture and again will stand out. Corner bricks are obtainable; material dealers know what they are and consequently charge good prices for them. The average brick fireplace would require about eleven corner bricks for each side to get to lintel height, so $3.00 or $4.00 each for corner bricks ($70.00 total) may be high on a per-brick basis, but for the entire fireplace the price is well worth the difference.

Techniques: Masonry Restoration

FORMULA FOR MIXING ONE BATCH OF MORTAR

For stonework: 20 shovels mortar sand (level)
                4 shovels portland cement
                5 cups yellow ocher powdered coloring
                Water

When you are mixing mortar for use when laying up stone, it is important to keep the mixture very dry. To test the consistency, squeeze a handful of the mix in your hand; it should hold its shape when you release your hand but should crumble when lightly tapped with a finger. The mixture may appear almost too dry but will set up to form a hard bond. The mix for stonework must be much dryer than that used for laying brick because the stone does not have "suction," whereas the brick will absorb a good part of the water out of the mix.

For brickwork: 20 shovels mortar sand (level)

                1 bag mason's lime
                1 five-gallon pail portland cement
                6 cups yellow ocher powdered coloring
                Water

Add enough water to make the mixture easy to work with the trowel, about the consistency of heavy sour cream. Always add water last.

Yellow ocher powder is purchased from a lumberyard or a mason's materials supplier. It is not usually kept in stock; therefore it will be necessary to place an order for it in advance. With this coloring your mortar joints will take on the appearance of clay. It is not necessary for all your batches of mortar to be colored, only those that will be used to build the firebox and to set hearths and those that are visible in the attic or above the roofline.

Repairing the Frame

In repairing the frame of an antique house, one should begin at the bottom and work upward in the sequence in which the house was originally built.

The Sills

A sill that has been damaged to the point that it no longer performs its function should be replaced. Such a replacement is made from the outside of the house and is a rather simple procedure.

First, remove from the affected area the water table and as many rows of clapboarding as may be necessary to fully expose the area to be replaced. If there is sheathing that is damaged, remove that as well. You will now be able to see the back of the plaster wall from the room where you are working and the studs (in the case of a studded house) to which the lath is nailed. You will not be able to get a clear picture of the ends of the first-floor joists where they are mortised into the sills; these can be examined from the cellar. Since these joists are attached to the inside of the sill, they must be supported before the defective sill is removed. They can be braced inside the cellar with temporary posts and cross timbers.

The studs as well must be held in place until the new sill is installed; nail a horizontal two-by-four to the studs, supported by vertical braces.

Now cut out the bad section of sill and slip in the new, which can be either another piece of oak of similar size (either new or old) or a sill built up from new lumber spiked together. Do not forget to treat this replacement sill by painting it with a wood preservative such as Cuprinol, Woodlife, or creosote.

Now that the new sill is in place, all that remains is to reattach the studs to it. If the bottoms of the studs are rotted, they can be cut, and new oak or fir pieces of proper length can be spiked onto them, or the sill can be built up to meet sound wood.

The ends of the floor joists in the cellar will be rotted where they entered the rotted sill. You can reattach them to the sill by spiking onto their sides new pieces, which can be supported by a ledger nailed to the new section of sill, or by the use of steel angles lag-screwed both to joist and to sill. For those who wish to accomplish this repair with the least possible cost, leaving the temporary braces in the cellar as permanent supports is a solution. If the cellar floor is dirt rather than concrete, the supporting

161

161. Termite damage.

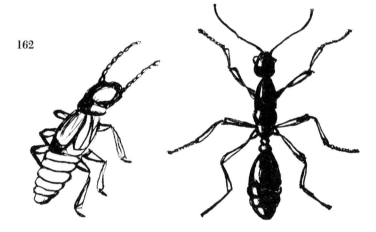

162

162. (Left) Winged termite (shown without wings). It is useful to know the differnce betwen the ant and the termite. Both swarm in the spring, and it is not uncommon to see them inside a house. (Right) Winged ant (shown without wings).

163

163. Powder-post beetle damage. The beetles work slowly over the years but eventually reduce large timbers to powder.

posts should be of the metal telescoping type sold at any lumberyard.

Posts

In the case of a rotted post on an outside wall, the same procedure can be followed. Expose the foot of the post from the outside of the house. Hold it in place while it is cut and a new piece of sturdy, treated material is substituted for the defective piece either by a half-lap joint or by the introduction of steel plates lagged to secure the two sections. While you have the old sill or post out, you have the opportunity to patch any defects in the top of the foundation wall.

Inside posts will most likely be damaged in the cellar where their bottoms are visible. It may be necessary, if the damage is extensive, to remove the casing from them to expose them for repair. There is, however, a tendency to make repairs where they are unnecessary. A sill or post timber may have many good years left in it even though there is some surface damage. If you remove the cause of the damage and stabilize the condition, it may be quite unnecessary to make any repair at all.

Girts and Summer Beams

These structural members occasionally require repair on an outside wall over windows and doors where water has entered. Unless there is an obvious sag or cracking of the ceiling plaster, a repair may not be necessary to the girt, and if you merely prevent further leakage of water, the trouble will end. Where the tenon of a summer beam, for example, has slipped out of the mortise in an end girt, it will be necessary to remove the summer beam casing (if cased) and a section of the lath and plaster in the ceiling as well as the girt casing. The casing can be removed by the use of a flat bar and gentle prying; it is better to cut the nails than to force a stubborn piece of wood. When one is removing trim, too much haste usually results in damaged wood. Make sure you get a good bite with the pry bar; catching the edge of the trim will result in torn wood. Steel braces of various shapes can be made up by your local welder to reinforce timbers and hold them together.

Joists

Occasionally a joist will be found that has cracked in the middle. If the location of this timber is such that it will be exposed to view in a ceiling, it must be replaced in its entirety. In order to do this, one must cut the bad timber, raise the flooring that was nailed to it, and insert the replacement joist in the notches of the girts. This process sounds easier than it is to accomplish, as the flooring is generally one length from wall to wall and is under the mop board above. It may very well be necessary to remove the entire under floor and the finished flooring of the room above to reinsert the joists. Where the ceiling joists of a room are to be lathed and plastered, a new joist can be spiked into the broken one, adding the required strength—it won't be seen. Replacement timbers are not hard to find. They can be purchased for about $2.00 per running foot from buildings that are being demolished.

Flooring

In a room that has had its flooring completely removed, a new "old" floor must be found to be installed. Flooring can be bought in wide oak, chestnut, or pine from about $5.00 per square foot with paint on it, to $7.00 unpainted. Remember, you must use the appropriate material for the age and room of the house that is being worked on. Lay the flooring out, preferably outdoors. Remove the paint from it with a solution of lye and cold water brushed on and then hosed off. If it is unpainted, a solution of commercial laundry bleach and water will remove most of the stains.

The flooring is laid out in the same manner in which it is to be installed in the room and is cut to proper length. The underflooring (or *slitwork*, as it was called) is laid down in areas where the flooring will be seen from below. Where the ceiling below is to be plastered, an underflooring of plywood makes a much better base. Over the plywood lay a cover of 15-pound felt (roofing paper) before the installation of the finished floor. This will provide a cushion between flooring and plywood and will also present a dark background to the eye should the flooring shrink and separate. Fit the flooring one board at a time, drilling pilot holes for the nails. You can draw each succeeding board tight against its neighbor by wedging until the nails are driven home. Remember the floors are laid in panels of even-length boards; only the end joints are staggered. You will need a good, sharp blade in your saw when laying oak flooring.

Where an occasional board in a room has "popped" its nails, you can often snug it down again by drilling new holes and renailing. Where a board has buckled, the offending board is first removed. Set the electric saw to a depth about half the floor's thickness, and turn the board over. Make multiple saw cuts (scoring the bottom) with the grain. The board can now be turned right side up, and the nails will snug it down flat.

Insect and Dry Rot Damage

The damage found to the wood timbers of an old building, especially the sills, is of major concern to most

164

164. Dry rot.

165. The badly rotted sill and sheathing boards on one side of this Cape house required major surgery in the form of a new treated sill, wall-framing members rebuilt to windowsill height, resheathing, and reclapboarding. The entire repair was made by three men in one day. Then an exterminator treated the house against termites. Not many houses are too far gone to be saved.

165

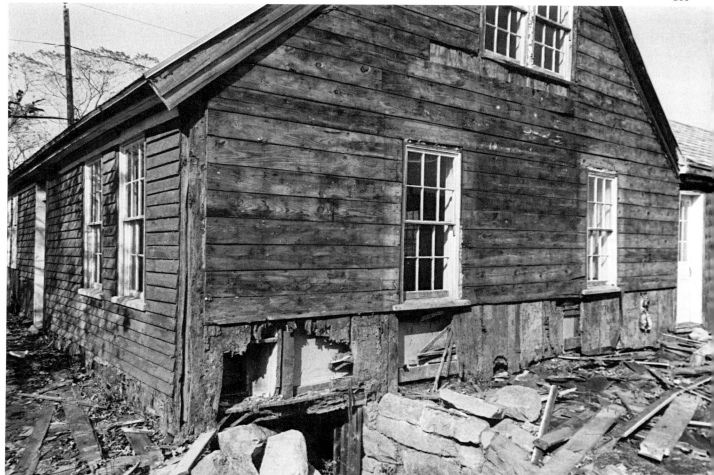

166. Major sill replacement such as this is rarely encountered, but even this looks worse than it really is.

166a. Close-up showing the house jacked up while a new sill is substituted for a rotted one.

167. New treated, built-up sill as seen from the inside of this plank-constructed house. The large rathole near the post will be covered by lath and plaster.

168. A new sill made of three layers of new two-by-six lumber spiked together. A sill of new-sawed oak can also be used. In both cases the new wood should be treated with a perservative.

169. Here is a common condition: the sill under a corner post is completely rotted leaving the post hanging in the air.

170. A post splice may be required if the bottom is rotted beyond supporting strength. First expose the post to sound wood. The repair shown here (side view) is a one-half lap joint firmly bolted.

171. Corner-post splice (front view). The bolts are countersunk so as not to interfere with the addition of corner-post casings. This splice will last as long as the house.

purchasers of old houses. It is rarely so extensive as to make the house unrestorable, however. This damage is of three major types: damage caused by insects and animals; damage caused by water or dampness; and wear and tear. Almost every old house shows evidence of one or more of these.

Insect Infestation

Termites and powder-post beetles are the two insects that do the most damage to the wood parts of buildings. Termite damage can be readily distinguished from that caused by the powder-post beetle. The termite leaves characteristic tunnels, which run with the grain of the wood. Often the exterior of a timber will show no signs that termites have been at work, although just below the surface the tunnels have made the timber almost hollow.

The worker termite, which does the damage, looks like a thick-bodied white ant. In order to survive, it requires access to moist soil. Consequently the first step in ridding a house of these pests is to dry up the cellar, cut off any contact between wood and soil, and provide ventilation. No wood should be within eighteen inches of soil.

All too frequently one finds firewood, wooden posts, storage bins, and other lumber in direct contact with an earthen cellar floor. These must be removed. Very often, too, cellar windows have been permanently sealed; these should be opened and repaired. If enough ventilation is not present in the cellar, additional louvers can be installed in the foundation wall quite inconspicuously. They can be purchased at any lumberyard for a few dollars and can be placed by the mason or the carpenter.

Wood posts in contact with the ground should be replaced by metal columns.

The single biggest offender in bringing moisture into a cellar is the manner in which the land directly outside the foundation walls is sloped. Since early foundations were laid up in dry stone, water, whether shed by the roof or running on the surface of the ground, will surely find its way through the joints between stones into the cellar, providing the termite the moisture it requires. A slope of a quarter inch per foot for a distance of sixteen feet from the house (a four-inch drop in sixteen feet) will keep water away. Once the cellar has been dried up, the wood has been removed from contact with the soil, and proper ventilation has been provided, the business of ridding the house of active termites can begin.

Powder-post beetles produce an altogether different result. The surface of the wood reveals tiny pinholes through which the "worm" has entered. Once inside, the insect literally pulverizes the wood, turning it into a fine wood powder. Powder-post beetles appear most fre-

quently in basements where the early builders installed floor joists with their bark still on.

Termite and powder-post beetles can best be dealt with by professional exterminators, who will not only perform a thorough job but will provide a guarantee and a yearly inspection service to see that these pests don't return. These people have special equipment with which they are able, under pressure, to inject pest-killing chemicals into the soil around foundations and in the floor of the cellar, including the interstices between the stones of the cellar walls, assuring a 100 percent effective job. They are equipped as well to spray the timbers and the underflooring in the basement, eliminating working powder-post beetles. The cost for the treatment of a house is around $650 with a small additional yearly charge for the inspection and the guarantee.

If, on careful inspection, no signs of active termites are found, you may wish to treat the house yourself. Chemicals can be purchased from local chemical companies in quantity or from hardware stores. The chemicals come in various strengths and are combined with water. They should be used in accordance with the directions of the manufacturer, and care should be taken to avoid contact with the skin and the eyes. Avoid breathing the vapors.

The method of treating a house is quite simple. A narrow trench three or four inches wide is dug completely around the outside perimeter of the house up against the foundation wall to a depth of eighteen inches. A similar trench, but to a depth of eight inches, should be dug around the interior of stone walls, including the chimney stack foundation. These trenches are then filled with the solution, which will seep into the ground. The trenches can then be refilled with the dirt taken from them, and another dose of solution can be poured on top.

Cellar timbers and underflooring can be sprayed with the chemical solution with the use of a pressure garden sprayer. This will help control powder-post beetle infestation. It will be necessary to wear a mask and gloves for protection.

The spaces between the stones on the inside of the cellar walls can be pointed up with cement mortar to help seal out water. This is best done after treatment has been accomplished, since the solution must be allowed as much freedom to penetrate between the stones as possible.

Dry Rot

Dry rot is a condition caused by a fungus of the mushroom group. The wood becomes quite brittle, often cracking at right angles to the grain; it loses a good deal of its resiliency and becomes much lighter in weight.

The treatment for dry rot consists of removing wood debris from the area, especially any that is in direct con-

172

172. Gusset plates in T and cross shapes are easily made by a welder. When spiked over the joints of abutting timbers, they prevent further separation of mortise-and-tenon joints. Other shapes can be made to suit special problems. In nailing into old oak, it is best to use concrete nails.

173

173. Here is a badly termite-damaged floor joist as seen from the basement. The source of termite infestation was first eliminated; then new joists were added between the old ones. All the new wood was treated with wood perservative.

174. Here a gable-roofed house is being brought back to its original 18th-century gambrel shape.

174

174b

174a. Since the gambrel shape was smaller than the later gable, it was possible to do most of the work within the enclosed attic. The late work is shown being removed.

174b. The house now has its original roofline. Privately owned; Old Wethersfield, Connecticut.

4c

174c and 174d. The side and front of the house nearing completion.

174d

175. These floorboards were laid out on the grass, cleaned, measured, and trimmed to size before being brought into the house for installation. Restoration by the author.

175

176. When this restoration was in progress, boards long enough to span this room in one length were not available. A single board was therefore nailed parallel to the far wall in this photograph to make up the difference. Once the room had been furnished, the one board running in the opposite direction was hardly noticed. This, I feel, is a neater method of solving the problem than adding a small piece to the end of each board.

FELT PAPER

176

177. Drilling "pilot" holes for flooring nails prevents the boards from splitting. Most boards take two nails across their width; boards wider than 18 inches should have three. When nailing, don't "snap a line"; use your eye. Use wood shingles for leveling.

177

tact with the soil. The spores become active when the humidity is high, and they become dormant when the humidity is low. Provide ventilation.

FLOORING

It will be found that in most antique houses the flooring on the ground floor is in much poorer condition than that of the second story or attic. The reason for this is twofold: greater traffic in the downstairs rooms and proximity to the dampness of a dirt-floor cellar or crawl space.

If the old flooring has been replaced by modern boards at some time, there is only one remedy available; replacement of the new flooring by old flooring of the proper vintage and type.

In the reinstallation of old flooring you will want to use the best boards in the most prominent part of the room; thus you may wish to place a particularly wide, close-grained board directly in front of a fireplace hearthstone, using narrower pieces close to the walls.

Original replacement flooring can be purchased from dealers in antique house materials, or you can scour the countryside for an old house that is about to be demolished. The use of attic flooring is a last resort, as attic floorboards were often of inferior quality, being those remaining after the best ones were used elsewhere.

Replacing flooring on either the ground floor or the second floor of a house entails removing the baseboards (mop boards), as these are set on top of the flooring. If one finds that the floorboard runs under the planks of a parallel plank-wall partition (I can never remember this *not* being the case), then the procedure to follow would be to replace all the boards in the room except those on which the partition rests. If it is found that these boards are in very poor condition they can be cut as close to the wall as a saw will allow.

Where a modern floor has been installed over an existing original floor, remove the new floor and inspect the old one to determine if it is worth retaining. If the spaces between boards seem excessive, they can be "lifted" and reset tight. An additional piece may be required to fill in the space left by the shrinkage. New floors are put down with cut nails that are "toenailed" every twelve to sixteen inches. When this flooring is removed, it will leave the old boards pockmarked with hundreds of nail holes, a situation often not as serious as it seems. These holes can be filled with wood putty or a mixture of sawdust and glue and then stained to match.

Where boards have shrunk, leaving wide spaces between them, the simplest method is to cut strips of the same wood, stain them to match the color of the old floor, and drive them into the cracks. An occasional small finishing nail will hold the insert in place. I have been unable to discover a plastic material that will harden and stay in place permanently to fill these cracks. I have tried sawdust and glue, wood putty, and a variety of materials made for use on boats. The constant expansion and contraction of the flooring soon forces these materials out.

Replacement flooring should be laid down as described on page 56. It should be laid in panels of even length. Each successive board is first laid down and wedged tight against its neighbor before it is drilled and finally nailed.

Should flooring the full length of the room not be available, the best solution is to install one or two boards running in the opposite direction against the walls to make up the difference rather than to use many small pieces.

Unevenness or irregularity in the thickness of under-flooring, which will result in waviness of the surface (one board being slightly higher or lower where boards join), can be corrected by the use of wood shingles as shims where necessary.

In existing flooring one occasionally encounters a hole or an imperfection small enough not to spoil the entire board yet large enough to require a patch. In this situation a *dutchman* is installed. This is a piece of wood of the same material as the flooring. It is cut in a square, a rectangle, or a "bow tie," and a scribe mark is made. The imperfection is then cut out carefully and the patch should slip exactly into the space. The grain of the wood of the patching material must, of course, run in the same direction as that of the boards.

New material for the replacement of flooring in an antique house is always a second choice but must be resorted to when the old is unobtainable, a condition that is becoming more and more frequent. Because of the many restorations taking place, not only has original material become hard to find, but the prices have risen astronomically.

In a room of *old* material a replacement board should always be of *old* material too, as a single new board will stand out and will be easily distinguishable for what it is.

When an entire room requires replacing, new material can be used. New oak or pine flooring can be obtained from local sawmills as a rule, but the use of new wood presents a number of problems.

It is the nature of all wood to expand and contract with the seasons because of absorption or loss of moisture from the air. The amount of shrinkage across the grain of a one-inch-thick, freshly cut, sixteen-inch-wide oak board brought into a heated house is truly remarkable; within a few days it can lose half an inch or more in width. Therefore when you are using newly cut material, have it air-dried for six months at least before attempting

178. Some people are disturbed by cracks between their floorboards. This flooring shows the way old flooring appears during low-humidity periods.

179. A "dutchman," or insert, is used to fill a hole where a knot fell out. After staining, the repair is barely noticable.

180. A new "saddle" or threshold hand-planed to show "wear."

178

179

180

to use it, and then use it only after it has been brought into the house for a few weeks to become adjusted to the atmospheric conditions. Better still, purchase kiln-dried lumber, the moisture of which has been reduced (and measured) under controlled conditions.

An equally difficult problem is obtaining material twelve inches or wider and getting it long enough. It is no problem to find sixteen-inch-wide boards eight feet long; the trick is to locate sixteen-inch boards sixteen feet long. Most of the trees harvested today are not old enough to be sixteen inches wide as high as sixteen feet above the ground. A good deal of the material being using today is being imported from Canada and Maine. It comes down rough-cut and must be dried and planed on one side by a local mill. It is really not expensive lumber. A good source other than lumber mills for very wide boards is the custom kitchen-cabinet maker, who often has his own sources.

When you are laying down new-cut boards, the appearance of the flooring can be enhanced if you have the carpenter "soften" the sharp upper edges by running the hardwood of his hammer handle down the edges for the length of each board, a process that will slightly round the edges.

The finish of your flooring is a matter of personal preference: there are those who like their floors to shine and to have a deep, rich brown tone not unlike the finish one would expect to find on a antique chest of drawers; others want their floors to have a gray "scrubbed" look. No matter what finish is chosen, the old flooring must be first cleaned of its paint, stains, or grime.

REMOVAL OF PAINT
FROM FLOORS

Lye and Water

The simplest method of removing paint from floors is with a solution of lye and cold water. The work should *only* be done outside. Precautions must be taken to protect both yourself and the house. It would be wise to wear rubber boots, rubber gloves, and protective goggles.

The floors are laid out on the ground and the lye solution is brushed on. Work in a shady area, keeping the wood wet by adding more solution from time to time. Don't be in a hurry. Give the lye a chance to penetrate the paint before hosing it off. The brush used should have a long handle and be stiff. By testing with the brush, you can see if the paint is melting. When most of the paint has

been loosened, it can be washed away, and then another brushing of lye can be applied. When the final paint is off the wood, a complete washing with clear water (a hose is ideal) will get rid of the lye. The floorboards must now be stacked under cover with wood shims separating them. Under no circumstances let the boards dry in the sun, as they will warp very quickly.

The big advantage of lye is the relatively large area that can be covered quickly and the low cost of the materials. Make sure you have proper ventilation.

Paint Remover

Paint remover is a safer material to use than lye, but here again be careful. Don't smoke near the work and don't have a fire going in a fireplace. It is a wise precaution to keep a fire extinguisher handy. Do a small section at a time. Lay on the remover according to the directions of the manufacturer and give it the full measure of time to do its work. When all the paint has been removed, a mopping with a solution of washing soda and water will stop further action of the remover.

Dry Scraping

Dry scraping of floors is a slower process than the methods already mentioned, but it is far safer. The tool used is a carpenter's scraper, which is no more than a rectangular piece of saw-blade steel; these blades can be purchased from makers of fine carpentry tools and usually come with directions for sharpening. The edge desired is merely a curl of the metal, so that the tool does not actually cut into the wood but merely scrapes the surface. You could get the same result by scraping with the edge of a piece of glass, but the use of glass as a scraper is too dangerous.

Sanding

Using a commercial sander on old floors is a common error made in restorations. The rotating motion of most sanders is contrary to the direction of the early plane marks and wipes them out, leaving instead circular ridges and valleys. Few old floorboards are dead level because they have been worn unevenly over the years. The powerful sander will cut the high areas down to the low ones, giving a mottled effect. The patina of the old wood is only skin deep and took years to develop. The power sander will quickly remove this patina and get down to "yellow" wood. One might as well have new boards. Should one inherit floors that have already been sanded, the remedy is to scrape the rotary sanding marks off with the carpenter's scraper parallel to the length of the board (never across the grain). Once the board has been scraped, it can then be stained and refinished so that it will look pretty close to the original in color and surface texture.

The Finish

If you are one who wishes to give your floors the look of the gray brown "sanded" finish, a few coats of hard floor wax will do the trick over a washed floor. When lye or bleach has been used to remove paint or stains, a bit of color may have to be put back into the wood before waxing. Experiment with a piece of wood and one of the stains supplied by your local lumberyard or hardware store. When you have found the color you wish to achieve, stain your floor, allow it to dry, and then wax.

One of the loveliest natural finishes for oak and chestnut flooring, and for pine floors as well, is that achieved when the flooring is fed with raw, warm linseed oil and turpentine mixed half-and-half and flowed on with a paintbrush. Be cautious in heating the mixture as it can ignite if allowed to get too hot. Flow on the solution until the wood won't take anymore and retains a wet appearance; then wipe off the excess. Caution: dispose of oily rags, as they can ignite through spontaneous combustion. After a day or so repeat the feeding, again wiping off the excess. This feeding of raw linseed oil and turpentine can be used as a finish in itself or as a preparation to bring out the grain of the wood where a further finish is to be applied. It works best on floors that have required only washing or that have been dry-scraped.

Modern floors are usually finished with shellac. I prefer the use of a harder substance such as a polyurethane floor finish, which is applied according to the manufacturer's direction after the color you want is achieved. Once the finish has dried sufficiently, the floors can be waxed. Aesthetically I find a dark floor more pleasing than a light one, especially in a room where the ceilings are plastered. It gives one the sense of standing on a solid base.

INSULATION

One encounters crude attempts by early builders to insulate their houses against the cold by the use of rye huskings poured between floor joists in the attic, by the stuffing of corncobs in knotholes of planking boards, or by "papering" the cracks of exterior wall sheathing boards with newspaper. By the way, these newspapers are often of great help in dating an old house.

Today we have more efficient methods of insulating. In the old days the few insulation attempts were no doubt meant solely to keep the cold out; today we think of protecting ourselves from both cold in winter and heat in summer. Modern insulation is sold by R factor, which is its measured resistance to the passage of heat in one direction. The higher the R factor, the greater the insulating quality. Besides restricting the "flow" of heat, modern insulation is designed to restrict the flow of moisture by the addition of a "moisture barrier" in the form of an impenetrable membrane attached to the insulating material. Some insulations use for their moisture barrier aluminum foil, which protects the house from another way that heat penetrates, radiation. In northern climates the minimum recommended R factor for modern houses is R-11 for the walls and R-19 for the attic (it has been discovered that most of the heat loss in a house is through the attic).

Insulation comes in different materials as well as with different R factors. The most common materials are fiber glass, in the form of "bats" or rolls, and styrofoam in ridged sheets. Both of these are installed by hand.

Insulation can also be mechanically "blown" into the walls through small holes made in the outside clapboards. Unfortunately a studded antique house frequently has diagonal bracing at the posts as well as having unconventional stud spacing, making the blowing of insulation less than 100 percent effective. Over the years mice, rats, and squirrels have deposited nutshells and corncobs haphazardly within the walls; these block the flow of blown insulation, which must fill all the voids to work properly.

In a studded house insulating the joists under the attic flooring with eight inches or more of fiberglass insulation will greatly reduce heat loss. Wherever an outside wall is opened for construction, insulate, but don't purposely destroy old plaster to insulate the walls.

Insulating a plank house is another matter. Again, the attic floor can receive full insulation, but the walls are only about four inches thick from the outside of the clapboards to the inside of the plaster and do not have the dead air space that is a "natural" insulation in a studded house. The best procedure with a plank house (short of opening the walls) is to make sure that you have a tight house on the outside; that is, caulk the windows with the best grade of caulking and make sure that the clapboards are tightly nailed. Install fiberglass insulation on the inside of the sills in the cellar between the first-floor joists. And keep the house well painted. A good paint job will do a lot to keep a house warm. Remember, dark colors absorb heat, and light colors reflect.

A great deal of heat loss takes place through the glass areas of the windows. The decision to install storm win-

181. Four-inch fiber-glass insulation with an aluminum reflective-vapor barrier. The vapor barrier always faces the heated interior.

dows is an aesthetic one that only you can make. If you are going to use storm windows, be sure when you order them that the meeting rail of the storm window is the same as the meeting rail of the sash; otherwise you will have an extra horizontal line running across each window opening. Storm windows can be made with colors baked on to match the color of your house.

If, in a plank house, your restoration necessitates re-plastering some or all of your exterior walls, it is possible to use FR styrofoam insulation instead of wood lath. You can put plaster directly over this material, which comes in ridged sheets two feet wide by eight feet long and can be cut with a sharp blade. In thickness FR styrofoam insulation comes in 1-inch, 1½-inch, and 2-inch thicknesses. Each inch provides an R factor of 5.4. Two inches will give the recommended R-11 but may be too thick for your trim. It may be necessary to compromise. This is a special material not to be confused with ordinary styrofoam insulation.

Insulation information is readily available from your building materials dealer, who will give you the recommended installation instructions and R factor for your area of the country.

When you are installing insulation in exterior walls, it is important to stuff the material in every crevice, being most particular around the window frames and especially behind the electrical convenience outlet boxes.

MECHANICAL TRADES

In the restoration of an antique house the major mechanical jobs—that is, the plumbing, heating, air-conditioning, ventilating, electrical, and telephone systems— often require treatment different from the same systems as installed in modern houses. In old houses it is desirable to hide from view the greater part of these systems, leaving visible only those parts that work the system: we conceal the pipes but are forced to expose the lavatory; we conceal the wiring but not the switch.

Because of the post-and-lintel construction of these homes, we are faced with heavy girts and columns, which lie as obstacles in the path of pipes, ducts, and conduits, and interior partitions generally no thicker than two inches. As a result we are forced to take special measures.

In order to obtain permission from your town or city to occupy your house as a dwelling, you will be required to install at least some of these services in your home. The work must also be accomplished as prescribed by the building code, and it must win the approval of the fire marshal, the utility company, and the department of health. The trick in restoring an antique house is to make these installations in the manner that will least disturb those qualities of the house that you wish to preserve.

Each mechanical contractor must be told what is expected from him *before* he submits his bid. It must be emphasized that the wood trim and the paneling of your house are sacred and must not be cut without special permission; that where your timbers are to remain exposed to view, he must run his lines somewhere else; and that he must conceal all of his conduits, pipes, outlets, fixtures, etc., as much as possible.

Mechanical systems are installed in two phases: the *roughing* and the *trim* or *finish*. Roughing includes the running of lines or wires, which, for the most part, are to be concealed within walls, floors, or ceilings. The trim, or finish, work consists of hanging plumbing or lighting fixtures, hooking up kitchen appliances, and installing grilles, registers, convenience outlets, etc.

The Electrical System

The electrical system, running as it does to every room of the house, can cause more difficulty than any other mechanical job. The roughing includes the service and wiring; and the trim is comprised of the installation of kitchen appliances, lighting fixtures, outlets, exhaust fans, etc.

The Service

The capacity of your electrical service will depend upon the number and kinds of lights, appliances, motors, etc., you requre and will be determined by your electrician after he discusses your needs with you. The service may be installed either *overhead* (exposed) or *underground* (concealed). The latter is much to be preferred, although it is more expensive. In an underground service installation the owner must have a trench dug from the house to an energy source specified by the utility company (usually the nearest electric pole). Some companies require that a bed of sand be placed on the bottom of this trench and a conduit laid on the sand. The company will then install a special cable through the conduit. At the same time the electric service wire is being placed, the telephone company will install its cable in the same trench, thus relieving the house from all unsightly exposed wires. A meter panel will still be required against the outside of the house, but the conduit will run downward from this panel into the ground rather than from a mast near the roof.

The Wiring

How does one wire an old house in the least objectionable manner? There are two methods of wiring: the conventional method and the low-voltage method. The latter is a more expensive installation but is by far the best solution to the concealment problem. Not every electrician has had experience with low-voltage systems, and it would be prudent therefore to inquire at a local electrical supply house for the names of electricians in your area who have made installations of this type.

In essence the low-voltage system brings the power source to convenient and easily accessible locations, from which points low-voltage circuits utilizing solenoids and small-diameter bell wire energize the outlets, switches, and fixtures. The wires are so small as to allow them to be embedded in grooves cut into the plaster. In plank-constructed houses low-voltage systems are particularly desirable, as running wires on exterior walls is almost impossible without the removal of the plaster on the inside or the clapboards on the outside of the house. The conventional method of wiring as used on new construction can be modified somewhat to overcome the obstacles of old house construction. Slimmer boxes and switches can be obtained. The threading of wires under the lath between the spaces of adjoining planks of the partitions can greatly reduce exposure.

Crossing a room horizontally is more difficult than running wires from floor to ceiling in all but low-voltage systems. The best location for a horizontal run would be directly above the mop board, where a plaster patch becomes undetectable. To get around door openings the wires can be run along the door casings, the lath and plaster being cut back to accommodate them. Switch plates and outlet plates if painted to match the wall in which they rest can almost disappear from view. It should be borne in mind that once a room is furnished, the eye is distracted a good deal from concentrating on outlets, switches, etc., whereas in a bare room they are emphasized.

By far the least expensive method of wiring an old house is by the use of Wiremold, an extruded-metal channel that has wires inside and frequent positions to plug into. This installation is recommended for only those restorations in which a very tight budget must be adhered to; the wiring is completely visible, but you can camouflage it by painting it to match the wall behind. The least conspicuous place to run these channels is along the floor line attached to the mop board or directly on top of the heating convectors in houses with baseboard heating systems.

Where paneling occurs, such as a wainscot around the base of a room, two options are available. If the outlets are to be kept close to the floor, then the paneling can be removed, the wiring placed behind it, and the paneling reinstalled with the convenience outlets cut into the lowest rail (the mop board).

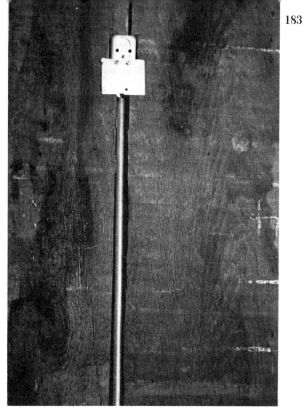

182. Underground service installation. If there is cable television in your area, it may also be possible to bury those wires in the same trench. An underground service may save you an "outage" in times of snow or hurricane.

183. Rear view of a metal conduit and a thin, convenience outlet box installed in a 2-inch-thick plank partition.

184. Front view of a similar installation. The lath has been cut on both sides of the partition to gain maximum concealment.

185. Provision for television outlets and smoke detection and burglar alarm systems can be made by the electrician at the same time he does the wiring.

186. Crossing over a doorway can be accomplished by removing the casings and running the wires behind them.

187. In paneled wainscot convenience outlets are cut into the lowest rail. Cover plates can be painted to match the woodwork.

188. Installation above heating convectors in a feather-edged boarded wall with baseboard heat.

187

18

Some people don't object to the outlets of a room being in the plaster at a height of about 2½ or 3½ feet above floor level. If the building code allows this, the wainscot paneling can be spared completely from the carpenter's saw.

Floor outlets—that is, those set faceup in the flooring— are a fire hazard; dust and other objects can short the wires, and they should be avoided.

In the long run it is up to the electrician to use his ingenuity; once they understand the problem, most electricians welcome the challenge and this departure from a routine job.

TV, Telephone, Fire Detection, and Burglar Alarm Systems

The time to install these systems is while the walls are open and the electrician is on the job. TV conduit run to specific locations at this time will be appreciated later. A massive antenna on the roof of a well-restored early house is a sad sight. TV antennae can be placed inside the attic; a signal booster will make the reception as good as it can be, and the house will look much better.

Lighting Fixtures

What does one do about lighting fixtures in a seventeenth- or eighteenth-century house? Floor and table lamps with an "antique flavor" can be purchased or made from an assortment of objects that are relatively inoffensive, such as bottles, crocks, hitching posts, wooden turnings, etc. Overhead lighting fixtures are generally used in bathrooms and modern kitchens. A chandelier in the dining room may be desirable. Good reproductions can easily be found and can be wired by a competent lamp store or electrician. Many people prefer to use floor lamps around the perimeter of a room with nonelectrified (candle) sconces on the walls and a chandelier overhead.

Wiring an electrified chandelier hanging from a summer beam or from the plaster ceiling in the center of a room may pose a problem. One solution is to remove one or two floorboards from the room above and cut a groove in the top of the summer beam or drill through the floor joists. The wire can then be brought directly above the chandelier and snaked down to it, and no wires will be visible.

Heating Systems

A variety of heating systems are available to the home buyer, some more adaptable to the antique house than others. Most houses are purchased with an existing system of one type or another. Houses that have not been "modernized" since the 1930s will probably have steam heat. The main drawbacks of this kind of heat are the large radiators in each room and the heavy-diameter piping leading to them. Plumbers who installed steam systems in early houses invariably avoided going through the girts by the only method available to them— exposing the risers in the rooms. Most steam systems are eventually replaced; new installations are not recommended even though more modern radiators of the baseboard type are on the market.

Circulating hot-water systems are in great demand since they provide even, nondrying heat and utilize piping of small diameter. Boilers can be obtained for these heating systems that also supply the domestic hot water for the house, obviating the necessity of a separate water heater. Radiation of the stand-up or baseboard types are available, the latter being preferable in most instances, since when run along the floor and painted they look somewhat like baseboard moldings. If such an installation is to be made in your house, insist that the radiation covers be the full length of any wall they are on, even though the actual amount of radiation within these covers is only a few feet long. Covering only half a wall with radiation covers calls attention to it.

Electric Heating

The installation cost for electric heat is less than for the other types, but in all but a few areas of the country it is more expensive to operate. In an old house without proper insulation, not only may the cost be prohibitive but the utility company may refuse to allow its installation.

Electric heat utilizing baseboard convectors is the most frequent manner of installation. Wall panels with or without fans are available and are sometimes the only practical way to heat a small bathroom. Although radiant electric heat is sometimes used in modern homes, its application to post-and-lintel houses is not practical.

Forced-Warm-Air Systems

This type of heating system allows for the house to be centrally air-conditioned if the ductwork is sized for this purpose. The problem with forced-warm-air heat is getting the air ducts from one place to another. Remember that it is not the shape of the ducts but the cubic area that is important when you are looking for space to install ducts. Thus a duct one foot by one foot will take up one square foot of floor area; a duct six inches by two feet provides the same area and may take up less room in a closet. Round ducts can also be used. There are forced-hot-air systems today that provide outlets in the rooms only a few inches in diameter, the airflow being forced at greater velocity than that in the larger duct systems.

189. What does one do about lighting fixtures? Electrified antique lanterns and chandeliers look better than modern "Colonial" fixtures. "Candle bulbs" are available, which would have made this lantern appear more authentic.

190. Don't forget a ceiling hook for a chandelier.

191. The real thing—an unelectrified tin sconce.

192. All manner of things, such as this brandy jug, can be made into lamps. Concessions to modern living must be made; there is no such thing as a "pure" restoration.

191

192

193. An antique chandelier that has been electrified.

194

194. An 18th-century lantern can be energized with gas or electricity.

193

195. Baseboard-heating convectors painted to match the wall.

196. When there is no way not to expose the piping to view, it may be best to "loop" back and go the way you came. The convector cover should have continued empty to the left wall.

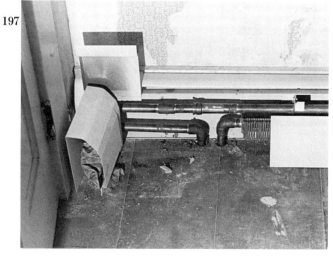

197. A convenient spot has been found to return hot-water pipes downstairs.

198. Once the room has been furnished, the heating is camouflaged. If you want the advantages of baseboard water or electric heat, what else can you do?

199. In a large room with lots of furniture baseboard heating almost disappears. Old kitchen, restored by author, Lisbon, Connecticut.

200. A small floor register painted brown to disguise it will direct the air in this warm-air system. Similar grilles, painted white, can be placed in the ceiling plaster of second-story rooms.

200

201. A concrete pad is required to support your boiler. Locate this as close to the flue as possible, as long runs of pipe are less efficient.

201

The most satisfactory method of using a forced-hot-air system in an old house is one that feeds the warm air up through the flooring on the first floor and down from the attic through the ceilings of the second-story rooms. Either a single blower in the cellar will heat the air or two separate units can be used—one in the cellar and the other in the attic. Provision must be made for one or more "returns" to carry the warmed room air back to the heater to be reheated. In a system with a single heating unit in the cellar, it will be necessary to sacrifice part of a closet or to build a false post in some out-of-the-way place to house the main second-story duct as it runs from cellar to attic. Once the attic is reached, the ducts can be held close to the rafter feet, making for a neat installation and leaving the bulk of the attic space free.

Other Systems

More elaborate and expensive heating systems can be purchased that combine two systems. A typical example would be a system that utilizes a "heat exchanger" in the attic to convert hot water to hot air. Hot-air systems, like hot-water systems, may be "fired" by oil, gas, or electricity.

Plumbing System

Bathroom installation on the second floor of antique houses causes the primary difficulty for the plumber. The *risers*—that is, the vertical piping—are of small enough diameter that an inconspicuous place can usually be found to get them to the second story. A false, cased column, within which the pipes run can be made as a last resort. However, it is the traps and *lead bends*—the waste lines running from water closet and bathtub—that cause the problem, as they will protrude below the ceiling line of the first-floor rooms in a normal installation. Where upstairs bathrooms are directly over downstairs bathrooms, or kitchen, there is no problem as these pipes can be concealed behind cabinets or inside "hung" ceilings. Many restorers have found that the most satisfactory manner to overcome this frequent problem is to raise the upstairs bathroom floor to a height that allows the hiding of all pipes. If your house is getting a new chimney stack, it may be possible to hide the piping in *chases* (channels) left by the mason for this purpose. It is imperative that the plumber plan his work knowing beforehand what is expected of him; redoing this work is expensive.

TRIM

Repairing the interior trim of a house calls for the highest degree of woodworking skill. If you will be doing the work yourself, you must invest in a few beading planes (your restorer will no doubt have his own tools). These come in various radii. Old ones can be purchased from antiques shops; new ones, made very much like the old, are sold today by some of the better manufacturers of woodworking tools. It will not be difficult to find beading planes that will match the beads on your corner-post casings, beaded boards, or other cased trim. Finding planes that will match exactly the more sophisticated moldings of your house, such as chair rail, crown molding, bolection moldings, etc., is another matter altogether; it will be best to have these moldings made for you by a woodworking shop or a kitchen-cabinet manufacturer. Special blades must be made for the shaping machinery that is used to turn out these moldings. Although it is possible to find "Colonial" moldings in stock in most lumberyards, an exact duplicate of your old moldings will be impossible to find. There are a few makers of reproduction trim who will be able to give you a price per foot for making moldings, paneling, doors, windows, and boards in the old manner. It will be necessary for you to supply a sample of what you want duplicated.

Most good trim carpenters can run out new feather-edged or beaded boards for you if you cannot obtain the old material at a price you can live with. New wood is machine-planed dead smooth and must be surface-planed (scrub-planed) by hand to give it the ripples that hand planes gave to old work. Examine examples of original work before you surface-plane, as there is a tendency to overplane new wood. New wood requires distressing as well as surface planing. Hitting boards with a light chain, gouging, and denting are the only ways to add "years of age" to them quickly; but one must use common sense with these methods. Wood that is to be located in areas of high use or traffic, such as door casings or hall woodwork, would be more likely to have suffered bruising than a corner-post casing at the ceiling line. Doors are "chewed up" more around the latches than elsewhere; and mop boards take more punishment than crown moldings. If the new wood is to be painted rather than stained to a natural finish, a secondary grade of wood can be used; hemlock or spruce can be substituted for clear pine if you want to gain a rougher texture.

Complete walls of paneling must at times be built in houses where they have been removed. A first-rate restoration carpenter can make these either in his shop or right on the job. Commercial trim houses will also make up paneling for about $150 per running foot at this writing. Again it will be necessary to instruct the one making the wall to surface-plane all the new wood. Wood without the plane marks will never appear to be old.

Remember, there is no old woodwork that cannot be

202

203

202. False walls of modern lumber hide plumbing piping. The final wall finish is up to you—ceramic tile, plaster, wallpaper, barn boards, etc.

203. A false beaded corner post conceals pipes going to the second floor from the "wet" bar.

204. Where ceilings are exposed below an upstairs bathroom, it is almost mandatory to raise the bathroom floor to conceal the plumbing; otherwise the piping must be "boxed" (covered) from below.

204

205. Making paneling on the site. These boards have been measured, cut, and fitted. The paneled fireplace wall took two men three days.

206. A modern "heat-a-lator" was removed from this fireplace, which required extensive panel repair. The large overmantel panel had been cut and has now been brought back to size. Two new stiles and a roll-bolection molding were made up from new lumber. House in Hanover, Connecticut.

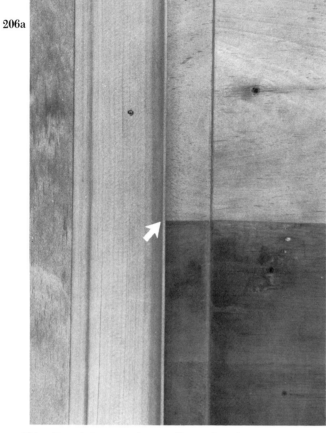

206a. Detail showing the excellent splice that pieces out the large panel in figure 206. A coat of paint will make the repair undetectable.

206b. Detail showing splice in bolection molding at hearthstone.

207. New corner-post casing at ceiling. The bead matches another on a post in the same room. Note the "power nails" used as a substitute for old nails.

207

208. Here the paneled dado has been raised to provide room for baseboard heat convectors.

208

209. The window casing and one or two of the panels in this room are new; the remainder of the dado is original to a house that had been demolished.

209

210. The same dado now finished and furnished; the baseboard-heat convectors are inconspicuous.

210

211. The trim in this room is old with the exception of the window casings; however, the dado came from one house, the overmantel panels from another, and the two doors were found in place. Late 18th-century house restored by the author.

212. The rear staircase in this kitchen of c. 1760 was rebuilt slightly wider than the original to permit modern furniture to be carried upstairs. Not completely "pure" but a very practical adjustment. Restored by the author.

duplicated by a good workman today with the proper tools and an understanding of what it is he is doing. Your local lumberyard can tell you who in your area has the equipment to reproduce woodwork for you.

The most frequent repair in house-trim restoration is fixing the panel over a fireplace wall through which a stovepipe was installed. If the wall is to be painted, a patch of similar wood can be made; if the wall is to remain "natural," it will be better to make a new panel to replace the old one.

Mantels were frequently updated in the 1830s or 1840s. Late mantels can easily be removed and replaced with mantels of the appropriate period.

Paint Removal

It is much easier to remove paint from your woodwork when that woodwork is off the wall. Therefore, should you find it necessary to remove any trim for repair, take the paint off before it is renailed. Paint removal is a slow, tedious job no matter how it is done. There are many methods.

Dry Scraping

Dry scraping painted surfaces is the slowest but the best method to use if you intend to reach the original coat and save it with the least damage. The scrapers used must be kept very sharp at all times. It will be necessary to make scraper blades to fit unusual molding curves or beads; this can be done by filing. If standard, handled scrapers are to be used, file the corners of the blades round to prevent gouging the wood. Have a number of scrapers of different sizes, and files and a stone for sharpening.

The best scrapers for this work are carpenter's scrapers; these are flat pieces of saw-blade steel that are sharpened in a very special way. The edge to be sharpened is first "draw-filed" square, then honed smooth on a fine stone. Then the scraper is placed in a vise, edge up, and an edge is rolled with a burnisher to form a burr. Carpenter's scrapers can occasionally be found in old-fashioned hardware stores or can be purchased from quality manufacturers of woodworking tools. Burnishers, files, sharpening stones, and instructions for sharpening can be obtained. These scrapers can be bought with one concave and one convex side for scraping curved surfaces.

The burr formed on the edge of the tool will scrape the barest skin of paint at each pass. If you wear gloves while you work, you will be able to exert greater pressure against the tool without its hurting your hands. The job will take patience, as the paint is removed very slowly; the cutting edges will require frequent resharpening. I

hesitate to recommend the use of glass as a dry scraper, as the danger of its breaking in your hand with serious results is not worth taking. The steel carpenter's scraper works very much the way glass does, but it is faster and of course much safer to use.

Paint Remover

There are many commercial paint removers on the market. I perfer to use one with the consistency of gelatin rather than the watery type, especially when working on vertical woodwork. Most people are too impatient to get the paint off to give the remover a chance to penetrate fully. Read the directions on the can and follow them to the letter. Be very careful to work in a well-ventilated area and, since most removers are highly flammable, do not smoke while you work or have a fire in a fireplace. It is a good idea to keep a fire extinguisher on the job at all times. If your woodwork is off the wall and you are working out of doors, keep the trim out of the sun, as the sun will dry the remover before it can do its work.

To avoid digging into your woodwork, round the corners of your putty knives (you may need one that has sharp corners). A stiff putty knife works better than a springy one. I recommend that you have three or four putty knives of different widths. You may find it necessary to file one very narrow to fit such areas as the feather of a raised panel, the fluting of a pilaster, or an intricate molding.

I find it helpful to have one narrow putty knife filed to a rounded end. Have plenty of newspaper to catch the debris. When almost all the paint you want off has been removed, a final coat of remover used with No. 000 steel wool will catch any paint your putty knives have missed. Finally, wash the surface with a solution of washing soda and water to stop the action of the remover, and then dry the surface. Never let wet wood dry in the sun, as it will warp.

Paint remover is messy but it is effective. If you are trying to get down to bare wood and you find that the original first coat of paint doesn't want to come off, try using Lestoil and steel wool. You may find that you must go back to the dry-scraping method if your remover or a commercial cleaner doesn't penetrate that first coat.

Lye Solution

There is no quicker way than the use of a solution of lye added to *cold* water for removing paint from large surfaces such as entire walls of paneling, doors, girt, post, and summer beam casings, chair rails, mop boards, etc., when these are off the wall and can be taken outside to be worked on. I use a solution of one can of lye to two gallons of water. However, the ratio can be varied

213

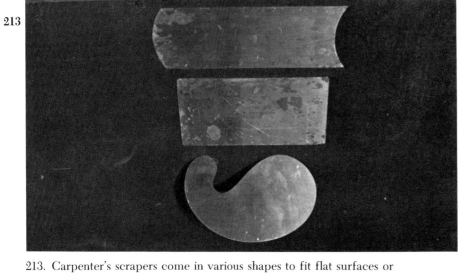

213. Carpenter's scrapers come in various shapes to fit flat surfaces or moldings. You can make your own from old files or saw blades.

214. Removing paint from paneling using lye and *cold* water. This work is best done outdoors. To avoid warping, the wood must not be permitted to dry in the sun.

214

depending on the tenacity of your paint. Safety precautions are necessary when you are working with lye solution. Wherever a drop of the solution touches you, it will burn. Use safety goggles, rubber gloves, long sleeves, and heavy shoes if you wish to avoid being "stung" by the mixture. The lye solution can be applied with an old paintbrush. From time to time after the trim has been wetted, test to see if the paint is becoming soft. Using a stiff, long-handled scrub brush, you can loosen the paint and then hose it off. If there are many coats of paint on the wood, repeat the treatment until you are down to the wood.

If the wood is wet for too long, there is a tendency for a strong lye solution to lift the grain, making the surface furry. From my experience this does not occur until the final coat is being removed and the watery solution penetrates the wood. I would therefore recommend a milder solution toward the end of the procedure. You may wish to experiment on a small piece of wood before tackling the major work to see how your lye solution works on your particular paint. Again do not work in the direct sunlight or let the wood dry in the sun.

This procedure is also excellent for the removal of paint from flooring that can be taken outside. Do not use lye in the house, as it may get between the cracks of your floors and will burn through electrical wiring, creating a fire hazard.

Heat

Burning paint off interior painted surfaces can be accomplished in one of three ways: with a high-intensity light, with an electric-coil burner, or with an acetylene gas flame.

The trick here is to remove the paint without scorching the wood beneath. It is entirely possible once the technique is mastered to remove all the coats of paint except the first one without in any way burning the original. The putty knives used must be sharp (with rounded corners), and one should wear asbestos gloves. It is wise to have a fire extinguisher and a bucket of water handy as well. The trick is to heat the paint until it blisters and separates from the wood or the first coat. It is a matter of timing. There is an exact moment when the paint will separate without leaving a scorch mark beneath—two seconds beyond this moment and the browning of the wood occurs.

High-intensity-light paint burners are available. They work more slowly than electric or gas burners, but they also present less chance of burning the wood. These burners must be used with special goggles to protect the eyes from the light.

Gas burners may also be used. For the removal of small areas of paint, use a hand tank with a wide-mouth flame spreader. For large jobs a full-sized tank of gas with a valve can be rented from your local welding-supply house, together with *at least* six feet of tubing and a welding torch with a wide tip. The large tank will supply you with flame for many hours of work, and the long hose will permit you to reach from ceiling to floor and from one end of a wall to the other without constantly having to move the tank.

Electric-coil paint burners can be purchased at any hardware store and do a good job once their use is mastered. Be careful not to set the burner down on a flammable surface.

When any of the heat methods of paint removal are used, the paint usually separates from the wood, leaving behind the original first coat of paint. If it is required that this coat be removed as well, it is often safer to do so with paint remover rather than burning, as there is a much greater possibility of scorching the wood in burning off a single coat than there is in taking off many layers at a time. Some of the early "milk" paints resist both burners and paint remover but may yield to Lestoil or other similar household cleansers. If neither of these methods works, dry scraping is the answer.

Commercial Paint Dipping

Almost every town or city has a paint-stripping establishment. Various chemicals are used, but in all cases they claim to remove paint without raising the grain. Most of these places are quite good for stripping doors or boards. These must be brought to their dipping tanks. The work comes out with an almost bleached look, and "life" will have to be put back into the wood with linseed oil, stain, or paint. In large quantities door stripping can be done for $20 per door. To strip a door with lye will take you or your worker about two hours. Burning the paint off a door to a finished surface will take at least two hours. Dry scraping may take even longer, depending on the tenacity of the paint. Some professional paint strippers can be persuaded to take the paint down to the original coat. Before giving all your wood to him, I would experiment with one door to see how it turns out.

Power Sanding

Power sanding of old woodwork with either a rotary or a reciprocating sander will kill it even if the woodwork is to be painted. Not only will the ripples of the hand planing be cut flat, but the surface will become too smooth. In short, the character of the old work will be lost.

In the case of floorboards, sanding will flatten the nailheads. The heavy rotary floor sanders will scratch a circular pattern across the grain, which will require hand

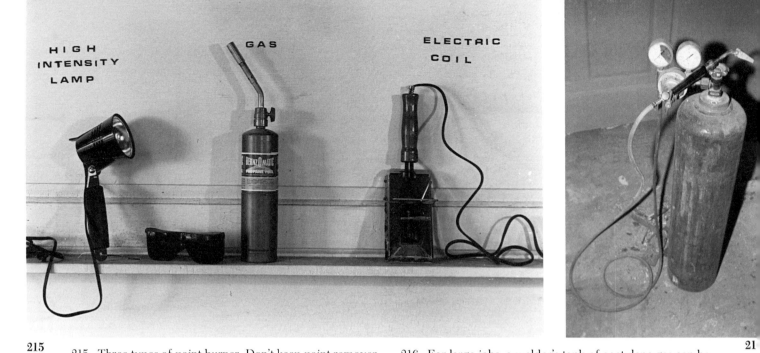

215. Three types of paint burner. Don't keep paint remover in the same room in which a burner is being used.

216. For large jobs, a welder's tank of acetylene gas can be rented, together with a welder's torch, long hose, and wide flame nozzle.

217. An original window frame (note the dowel).

218. A poor reproduction put together without doweling the mortise-and-tenon joint. Restoration by the author when he didn't know any better (1959).

scraping to remove. It is impossible to power-sand flooring without losing at least some of the patina of the old wood.

Window Sash and Frames

It is rare indeed to find an old house with all its original window sash intact. The original sash (and often the window frames as well) have been replaced two or three times. It is therefore usual to have sash of the right type made after ascertaining what was original to the house.

It takes a pretty skillful woodworker to make sash, and it is a time-consuming job. Unless you are set up with sophisticated machinery, you'd best leave this job to those who do this kind of work on a regular basis. The amateur making his own windows will find that in the long run (counting his own time) it is much more expensive than having a professional do the work. Trim houses, kitchen-cabinet manufacturers, and those in the business of reproducing old woodwork have the tools to run out rail, stiles, and muntins to your pattern quickly and accurately. It is important that whoever does this work for you be told that you want an *exact* copy of the sample given them; this may necessitate their making up special cutters. Naturally, if you find in the attic or elsewhere in your house an original window sash, that is what you will want copied. If, on the other hand, all the sash have disappeared, you can buy a sash to be used as a pattern.

When your window frames are also missing, they will have to be made. If possible, have the same person make the frames and the sash, although you may find that certain craftsmen will make only one or the other. The sash must fit the frames; your measurements must be accurate. Sash are always made a bit larger and are trimmed to fit on the job when they are installed. Do not forget to point out the dowels in both frames and sash when placing your order. Do not rely exclusively on your attic windows when choosing a size for your house, as attic windows were often smaller; thus many a house had nine over sixes in the attic and twelve over twelves elsewhere.

Sash come glazed or unglazed. Glazing is tedious work, and you will no doubt find it more rewarding doing other aspects of your restoration yourself, leaving the installation of the glass to the supplier. If you have "wavy" glass to install, the sash manufacturer can put these lights in for you. Ask for a price "glazed" before ordering. Window sash at this writing have been running about $5.00 per light of new glass supplied and installed (12 over 12 = 24 x $5.00 = $128).

It will cost the same if you supply the old glass to the manufacturer as it takes longer to install old glass. When I do not have enough old glass to do every pane, I prefer to spread out what glass I have, putting one or two panes of early material in each sash, rather than doing a few windows completely.

Plain doweled window frames cost about $135 each.

By and large, people restoring houses, whether they are craftsmen themselves or owners doing the work themselves, are happy to share their sources of materials with you. By asking you will soon discover who is making sash and frames in your vicinity.

It is not impossible to find old sash and frames from buildings being torn down or from "old materials" dealers or demolition contractors. The chances of finding enough of the same type to do your complete house are remote. Old frames and sash require work to put them back in usable condition. Windows taken from the "prevailing wind" side of a house are generally weather-beaten and the window sills, more often than not, require replacing, unless the house was kept up with regular painting. The wood should be stripped of its paint, all joints tightened, and then the wood should be treated with Cuprinol or another wood preservative. Don't use creosote.

You don't want to install windows that leak air or water. It is important therefore that the time be taken to do a proper job. In the *guillotine* (single-hung) window only the bottom sash moves and must be neither too loose nor too tight. You can increase the width and height of sash by gluing thin strips to the top or the side as required.

Doors, Door Trim, and Hardware

The most frequent repair that must be made to doors is to remove a late knob and lock. Even doors of a thickness of one inch were rabbeted out to take a lock. When the lock is removed, the hole remaining must be filled in with wood and glued. It is important that this splice be strong, as the reinstallation of an early latch must stand up to years of use and abuse. Most exterior doors retain their early strap hinges, but interior doors have often lost their HL hinges to butt hinges of a later date. Where this has occurred, the more modern butts can be removed and the two recesses filled in. Now replacement HL hinges can be surface-mounted and the door rehung. The original type of hardware should come to light when the door is first examined.

Door casings are frequently changed on one side or the other of an opening. A beaded casing can easily be reinstalled. An unbeaded casing does not seem as objectionable when the woodwork is natural; but once the wood has been painted, the unbeaded sharp corner of the casing seems to appear obviously plain and unattractive.

When you are installing hardware such as HL hinges, strap hinges, bean latches, etc., small squares of leather should be used under the nailheads just as they were in

219. After the removal of the modern doorknob and lock, a large graft was made before replacing the old wrought-iron bean latch. The door was made ½ inch wider by adding a strip of wood to the edge. As the door was to be painted, new pine was used in this repair.

220. This unpainted cupboard door was butt-hinged when found; the mortise for the butt hinge was filled in with new wood, which was later stained (it is barely visible under the right side of the H hinge in the picture).

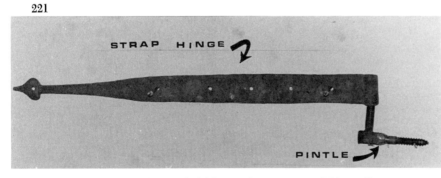

STRAP HINGE

PINTLE

221. An altered pintle may hold better than an original "driven" one.

222. A reproduction exterior door made from weathered, beaded material; old hardware and nails were used in its construction. A weathered look can be mimicked by *lightly* sandblasting new wood in the direction of the grain.

223. The right-hand door of this double door was missing from the house and a new one had to be made. It was created from old wood. House in Preston, Connecticut.

223a. Detail of figure 223. It is almost impossible to match exactly the texture of weathered wood. In time the door on the right will become more like the original. A light sandblasting would have produced the weathering effect but the patina would have been lost, and the owners wished to keep the doors unpainted.

223

223a

224. Some time after 1800 the original double doors and their frame were removed from this 1760 center-chimney house in Old Wethersfield, Connecticut, and a single door substituted. Here a doorframe of the original type is being made on the job.

225. New double doors and a frame are in the process of being handmade for this lovely house in Hanover, Connecticut, c. 1760. After their installation, the skimpy brick chimney will be brought back to its once massive size. The final step will be to paint the house in its original color.

226. This elaborate doorway of c. 1776 is on the Whitman House, West Hartford, Connecticut.

226a. Detail of figure 226 showing the "Connecticut rose" and fine Ionic capital.

227. The headpiece over this side door was water-damaged beyond repair. The new head, properly flashed, has been reset.

228. To prevent deterioration houses must be able to breathe. A wood louver has been placed high in the gable of this house to let air enter. When stained, it matches the reproduction red-cedar clapboards and is hardly noticed from the ground.

the original. These *washers* were not used for decoration but had the practical function of acting as a lock washer does, holding the nail in place and preventing it from slipping out.

On exterior doors where new pintles are to be installed, I find that a stronger installation can be made (especially if it is going into new lumber) if the pintle is altered. I do this by cutting the pintle shaft off, leaving a 1-inch to 1½-inch stub with the upright rod on it. To this I weld a ½-inch or ⅝-inch lag screw or bolt about 3 inches long, welding it on head and all. The pintle can now be screwed into the door framing, where it will grip well. The head of the lag bolt can be screwed right into the door casing and will not be seen, or it can be ground round on a wheel.

LATH, PLASTER, AND SHEETROCK

Lath

Although a good plasterer can simulate the look of old plaster on both wire lath and rock lath, best results can be obtained by the use of the original material or modern wood lath. Modern wood lath should be applied in the same pattern as it would have been originally, that is, in panels of even length. The joints were not staggered as they would be today. Each lath is nailed about a lath's thickness from its neighbor to permit the wet plaster to set in a proper "key."

Applying lath is an easy job not requiring a professional carpenter. The distance is measured between floor joists (for a ceiling) or studs (for a wall), and the required number of pieces are cut to length. A nail is "started" at each end of each lath before it is placed where it is to go; this is much easier than holding the piece while trying to nail at the same time.

An experienced plasterer will not find it necessary to cover the woodwork or flooring while he works, but the amateur will no doubt drop globs of wet plaster on chair rails, windowsills, floors, and his shoes. Before work begins, wood lath can be wet lightly to prevent its sucking the water out of the plaster, causing dry spots.

Plaster

If you are using a plasterer who has not done antique work before, it would be wise to show him the texture of the finish you want to reproduce. The three-coat modern method of plastering (scratch, brown, and white) is not necessary to achieve the job you want. Any of the one-step plasters on the market, such as Structolite, will be the material used. The first, or scratch, coat is applied and allowed to dry. The second coat is the final one, and it is with the application of this second coat that the finish is obtained. Keep in mind that the old-time plasterers tried their best to get a smooth, even surface. Some restorers feel that by making the surface very crude they are being authentic. Actually it is the ripples in the plaster formed by the wood lath and the coarseness of the material that make new work resemble the old. Another method of applying plaster is to lay on the scratch coat and then go back, before it sets up, adding the final coat. While still wet, you can "shock" the wall or ceiling by hitting the area over a joist or stud with a two-by-four, causing the whole panel to vibrate slightly. This will make the lines of the lath more pronounced through the plaster. The spots that were struck can now be repaired. The final painting or whitewashing will finish the job.

Sheetrock

Sheetrock is an excellent building material, although it was unknown in the early days. It doesn't crack and is easy to install. Where it is not important to be "authentic"—in bathrooms perhaps or modern kitchens or inside closets— it is the ideal material. In the interest of economy, where the budget will just not permit the luxury of a plaster job, sheetrock can be used and made to look as "original" as a new plaster wall.

If you desire to make a sheetrock wall look like an old plaster wall, you need only "plaster" the entire surface with the taping compound you used in taping the joints. Taping compound can be purchased in large quantities either as a powder, which you must mix with water, or in the more convenient premixed form. A two-coat job will look better than a one-application job. Allow one or two days for the first coat to dry before applying the second. Remember that if you are going to use sheetrock instead of plaster, you must apply the wood trim to the room *before* sheet-rocking, just as you apply the trim before plastering. In modern work the trim goes over the plaster or sheetrock; in the seventeenth- and eighteenth-century house the plaster was applied against the edge of the woodwork, the wood acting as a "stop" or "ground" for the plaster.

TRIM

Doors, like windows, are one of the few moving parts of the house. Unlike the windows, however, which are opened upon occasion, the doors are constantly in use. The original blacksmith-wrought latches were relatively quick to wear out and were replaced by cast-iron latches or, at a later time, by ceramic doorknobs. The surface-mounted H or HL hinges would be replaced by butt hinges.

When doorknobs were installed, the doors had to be severely cut to receive them; in going back to the old

229. Modern wood lath.

230. The lath is butted up against the corner post and other room trim in the old manner.

231. When new plaster is properly applied, as in this reproduction ceiling, the outline of the lath is visible.

232. Window trim, corner post and girt casings, chair rail, and mop board are installed *before* the room is sheetrocked.

232

233. Wall and ceiling joints, and nails are taped and spackled.

233

234. Joint compound is one of the handiest materials of the restorer. It can be used to make sheetrock look like plaster, fill in nail holes in woodwork before painting, repair old plaster, etc. It can be purchased in the premixed form illustrated here.

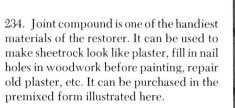

234

235. Bars and cupboards are attractive and useful items of built-in furniture in an antique home, where they are sometimes found in their original condition. When removed, at some time, their original shape and position can often be ascertained by telltale marks on floors, ceiling plaster, and corner post casings; reproductions can then be made. House in Hanover Connecticut, c. 1760.

236. Pewter cupboard.

latch it will therefore be necessary to make a sizable patch, filling in the mortising with wood of the same type.

The exact size and position of original H or HL hinges can be determined if you closely examine the door surface for a line of nail holes or the outline in the paint of the old hinge. Again the mortise cut for the later butt hinge must be filled in before you install a surface-mounted wrought hinge of the proper size and type.

The nails used for the installation of both hinges and latches are set with a small square of leather under their heads as a washer, or else they should be sufficiently long to protrude from the opposite side of the door, where they can be clinched.

Long strap hinges were used to support doors of great weight, the pintles on which they rotated carrying the entire burden. These pintles were originally driven into "new" oak studs. In rebuilding a doorway today, we use a soft wood for framing, a material that does not hold a driven pintle as securely as oak does. I find that if I alter the pintle by cutting it just short of the end that will be visible and welding on a lag bolt of suitable size, this can be screwed into the new wood and will hold firm.

It is sometimes necessary to make an entirely new door or to patch part of a door that has been cut. The most frequent addition one encounters is at the top and bottom of a door. As a doorframe settled (generally at an angle), the door had to be cut and rehung. The door was usually cut at the bottom and a strip nailed to the top to fill in. This patchwork was frequently very poorly done and it may be desirable to remove the door, repatch it properly, and fit it again.

The important thing to remember is to use a material similar to the one on the door if the work is to remain unpainted.

PAINTING

When our antique houses were first built, the woodwork, both structure and trim, was created from new lumber and consequently was yellow in color. The builders of that time covered this new work with paint or stain. One finds an occasional room that escaped the paintbrush, but such examples are rare indeed; I believe they occurred only because the builder didn't get around to completing his job. (*Note:* Having spent some twenty years in inspecting over twenty-five hundred 17th- and 18th-century New England houses, the writer has yet to discover one in which the *original* woodwork was not painted a strong color and with the walls whitewashed. Although others have found tinted plaster, I have as yet found no evidence of this having been done. I have, however, found many walls with their original wallpaper still in place and have found rare rooms in which the builder had not painted the woodwork. After a few years of exposure to the air the wood darkened thus making painting unnecessary.) As a matter of fact, painting must have been considered vital to the preservation of the house, as many roofs were painted as well as the body of the house. From what I have discovered by scraping down to the "original," most eighteenth-century houses were painted entirely in one color—the sash and window frames, the corner boards, vergeboards, clapboards, water table, crown moldings, cornice—everything on the outside of the house was the same color. On the inside of the rooms, all the woodwork of each room was painted, and the plaster walls and ceilings were whitewashed.

Any good "bone" white paint can be used on walls and ceilings. I prefer a latex paint, as cleaning brushes and drips is much easier than with oil paint. Painting an old room is generally more difficult than painting a new one, as there is a lot of *cutting in* to be done—that is, fine lines to be drawn where the white walls come in contact with the protruding corner post and door and window casings. The edges of door and window casings that protrude into the room should be painted the same color as the face of that trim; however, on occasion the plaster line is so uneven that it is preferable to paint these narrow reveals as part of the white wall.

The color most frequently used in both the seventeenth and the eighteenth centuries was Spanish brown, a dark brownish red. This color was so popular that it persisted right through the eighteenth century, being used on furniture as well as houses. Sometimes it was employed as a ground, or first coat. Although the front and the sides of a house may have been given another color, the rear was almost always painted in the "old red."

Other popular colors found in eighteenth-century rooms are mustard, blue, green, olive, pumpkin, and gray. In all cases strongly pigmented paints were used that contrasted boldly with the dead white of the walls. White paint, as an outside color, seems to have been infrequently used. In the last few years a number of paint manufacturers have come out with reproductions of early colors that are accurate copies of original colors found in the rooms of museum houses. However, color matching has become a science in recent years, so there is no reason not to duplicate the original colors of your own house if they are pleasing to you. All you need is a small sample to take to your paint store.

There are two schools of thought about paint restoration. The first suggests that we repaint our houses as they would have appeared when newly built. The other tells us that we must paint "old," to appear as paint would

237. A room in process of being restored. Note the paint-scraping of the corner cupboard to discover the original color. The window sash, which are reproductions, have been primed for protection; their final color will be applied later.

238. The prime coat has been applied to a wall of new paneling and room trim. This room was painted "new," rather than being antiqued to make the paint look 200 years old. Restoration by the author.

239. Magnificent door for a church pew found in a house in Stonington, Connecticut. Although this door was originally painted, it is always difficult to decide whether or not to repaint, when you can achieve a warm color like this by stripping to the bare wood. Notice the very rare pair of butterfly strap hinges. The door dates to c. 1725 at the latest; it may possibly be late 17th century.

look after 200 years of aging. Neither way is the "right" way, of course. It is my own preference wherever possible to strip the woodwork down to the original first coat of paint. However, if extensive new woodwork has been required in a room, it will be necessary to match the new to the old or to repaint the room in its entirety.

Antiquing New Paint

When matching old surfaces or in repainting something to appear aged, the object is to get away from the fresh-painted look. If you examine an example of old paint, you will notice that the years have altered the surface both in texture and in color. Take for example a feather-edged board in the old red. You will notice that not only has the paint surface lost the fresh, clean, even look it had when first laid on but it has aged unevenly. One can find two or three different shades of red. Many of the indentations in the wood, the distress marks caused by use, and the lines formed by the joining of the feather to the bead will be black or dark brown. Here and there, too, bare wood may show through where the wood was frequently touched. How can this effect be reproduced in new work? Antiquing kits are sold in paint stores; or one can mix a pinch of lampblack with turpentine, rub it on the newly painted surface, and then wipe it off again immediately, thus "dirtying" the new paint. The entire surface will darken when this is done, and it is best to experiment on a sample before doing a whole room. It may be necessary to begin with a lighter color.

Another method of achieving the "antique" look is to daub another color here and there on the new paint and then wipe it off. Experiment.

Reproducing the Old Red

Since the old red must be reproduced so frequently in restorations, I will give my own formula for mixing that color and two methods of making it appear very old. The colors I have used in matching the old reds are Venetian red and Prussian blue. Only a small quantity of blue is needed. Add the blue pigment little by little to the Venetian red, stirring after each addition. The red will slowly darken. Eventually your red will match pretty closely one of the old reds so frequently found. If you wish to darken the color even more, a small pinch of lampblack can be added to the mixture.

Painting Old

Method #1. Paint the woodwork a dark brown using either oil- or water-base paint, leaving bare wood where

signs of wear would have been "natural." Use a flat rather than a glossy paint. Do not do a very smooth job of laying on the paint; lean toward a rough job. When this first coat has dried, apply a coat of red paint (made by the formula above), and after a few minutes wipe it off lightly with a rag, allowing some of the red to remain. The brown will "show through" the red, giving an old look to the wood when it dries.

Method #2. Here is a surefire method of adding 200 years to a new paint job. After mixing your paint to arrive at the desired shade of red, paint the surface. Be generous with the paint and do a rough job. Take an old brick and scrape it until you accumulate enough brick dust to fill the foot of a woman's silk stocking. When the paint is almost dry but still tacky, beat the surface until it is entirely powdered. Allow the paint to set up completely. Now lightly steel-wool with No. 000 steel wool. The paint will have the chalky appearance of "old milk paint."

Old Milk Paint

In the earliest houses, when one scrapes down to the original color one finds a paint that is chalky in texture rather than glossy or semiglossy. One hears these paints being referred to as "milk" paint or "buttermilk" paint. I have never run across a formula in writing that describes how these "milk" paints (if, indeed, milk was used) were formulated, although an old-timer once told me how his grandfather would mix paint by using a "bucket of blood, a bucket of milk, and some urine to set the whole thing." I daresay it would be best to leave town for a week after using such a mixture.

Milk paint can be created either by the use of dry pigments (earth colors) or water-soluble dyes of the desired color. Either can be mixed with powdered milk to give them "body." The dry colors can be mixed with skimmed milk instead of water. The results will be a chalky "milk paint" look, closely resembling the early texture. I will not give a formula here because I have not been able to repeat exactly the same results twice. Experiment for yourself and mix a large enough batch of paint to do the entire job at one time. A setting agent such as casein glue will prevent "chalking."

When you are painting over existing paint, it may be quite unnecessary to remove that paint before applying the new. If the panels, moldings, and beads are well defined and sharp rather than being filled with paint, you may want to avoid having to scrape off the existing paint. In this case give the woodwork a light sanding and then "size" it with shellac cut thin with denatured alcohol.

CHAPTER 4

THE JOHN PALMER HOUSE: A RESTORATION LOG BOOK

5/28: Tomorrow, I will take title to the property at 9:30 A.M. at the bank. I am impatient to get started and have arranged for a truck and three men to begin cleaning up the mess created by the fire. Only after the debris is gone will it be possible to get a full picture of what restoration must be done.

5/29: Title closed. Cleanup and demolition work began today. One man and two boys. Sent two full truckloads to the dump, most of which were wet furniture, rugs, and charred lumber (figs. 240, 241).

5/30: Removed some of the smoke-blackened window sash from their frames so the men could see to work. Still can't assess the extent of the fire damage but believe it was confined to the sitting room. Continued all day sending truckload after truckload to the dump with everything from loose plaster to a few hundred jars of home-canned vegetables from the basement. Removed some of the asbestos shingles from the outside of the house and was surprised to find wood shingles plus some old-fashioned insulating board over the original clapboards. As soon as the interior is broom clean, will strip the house down to its first outside covering—clapboards.

6/2: By early afternoon the inside of the house was free of debris from attic to cellar. Two-and-a-half days' work for three men. Began to strip the outside. Am having the men save the wood shingles as they come off; they make the very best kindling wood. While the work progressed outside, I investigated inside. No reason to remove any more of the building than is absolutely necessary. It is still so dark inside that I find I must use a flashlight most of the time. A new kitchen of sorts and a bathroom with metal stall shower were built in the little bedroom off the kitchen; both must be removed. There is a plastered wall built across the entire length of the old kitchen fireplace wall and another over the parlor fireplace wall so that neither fireplace is visible. These walls must be removed. There is new flooring in the old kitchen, but there may be original floors underneath. Have decided to remove the plaster ceilings from all downstairs rooms as the water from the firemen's hoses loosened the plaster. The dormer is about a hundred years old and should come off; square-cut nails. Made telephone calls this evening to stonemasons, carpenters, brickmasons, electricians, and plumbers; will meet with contractors on the job when it's clear which direction to go.

6/3: Today shifted work to the inside of the house again and began removing the new kitchen and bathroom, opening up the fireplace walls and taking down the ceilings. I enlisted Joan's help in saving the old nails from the ceiling lath, which she placed in a separate pile (fig. 242).

Three interesting discoveries! On the outside wall of the old kitchen there is evidence of some horizontal dado made of two feather-edged boards with a chair rail over them. The big surprise is a dated stone found *upside down* above the fireplace in the parlor. It has what appear to be two turtledoves facing each other, a dog and a cat, and the date 1784 cut into it (figs. 243a, 243b)!

Where does it come from? An older house? And why placed in the fireplace breast upside down? Every restoration has its surprises, but this is a real mystery. It certainly is a domestic scene. Was there a marriage in the house? Surprise number 2 was finding two small mustard-colored (original color) panels cut off over the door to the stair passage. The entire wall must have been paneled. Yes, and right over the dated stone. Impossible! The fireplace seems too narrow (fig. 244). There must have been major work done here at one time, as the chimney girt is cut as well just where the cupboard begins.

6/4: Met the stonemason at the house and had him go over the foundation walls; there must be more light and air brought into the basement. Therefore, the mason will install basement window openings and a few louvers (ventilators) through the cellar walls so the area can breathe. We are also providing an exterior cellar doorway with steps from the rear of the ell. Began to uncover the old kitchen fireplace.

The old kitchen fireplace and its wall are most interesting. The crane is still in place, and the original sheet-iron bake-oven door was found covering the opening to the bake oven. Both of these have been removed temporarily from the premises for safe-keeping. It appears that a two-part wood door was installed to cover the bake oven and its storage niche; this is of later date than the paneling above, which consists of two long panels. Both these panels were fire-scorched and might be better replaced by new paneling. On the same wall the feather-edged boarded dado continues to the right and left of the fireplace and bake oven. Found no pots in the bake oven itself.

6/5: The fireplace in the old kitchen, including its bake oven, is nine feet long. The hearthstone was made in three sections, two of which are in front of the fireplace and measure three feet each; the third piece is missing and lay in front of the bake oven. It also was three feet long.

The entire kitchen fireplace is of gray granite except for three bricks, one on top of the other three-quarters of the way up the rear wall of the fireplace. These bricks are evidently of later vintage. On removing them, I was surprised to find a small square wooden door behind leading to a flue of some sort. Strangely, this flue ends at the opening and goes downward toward the chimney base! Why down? Is this an ashpit, perhaps? There is a hole in the chimney base in the cellar about one and one-half feet square, behind

which is a large cavernous space approximately in the center of the stack (fig. 245).

Upon investigation of the cavern within the chimney base I found no signs of ashes, nor is there evidence that a fire had ever been made here. The small flue from the kitchen fireplace leads into the ceiling of this cavern. Could this small flue, which is about eight inches square, draw smoke into the basement, and if so for what purpose? To drive out mice and insects perhaps? Sounds ridiculous. Must give it more thought. Nothing in the books about it.

The parlor fireplace seems much too narrow. It appears that the stone lintel was cut on the left side and the left cheek stones have been replaced with square stones instead of angle stones. This indicates that the closet under the stairs was not in its present location and that the fireplace was made narrower when the closet was installed.

Inspected the fireplace in the south front room and found that the same situation exists here. The fireplace has been cut down in width. At first I believed that the stairs had been changed—made wider—necessitating a narrowing of the fireplace. But since the hearthstone has not been cut, it is obvious from its length, running well past the center of the stairs, that the stairs couldn't have been here originally (fig. 246).

Checked the stairs thoroughly and have concluded that they were put in about a hundred years ago. The dormer, even though it has two early 9/6 windows in original window frames facing the front, must also have been built when the stairs were. A major modernization took place somewhere about the time of the Civil War.

6/6: Arranged with the electrician to set us up with temporary electric service so that we can have drop-lights and power for saws and other tools. Swept the floors of the entire house for the tenth time. Removed the remainder of the new bath and "new kitchen" with its blackened cabinets. The inside is beginning to look better. Time to make some decisions. Cleanup cost $230 more or less for a week's work part time. Took a bid from a local kitchen-cabinet firm to include a new kitchen complete with dishwasher, cabinets, refrigerator, stove, oven, exhaust fan and hood. The same to be installed in the back part of the ell. Will take a few more bids before giving it out.

6/9: Cleaned the remaining debris from around the outside of the house and had same carted to the dump. Six full truckloads to date and still more to go if the

240. House as purchased (front elevation).

241. House as purchased (side elevation).

242. Removing 18th-century nails from lath.

243a. Date stone found over parlor fire-place.

243b. Two turtledoves, a dog, and a cat, and the date 1784; what is the significance of all the images?

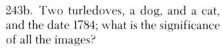

244. Cut chimney girt (right) and tenons on panelings (left) prove paneling continued on.

245. Draft hole in the base of the chimney stack in the cellar.

246. The fireplace was cut to make room for the stairs.

247. The dormer and stairs are gone.

248. Now it can be seen. About two feet of masonry was cut off the stack to make room for the stairs.

249. The completed new chimney.

250. The new chimney is twice the size of the old one.

250

251. A mason rebuilding the fireplace and flue.

251

252. Roofing begun.

252

stairs and the dormer are to be removed. Contracted with a mason to rebuild the chimney stack from the attic floor up through the roof to make it firesafe. It had been made smaller when the dormer was added on. I designed the stack and its corbeling and drip course to a measurement I think will be pleasing in size and shape for a house of this size. Had to explain what I wanted and took the mason to an old house nearby. He took notes and I supplied him with a couple of photographs. I have enough hard-burned brick to do the outside work. He supplies his own mortar. If we remove the stairs, he will do the fireplaces downstairs over, on an hourly basis (there's no way to figure what we'll run into): $10 per hour for himself and $10 for his helper.

6/10: Made the decision to go all the way! Both the stairs and the dormer will be removed and the fireplaces put back to their original width. Tomorrow, off comes the dormer and the stairs will soon follow. The rear stairs were the only ones the house ever had.

The partition separating the old kitchen from the little bedroom will be removed so that one large room will run almost entirely across the rear of the house. An extra window will be added in the back wall to increase light and ventilation. Leaving the bedroom as a separate room may be more authentic, truer to what the house used to be, but it is a much less practical arrangement for modern living in this particular house, chopping the back of the house into three small compartments: little bedroom, old kitchen, and buttery. The buttery, not having its original shelves, lends itself to being converted into a modern bath and allows for another full bath to be installed directly above it on the second floor. The new kitchen will fit well into the very back of the ell and will be a working kitchen as opposed to an "eating" kitchen. The main part of the ell will become a fine, large dining room with access to a terrace. All in all a very satisfactory arrangement of rooms.

6/11: The windows, two of which are still in the dormer, are 9/6. Windows take a long time to get, so I must make a note to order them tomorrow or the next day. Will require eighteen in all. The front entrance is a later one than the original and must be rebuilt; it was probably put in with the dormer and stairs. Three more decisions to be made: (1) Retain the clapboards, which are not original on three sides of the house and are full of nail holes from the many skins that were added to the house, or replace them? (2) And if they are to be replaced, will the house be painted or left natural? (3)

Shall I use plaster or sheetrock on the interior walls and ceilings that require rebuilding?

6/12: Today the dormer literally hit the dust (figs. 247, 248). The house looks ridiculous with the shortened chimney sticking out of the roof, but already the lines of the finished house without its dormer are apparent. It is an improvement. The stairs are out as well. Didn't think both jobs could be done in one day. It is easily seen where the chimney was cut back from the first floor to the second to make room for the stairs.

6/13: Made up my mind to compromise on the clapboards, replacing the newer ones and retaining the original ones, which are all on the rear wall of the old kitchen. I'll paint the rear and leave the other walls natural; the house can always be painted at a later time if a purchaser wishes. It is necessary to make this decision now as it will govern the kind of material to be used for the trim. Natural redwood trim blends well with red cedar clapboards; if the house is to be painted, then pine trim can be used. In the interest of economy I have decided to use sheetrock instead of plaster; it's a good material and can easily be made to resemble plaster. If price were of no concern, I would plaster. Ordered windows. Three week delivery—not bad.

6/18: The mason has removed the top of the chimney stack to a point below the ridge from which he can reconstruct it to the dimensions we have agreed upon— five full bricks across the front in width—and has begun to rebuild. Roughly 42″ wide by 42″ deep by 42″ high.

The exterior of the house looks its worst at this point. From now on it will be looking better each day. Covered the roof opening with a large canvas, and we are rushing to close up as quickly as possible, as rain on the old floorboards will soon cause them to buckle.

6/24: The mason is through the roof with the new chimney; contract price is $400, with sand and water supplied by mason and brick and cement by me. Gave out contract on red-cedar shingle roof, work to begin at once. Main roof 1,440 square feet, dining room about 300 square feet, and kitchen roof about 200 square feet (figs. 249, 250).

6/25: Chimney complete. Looks fine. Received bid on oil-fired circulating hot-water heating system with two zones and baseboard convectors. If it doesn't rain, the roof will be started tomorrow. Materials have arrived on the job. Mason has begun opening up the fireplaces in both the parlor and sitting rooms, and they will both be rebuilt to their original sizes, dampers will be installed, and their respective flues will be rebuilt to the first-floor ceiling (fig. 251).

6/26: The mason has begun the rebuilding of the fireplaces and their flues. The roofer has begun the roof by framing the opening where the dormer was with two-by-eights of new lumber, since this area will be a closet and the rafters will not be seen. So the shingles can breathe, we are going to use furring strips on the old roof rather than nailing them directly to the old roof; this will provide a bit more insulation as well (fig. 252).

6/27: The carpenters (three men) began work on replacing rotted sills. Water table and four or five courses of clapboards were removed so that the plank and the sills are visible. Will replace sills with fir, not oak, well painted with Cuprinol. Here and there the planks are rotted near the bottom, so will build up the sills until there is enough backing to nail the cutoff planks to. Ten men working, all but three on contract.

The fireplaces are taking shape in the two front rooms. Also the front of the roof of the house (not the ell) is half finished. The rough-framed opening for the windows is 27 inches x 54 inches, outside dimensions. Since this is a plank-framed house, I have decided to stud the exterior walls on the inside to provide extra strength, insulation, and space for wiring. The plaster on the inside was in bad shape. Might as well have a tight job. The carpenter is studding the outside walls and framing for the windows when they arrive (fig. 253).

7/3: Called bank for first payment on construction mortgage. All new lumber is treated with Cuprinol wherever it comes in contact with old wood, is near the ground, or may be susceptible to insect invasion.

7/7: Front half of roof completed using 16-inch red-cedar shingles with five inches exposed to the weather (fig. 254). Most of the cost is in the labor not the material. Took up the flooring in the old kitchen, revealing the crawl space (fig. 255). The timbers look good but there is a very bad piece of sill in the rear wall that we have replaced from the inside with built-up two-by-eights treated with Cuprinol. Covered the crawl-space floor joists with half-inch plywood, leveling a bit. The plywood is only tacked down, as the plumber must get into this space, and it will be less difficult to work from the top than to crawl under the floor. One carpenter and two helpers.

7/10: Found the original hearthstone that went in front of the bake oven lying in the crawl space and have pulled it up using a borrowed chain hoist. It must weigh 500 pounds. It is now set back in its original position (fig. 256).

7/15: The rear roof is going along nicely. I splurged and used copper flashing (20 lineal feet, 16-inch width) instead of aluminum. Carpenters moved to the left front room (the sitting room) and I had them remove the entire floor. This is where there had been considerable fire damage and the flooring was badly buckled from the water.

The mason has finished the two fireplaces, which are now back to their original sizes and have dampers and safe flues. No new material will be visible after the paneling is installed. The mason called for a payment as his youngest daughter (his "baby") is getting married on Saturday. Gave him $500.

7/18: Carpenters have replaced rotted joists in front left room and have laid down plywood. This is the room in which the fire started. Most of the floorboards are salvagable, although they are buckled. Couldn't resist making a fire in the old kitchen fireplace. Drew very well. The house looked great with smoke coming out of the stack. Will wait a day more to let the mortar set up fully before firing the other fireplaces. The roofer tells me he should be finished in two days.

Carpenter is studding the outside walls of the parlor (front right room). It will make insulating easier, but we shall lose some of the post projection within the room. Electrical to start tomorrow. Also two stone wall builders to patch the foundation walls in the cellar.

7/24: Hired a small backhoe to dig out around caved-in stone foundation in the ell. Found live termites in the rear and called professional exterminator who made short work of them. Treated the entire area. Electrician began installing his receptacle boxes. Discovered old well in back of house. The water is clear and tastes very good. It needs a new well cover.

7/28: Masons began rebuilding foundation under ell adding new cellar windows. It rained heavily, and the roofer couldn't finish. Also adding outside entrance to cellar (figs. 257a, 257b, 258, 259, 260).

7/31: Still wet—no roofer. Masons continue with foundation work. Set new cellar windows for light and ventilation in ell. Carpenter framed out bathroom walls downstairs in old buttery and in small room above. Stonemasons' work will come out to about $1,000.

253. Studding up the outside walls.

254. The front of the roof is finished.

255. The floor joists have been removed, the new sill installed, and the crawl space dug deeper.

256. Raising the hearthstone from the crawl space.

257a

257a and 257b. The masons begin rebuilding the caved-in ell foundation.

257b

258. The ell wall completed.

258

259. Outside hatchway (outside view).

259

260. Outside hatchway (inside view).

260

261. Planking exposed.

261

262a

262a. A framed opening to the size of the original windows.

262b. Placing the new window.

262b

263. New clapboarding begun.

263

264. The new window is set in the new clapboards.

265. The side of the house is now reclapboarded.

266. The house is beginning to look good.

267. The modern kitchen is trimmed out and sheetrocked (in the ell).

267

268. Heat convectors and covers installed in the dining room (in the ell).

268

269. Insulation going in. Note the charred summer beam and joists overhead.

149

269

270. The trim takes the longest time as it requires careful fitting.

271. The raised-panel dado for the sitting room being fitted.

272. The sitting room trimmed out and painted.

273. Parlor paneling going in.

274. Doors hung in parlor.

275. The parlor trim finished and painted with one coat.

275

276. The sitting-room chimney breast installed.

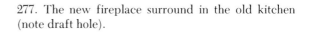

277. The new fireplace surround in the old kitchen (note draft hole).

278. The reinstalled crane and bake oven door. Kitchen panels have been painted.

279. Front door fitted with an old latch.

280. Antiques are brought in to dress up the rooms.

281. The sitting room is furnished.

282

282. The old kitchen fireplace outfitted with utensils, etc.

283. The restoration is complete!

283

8/5: Masons shifted to pointing inside and outside of stone foundation, first cutting away bushes growing close to the house. Found dated cornerstone: *JOHN PALMER BUILT 1790!* It was located in the front right corner of the foundation, top stone. A different date from the stone found over the parlor fireplace.

The roofer finished completely. Figures coming in on heat and plumbing. I must recap figures for complete estimate.

8/11: Stonemasons have finished installing new cellar steps. Waiting for the windows to arrive—no work. Electricians have roughed out as much as they can. Bought some very fine old wainscot (raised panel) at $40 per running foot, enough for one room—the parlor. Also bought a good 39-inch exterior door. Removed damaged clapboards on front and two sides of house (figs. 261, 262a, 262b).

8/18: Windows arrived and carpenter and his man are setting them. I Cuprinoled them myself. The clapboards were delivered—red cedar. Since the house is to be natural wood on the front and two sides, I had two boys paint on a coat of stain. The roofer will be doing the clapboarding and will start tomorrow. Gave out the plumbing with a promise that the plumber will start immediately. Carpenters framed out new kitchen and insulated exterior walls very well, as this room will be exposed to the weather on three sides. Reset front stone steps.

8/19: Believe it or not, the plumber sent two men and they've started. I have explained to them that they are not to cut without getting permission first. Also gave them a lesson on old construction and explained that some of the ceilings are going to remain exposed to view.

8/20: The clapboarding has begun, and the house is now beginning to look very good indeed, with the new windows and new clapboards. Since the windows are new wood, I am painting them red. The outside trim vergeboards, fascia, corner boards, and door casings are redwood. The carpenter cut in an extra window for the old kitchen area to provide a little more light. The vergeboards were made from one-by-twelves ripped to one-by-eights and one-by-fours. Beads were added to one edge of each, and the four-inch board was laid on top of the eight-inch board (figs. 263, 264, 265, 266).

8/22: Lots of work going on. The dining room's old flooring was installed and reproduction studded door with a diamond pattern was made by the carpenters on the job and hung. Bought 600 square feet of old wide pine flooring, 16-foot lengths, for only $.60 per foot. The carpenters will finish the ell—that is, the kitchen and dining room first—and then move to the main house. The plumber is going on with his roughing. We are going to sheetrock the kitchen and dining areas in order to save some money. Plumber hooked up to the existing sewerage system, which is of unknown quality. I'll see if it works before putting in a new system (figs. 267, 268).

8/27: The dining room and the new kitchen have been trimmed out and are being sheetrocked and taped. The kitchen is ready for the cabinets I ordered a few weeks ago. We laid a slab in the basement as a foundation for the boiler. The electrician finished the installation of the electrical service, and the lighting company has hooked us up.

8/29: Spent time with two boys doing the insulation myself (fig. 269). Six-inch bats in the second floor ceiling and the usual full, thick bats for the exterior walls. I also insulated the entire bathroom areas—walls and ceilings—for noise control.

9/4: Had small bulldozer to grade around the house sloping away from the foundation. The trimming of the parlor has begun, with the electrician working along with the carpenters (figs. 270, 271, 272, 273). It is important to hide the boxes in the stiles of the wainscot. We are getting baseboard hot-water heat. Work has begun on making the raised panels for the sitting room (the one that had the fire). I have some butternut paneling that can be trimmed to fit the parlor; it matches exactly the raised panel wainscot (figs. 274, 275, 276, 277, 278).

9/12: The entire week has been spent in trimming, but the place is really beginning to shape up. The boys made a new front entrance. I wanted a very simple arrangement, befitting a small house such as this, with a five-paned headlight over the front door.

9/15: Fitted the front door with hardware (fig. 279) and the raised-panel dado in parlor and trimmed out the side door. Every minute I have free I work on paint removal, trying to get the paint off the old wood before the men get to use it. I have a couple of young boys to help.

9/18: The plumbing and heating are now going on at a fast pace and the electrician is starting his finish. The sheetrock in dining room and kitchen has been completely "plastered" with taping compound, and it looks just like plaster.

9/22: I have begun to paint the paneling: parlor, olive green; sitting room, mustard. The trim has started going back on in the old kitchen. This will be red. Painted the outside doors red.

9/30: We are painting the walls dead white, and the house looks magnificent if I say so myself. Purchased a fine corner cupboard, which will be installed in the old kitchen area tomorrow. In a week the house should be ready for occupancy.

10/2: Flooring has been lightly stained where the lye bleached it. Tried out all three fireplaces at the same time. All work very well. The heating system is in operation and bathrooms all operate. Bad news!! We need a new septic system.

10/3: Gave out the contract for a septic system of 100-gallon capacity and leaching field.

10/8: Most of the work now is cleaning up, painting, floor polishing, etc. The stove, refrigerator, and dishwasher were delivered and will be installed shortly.

10/13: Made a pot of coffee for the boys on the new stove. I have been raking the grass seeding around the house and laying some stepstones to the front and side doors.

10/24: Moved in some antique furniture and pictures, etc., and will have an "open house" in about a week. I am happy with the way it turned out (figs. 280, 281, 282, 283).

CHAPTER 5

MOVING OLD HOUSES

Antique houses are moved in one of three ways: in one piece; by flaking; or by disassembly. Of these methods the first, *moving in one piece*, is practical for only the shortest distances. Highway departments govern the size and weight of loads that may be transported over the road. Weight poses little problem, as it can be distributed over a large area by the use of multiple wheels on the moving vehicle. Size, however, can be a serious obstacle. Permission to block traffic for long periods of time will rarely be granted, and low-hanging branches of trees, tight curves, and narrow country roads often make "one-piece" moves impossible.

The overhead utility wires present the biggest obstacle for a one-piece move of any length; utility companies will cut these wires for a fee, which can become astronomical in areas where there are many wires. I know of one instance where an estimate of $28,000 was given to cut and repair wires on an eight-mile route.

The second method, *flaking*, is simply a system of cutting the house into sections, which can then be moved and reassembled at the new site. The rafters are removed and the chimney stack taken down to the attic floor to lower the profile of the structure, which now looks like a rectangular box. The foundation is "needled" by steel beams after the building has been cut into sections of easily manageable size. The pieces are raised on jacks and placed on a wheeled flatbed trailer. The actual move is performed slowly and carefully; the contractors who do this work are specialists. They often boast that they can move an entire house or a flaked house without spilling a glass of water on a table within the house. Most one-piece house moves are made either within the bounds of the

same property or to a neighboring property; houses that are moved by cutting are usually moved within a few miles.

There has developed in recent years an increasing demand for houses to be shipped long distances. The only practical way to send a house from New England to California, for example, would be to *disassemble* it completely.

The steps involved in such an undertaking follow.

1. Before a move of this kind is made, a permit from the local building inspector must be obtained. In some areas a simple "removal" permit is all that is required; in others a "demolition" permit must be obtained, although strictly speaking the house is being "unbuilt," not demolished. The average demolition contractor is the very last person we would want to disassemble a house; these people generally work with a heavy hand and do not have the special knowledge required. They employ unskilled labor, who may be excellent at swinging a sledgehammer but are a disaster when it comes to removing paneling.

I have removed a number of houses by first obtaining a "building permit" to "disassemble and remove" rather than "demolish" when I explained to the inspector that the process was to be one of "unbuilding and reassembly." If it becomes necessary, a demolition permit can be obtained from the state. It may also be possible to work under the permit of a licensed demolition contractor—in short, to borrow or rent the license.

2. Photograph the house from attic to cellar, both

284. Mid-18th-century center-chimney house moved in one piece. A new foundation of concrete blocks is being built to support it. Glastonbury, Connecticut.

284

285

285. Before c. 1780 center-chimney house, Portland, Connecticut. Owned by the Lisbon, Connecticut Historical Society, Inc., and subsequently moved to Iowa. Probably now the oldest house in Iowa.

285a and 285b. The house as set up in Iowa, with the restoration in progress.

285a

285b

286. An exciting moment, discovering a wall of paneling hidden beneath sheet-rock!

286

287. Paneling painted Spanish brown discovered under three plaster walls of a parlor; the fireplace wall was fully raised-paneled, as one would expect. This is the only house that I have found in twenty-five years with all four walls of the room paneled. I have seen an occasional ceiling boarded in feather-edge or beaded boards.

287

288. Lath and plaster removal is the dirtiest part of the job. The average house can be stripped of plaster in two days.

288

289. A house from Enfield, Connecticut, that was sent to Westerville, Ohio. A section of front wall has been removed to allow the removal of the paneling in large sections. The chimney has been taken down to the attic floor, and measuring and photographing are taking place inside.

289

290. Marking begins on the very first day. Here red marks are sprayed on the paneling to identify it as belonging to "Room E." The paneling is to be stripped of paint later.

290

291. This board (as the circular roofer's tin at top right shows) is from "Room Q," west wall, column #1. Casing is marked in yellow crayon as well. The wood will remain natural.

291

292a. The frame as well as the trim must be marked and photographed.

292a

292b. Each stud, girt, post and summer-beam, plate, and sill has its identification. Note the small areas of water rot in the end girt. This area will be strengthened before being taken down and later repaired.

292b

293. After the chimney has been taken down to the first floor, the rear of the paneling is exposed for marking. The arrows denote "front of house" and "up."

293

294

295

296

294. The clapboards have been taken off; the rafters, the attic flooring, the paneling, and the stairs are stored in a nearby barn.

295. At least 210 years separate the new steel structure going up on the left from the timbers of the old house coming down on the right, yet the post-and-lintel method of construction was used in both. The old house gave way to a parking lot.

296. Opening up the kitchen fireplace is done carefully, as accurate measurements must be taken. This one (with the bake oven in the rear) was entirely bricked up.

162

297. Removing nails from the trim is work saved for a rainy day.

298. The sharp tips are cut off the nails so they won't bend under the hammer.

299. Nails must be removed from the timbers as well as from the flooring and trim.

300. The flooring is being taken to the barn for nail removal and storage.

301. An open cellar hole is dangerous. Cleaning up the site is usually part of the "deal" when a house is bought to be moved.

302. Freight cars must be ordered well in advance; to avoid demurrage the house must be at the tracks on time.

303. For ease of loading a boxcar with very wide "offset" doors should be requested. Special "soft-riding" cars can be specified. The average house, including foundation and chimney stone or brick will weigh about 100,000 pounds. The boxcar shown here (60 feet long) had a capacity of 190,000 pounds loaded and 74,000 pounds empty.

164

304. Many houses have single timbers 40 feet long; to avoid cutting them, "offset" doors are required. Timbers go on first, to one side; flooring boards and trim on the other; stone and brick directly in front of the doors. The stairs and cupboards are placed on top, and the entire load is securely braced to prevent "crawling" en route.

304

305. Loading stone in the center near the doors makes for easy unloading and keeps timbers from creeping into the trim as the boxcar bumps along.

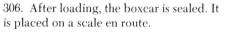

305

306. After loading, the boxcar is sealed. It is placed on a scale en route.

306

inside and out. Make sure you get a view of each wall. Remove all plaster from walls and ceilings, all modern partitions, wall finishes, flooring, etc. Before ripping into the walls, it is prudent to disconnect all electrical outlets except one on each floor, marking with a boldly lettered sign the fact that the outlet is "hot." You will no doubt require lights and perhaps power for electrical tools. Rephotograph. Color slides are easier to review than black-and-white prints, and prints can be made from the slides.

3. Remove the lath, saving the old lath for nail removal.

4. Now, with the entire structure exposed on the interior, examine the house in detail, both the trim and the exposed structure. Look for old materials, moldings, boards, nails that will give a clue to age, construction, and color. The checklist in Chapter 3, "Restoration Procedures and Techniques," may come in handy here.

5. The interior of the house is now measured. Special attention must be paid to the position of the fireplaces and hearths within the rooms, in the attic at the attic floor, and at the ridge, as well as to the size and position of the chimney base in the cellar. Since the timbers may not be true or level, it is wise to take more than one measurement in any direction. Thus, for example, in measuring the width of a room, it is not enough to measure at the outside wall; the measurement at the inside wall in the same direction may be off by two inches. Don't forget ceiling heights and the depth, height, and breadth of the fireplace openings. Now, from your measurements draw a plan of the house.

6. You are now ready to begin marking. You must devise a system and adhere to it strictly, noting on your plan the marks you have made on the wood. Keep the system as simple as possible. The system I have devised for myself is as follows. The front of the house is always called "south," no matter what the actual orientation of the house is on its land. All numbering is made from front (south) to rear (north), from left (west) to right (east), and from top to bottom.

For the purposes of marking, each story is assigned a color. Thus the basement may be white, the first floor red, the second floor green, and the attic yellow. I buy a few hundred "roofer's tins" at the lumberyard and lay them out on a piece of wood. I spray-paint some in each color. Each room is assigned a capital letter. Again working from front to back and from left to right, I mark the appropriate letter in chalk or carpenter's crayon on each wall of each room as large as space will permit, so that at all times I am aware of the room letter. Each wall in each room is further marked with a small *n, s, e,* or *w*

for the points of the compass—always circled—to fix the orientation.

It is now time to get down to the marking of each piece of trim by nailing on it a tin of the appropriate color. With a marking pen I mark on the tin the letter of the room and the directional letter, and so it goes until each piece of wood bears its identification.

The tins can be further marked to narrow the placement of individual boards within a room. Each floorboard should also be marked. Photograph the walls again, getting the marks into your pictures as best you can.

7. Once all the finish carpentry has been marked, it may be removed and the smaller pieces placed in wooden boxes made to fit. You are now ready to mark the frame, again using roofer's tins or yellow carpenter's crayon (keel).

8. Photograph the frame.

9. Take detailed photographs of the chimney stack and each fireplace. In the case of stone fireplaces, mark the corner stones, the lintels, and the hearths; brick fireplaces will require that wooden boxes be made to hold the corner bricks. The identification marks can then be placed on the boxes.

10. The chimney stack can now be removed to the first-floor level. Be careful that no one is below as the exterior bricks are allowed to slide down the roof to the ground. Once below the ridge, the brick can be allowed to drop through the flues into the fireplaces. From here they can be stacked neatly outside and covered.

11. The interior partitions are taken out next, nails removed, and boards stacked. When taking down the interior partitions, cut out each door together with its casing and frame, first nailing a brace across the bottom on both sides to keep the assembly steady and the door in place. As the work progresses, keep examining the timbers and other parts of the structure, noting how the joints were assembled. There was a system used to erect the house originally. One can figure it out by examining the method of joining the posts and girts. The house will be disassembled in reverse.

12. Each floor will now appear as one large space. The interior or the exterior walls will be exposed, and the flooring will still be in place.

13. All new flooring can now be removed revealing the old flooring. The roof will not be taken off until the last possible moment nor will the old flooring, since we require a platform to work on when unpinning the timbers.

If the pins (treenails, pegs) are dry, a good many of them can be driven out with a wooden mallet or

307. The new foundation can be built of poured concrete or, as shown here, of concrete block. In the cellar floor of this center-chimney house a reinforced-concrete pad has been poured to support the tremendous weight of the chimney.

308. The chimney base is being formed of concrete block to a size large enough to support the hearthstones of three first-story fireplaces.

309. A new oak sill is being fitted to the top of the block wall. It has been notched to receive the cellar joists and girts.

310. An original cellar girt being fitted to the new sill.

311. A notch has been made in the new oak sill to receive the cellar girt. Cuts such as this and mortise-and-tenon joints can be made quickly, using modern electric drills and sharp chisels.

311

312. The foundation is waterproofed and topped with stone above ground level before backfilling. Anchor bolts run through the stone to secure the house to the foundation.

312

313. Cellar windows (made up new to resemble the old ones) can be placed where necessary to provide ventilation; if the backfill comes above them, a "window-well" can be built to hold back the earth. House in Woodstock, Connecticut, c. 1690–1710. House moved from Massachusetts.

168

313

314. A termite-riddled sill on the left and its replacement on the right. Notice the chisel mark (X) on the new wood, just as it would have been made on old wood.

314

315. New replacement timbers are made to fit into the mortise-and-tenon joints of the original timbers. As these new timbers will be eventually cased, no attempt is made to cover the modern radial saw marks. If they were to be left exposed, old timbers would have been used or new ones hewn.

315

316. Tenon repair.

316

317. Old timbers repaired with new oak.

317

318a and 318b. The frame being erected on the new foundation. An occasional new piece is required, sometimes an entire new wall is needed. One would naturally pay less for a house that required a great deal of replacement of old parts with new ones.

318a

318b

hammer. I have devised a number of tools to facilitate this procedure. You can make a simple driving tool by using a pipe. (I have a set of various diameters from ½ inch through 1¼ inches). On one end of the pipe weld a round-head rivet, against which you can hammer. The pipe will fit over the tip of the "pin," taking hold lower down so as not to "broom" the end. A few sharp blows will free most pins.

If a pin won't move or if you run across blind pinning, it will be necessary to drill it out. Always use a drill bit at least as large as the hole. The barest shell of a pin left in the hole will be strong enough to hold the timbers together. Have a sharp chisel handy for chipping out or cutting any small pieces of peg left in the hole after drilling.

14. Now, starting in the attic, begin breaking the siding of the house away from the frame, allowing the pieces— clapboards, sheathing, and all—to fall to the ground, where it will be easier to work with. Take off any salvageable outside trim first, such as vergeboards, crown moldings, etc. The window trim has already been removed from the inside and the window frames have been taken out. Remove the studs of the outside walls if they will come out. You will soon have the skeleton of the house standing with a roof on it.

15. Now you must take off the roof, working as fast as you can to avoid bad weather. An entire roof and its rafters can be dismantled by four or five men in less than one day. Break the roof boards away from the rafters with long pinch bars, letting the boards and the roof shingles slide down to the ground. They rarely break when hitting the ground unless there is a great deal of rot, in which case they have to be replaced anyhow. Take the rafters down a pair at a time, unpinning them at their feet and leaning them over onto the attic deck. Then unpin and stack them, or hand them down to the ground. If they have *collar beams* (wind braces), don't remove these until the "truss" is lying down.

16. Now remove the attic flooring. The attic floor joists will already have been marked. They will slip out of their notches and can be handed down to the floor below and then to the ground floor.

The second-story summer beams can be removed by hand at this time, or if a crane is to be used to set down the heavy timbers, they can be taken down later.

17. Remove the second-story flooring and slip the joists out of their notches.

18. Now unpeg the remainder of the timbers and, using a crane, begin taking down the frame in the order planned: first the summer beams and then a pair of posts together with joining girts. It will be necessary to brace some of the timbers, as the post removal will leave them unsupported.

As the crane lifts the girts, the studs will fall away if they are not of the pinned variety. If they are pinned to the girts, they can be unpinned after the section is laid flat on the ground.

You will want to photograph the entire procedure as it takes place both as a guide to the reconstruction and also as an interesting story.

19. After the frame is down and stacked, the first-floor flooring can be taken apart, and the cellar framing can be photographed and marked. Usually a great number of defective timbers are found in the basement, many of which are not worth saving.

You will now wish to take any stones from the foundation that you will later use—certainly the cut stone at the top of the foundation and perhaps some of the better cellar wall stone or chimney base stones.

There are a few measurements that are critical to the making of a plan of your house. The first of these is the height to the top of the rafters from the attic floor; together with the depth measurement of the building, this will enable you to draw the pitch of the roof. I find that since the sills are so often rotted at the corners of old houses, this is not the place to measure to get a true figure of the length or breadth of the frame. Rather take your measurement at the first-story girts or at the plates, checking both front and rear of the building and both sides. Also measure the ceiling height of each story from the finished top of the flooring to the underside of the flooring above. With these measurements you will be able to draw a set of measured drawings of your building. Note your markings on your plan.

Transporting a building over long distances is most economically done by rail. Get the longest boxcar available, preferably with a wood floor and with ten-foot offset doors on each side. It is conceivable that your house will have three timbers forty feet in length. You will need a sixty-foot boxcar to get them in without cutting. If they must be cut, cut them over a post. You must reinforce long or weak timbers by nailing supporting two-by-fours (scabs) into them at the notches for strength. This will prevent them from snapping in two when lifted by the crane. Let the crane operator use a nylon choke set as far apart as possible.

The wood lath of an old house takes up a great deal of room in a boxcar, and you may wish to leave it behind if you are cramped for space. Load the freight car (and you will usually have three days without cost to do it) with the heavy structural timbers all on one side and the

319. Although on the surface this house would seem too far gone to save, there was enough sound material in the doors, flooring, stairs, etc., to make reworking the frame well worth it. It was priced accordingly, of course.

319a

319a, 319b, 319c, and 319d. More views of the same house: (a) before; (b) during; (c) during; (d) getting there.

320a, 320b, and 320c. Once again: (a) before; (b) during; (c) after. Now wasn't it worth it? It looked much worse than it actually was.

320a

320b

320c

321. In building the stack, *chases* are made to accomodate air ducts, plumbing, and electrical conduits.

321

322. One-room-deep plan with added lean-to and modern ell, c. 1700. This magnicificent house in Woodstock, Connecticut, was sheathed diagonally for added strength.

322

323. A saltbox house moved to Sharon, Connecticut, and restored by the owner.

323

324. A "three-quarter" house that was brought from Centerbrook, Connecticut, to Lisbon, Connecticut.

324

flooring and trim on the other, with the flooring on the bottom evenly spread out. In between, at the doors, place the stone and brick. The danger in a rail shipment is the "creeping" of the timbers and stone into the trim as the load vibrates en route. Construct wood bulkheads between the trim and the stone and the timbers using scrap material. This will keep them separate from each other. Certain states require insect extermination before the load is allowed to cross the border. Your rail dispatcher will be able to inform you of the regulations.

One of the great advantages of dismantling a house for shipment is the ease with which it can be inspected and repaired. The wood can also be treated for insect infestation. If it is possible to store your house in a barn or shed before shipping, it will give you the opportunity to remove the nails when the weather is bad. Spread a sheet of plastic or a tarpaulin on the floor under the area where the nail-removing operation is to take place. You will then be able to scoop up the nails from the ground without losing any. Save especially the blacksmith-made lath nails for use in hardware installation and for the hanging of pictures and sconces.

The cost of dismantling a 40-foot by 30-foot center-chimney house, filling in the cellar hole, and taking all the debris to the dump at this writing is about $14,000. This includes the hiring of a truck crane for one day. If you do not drill out or remove your pegs beforehand, you will need the crane for two days.

It is always best to have the same men dismantle and reassemble your house. However, this is not always possible. If you have marked it thoroughly, photographed it completely and in detail, and have drawn an accurate plan, you should have little trouble getting it back together again.

GLOSSARY

ARCHITECTURAL PERIODS

COLONIAL: 1620–1776
GEORGIAN: 1750–1800
FEDERAL: 1776–1830
GREEK REVIVAL: 1830–1850
VICTORIAN REVIVAL STYLES: (Gothic, Italianate, Tuscan, Queen Anne, etc.): 1850 on

HOUSE PLAN

ADDED-LEANTO: A house style beginning in the 17th century and ending about 1740; it is not to be confused with a true Saltbox that it closely resembles. The added-leanto house began as a one-room deep, 2-and-½-story structure. The rear rafters were later extended downward creating room for a new kitchen, bedroom, and buttery.

ATTIC: A garret or storage space under the roof.

BASEMENT: That part of a house which is partially under ground level and is sometimes used for living purposes as opposed to storage use (see CELLAR).

BEDROOM: A small first-floor room, usually off the kitchen, often mistakenly called "Borning Room" today; the latter term is not supported by documentation.

BORNING ROOM: See BEDROOM.

BUTTERY; Pantry; Larder: A place on the first floor where provisions are kept, almost always on the north or cool side of the house.

CELLAR: A space underneath the house that is almost completely underground and is used primarily for storage (see BASEMENT).

CENTER-CHIMNEY: A house plan with the primary chimney completely enclosed within the walls. The chimney need not be located precisely in the center of the house but may favor one side or another. Center-chimney plans cover a wide range of house types including Two-Room Plan, Added-Leanto, 1½-half-story "Cape Cod," etc.

CENTER-HALL: A house plan having two primary chimneys separated by a broad center hallway.

CHAMBER: A room primarily used for sleeping. In 2-story houses the largest rooms for sleeping were located on the second floor. The only room called a BEDROOM was a small room off the kitchen. Chambers took their names from the rooms beneath them; hence we find Sitting-Room Chambers, Kitchen Chambers, Parlor Chambers.

CRAWL SPACE: A low cellar, not high enough to stand up in.

ELL: An addition to a house—usually to the back. Ells come in many forms, viz. 1-story or 2-story; gable-roofed or shed-roofed. Many ells housed a summer kitchen, buttery, or woodshed.

ENTRY: A small stairless vestibule leading to the outside of a house.

FACADE: The entire exterior face or elevation of a building.

GABLE WINDOWS: Windows in the gable ends of a house.

HALL: The main living or all-purpose room in 17th-century houses; the term is taken from the great halls in English castles.

KEEPING-ROOM: A family living room of a house. The early kitchen is often mistakenly called the keeping-room, but early documents do not support this.

LEANTO: A small ell with shed roof (see ADDED-LEANTO).

PARLOR: A room used primarily for the reception and entertainment of guests.

PASSAGE: A narrow area inside the front door of center-chimney houses lying between the doorway and the stairs. This area has erroneously been called the PORCH in recent times, but research disputes this usage.

PEDIMENT: The triangular space forming the gable of a two-slope roof. Also an ornamental form used above doors and windows often in the form of a triangle, scroll, or broken arch.

PORCH: An enclosed entrance in the front of some 17th-century house plans. Rare. Original PORCHES have not been found in place, but reconstructions can be seen; for instance, The Hempstead House, New London, Connecticut.

SALTBOX: A type of house having two stories in front and one story in the back and with the rear roof sloping from the ridge down to the first floor plate on single rafters. To be distinguished from an ADDED-LEANTO plan.

SITTING ROOM: The most-used family room; family living room. Usually a first-floor room on the sunniest side of a house.

THE HOUSE FRAME, ITS COVERING, AND CARPENTRY TOOLS

ADZ: A carpenter's tool used to dress timbers.

AUGER: A carpenter's tool used to bore holes in wood.

BEAM: A large horizontal carrying timber; a Girt; a Plate; a Summer.

BEARING: That portion of a timber or lintel that rests on a post or wall.

BEARING PARTITION; Bearing wall: A wall that carries the weight of the structure above it.

BEARING WALL; Bearing partition: A wall that supports the weight of the floors and roof in a building. None of the walls in a post-and-lintel-framed house are bearing walls.

BRACE: An inclined timber running between a post and a girt to provide strength.

BROKEN-ARCH PEDIMENT: See PEDIMENT.

CHIMNEY GIRTS: Large horizontal timbers that pass at ceiling height close to a chimney stack. There is one on each side, one in back, and one in front of the stack on each floor.

CHIMNEY POST: The posts supporting the chimney girts. In a center-chimney house there would be six.

COLLAR BEAM; Wind brace, Tie beam: Horizontal attic timbers that tie a pair of rafters together, thus forming a truss. These are placed about six feet or more above the attic floor.

COLUMN: A free-standing post, as opposed to a pilaster that is part of a wall from which it projects.

COMMON RAFTER SYSTEM: Roof framing in which all the rafters are equal in size.

CORNER POSTS: The posts in a braced (post-and-lintel) framed house that are exposed in the inside corners of the rooms.

DIAGONAL BRACE: A small diagonal timber connecting a post to a girt or plate.

DOVETAIL: In carpentry or joinery, the method of fastening boards or timbers together by letting one piece into another in the form of the expanded tail of a dove.

DROP: An ornamental pendant hanging from the soffit of framed overhangs in 17th-century houses.

DRY ROT: Decay of seasoned wood caused by certain fungi.

DUTCHMAN: A flooring repair spanning two adjacent floorboards usually in the shape of a bow tie.

EAVES: That part of a roof which projects beyond the exterior walls of a building.

END GIRT: Those girts at the gable ends of a house. On a 2-story house there are lower- and upper-end girts.

EXPOSURE: That part of a roof shingle or clapboard which is visible—that is, exposed to the weather.

FLOOR JOISTS: See JOISTS.

FRAME; Framing: The name given to the rough wood-work of windows and doors, etc., as distinguished from the trim or finish. Also the entire timbering of a house.

FRAMED OVERHANG: The projection of the upper story of a house beyond a wall of the first story formed by extending the framing timbers.

FROE: A wooden-handled tool with a blade at right angles to the handle used to split shingles from a block of wood or a log.

FURRING: The application of thin wood strips to joists, studs, or other framing members to level the surface to receive lath and plaster, paneling, or other trim.

GABLE END: The triangular walls that enclose a building under a gable roof. The end of a gable-roofed house as opposed to the front or rear.

GABLE ROOF: A roof having two slopes that meet at the ridge, forming two legs of a triangle.

GAMBREL ROOF: A roof having two slopes, the lower slope being steeper than the upper.

GIRT: A heavy horizontal timber—a beam—that supports the floor joists. The attic girts that support the attic-floor joists and rafter feet of a house are called plates.

GUNSTOCK; Gunstock post: Corner or chimney posts that are wider at the ceiling than at the floor. They get their name from their similarity to an inverted gunstock.

HALF-LAP: The joining of two timbers or boards by halving one into the other. Used to join floorboards at their long edges.

HEADER: A short horizontal timber spanning an opening such as a window or door.

HEW: To shape a log or timber with an axe or an adz.

HEWN OVERHANG: The projection of the upper story of a house beyond the face of a first-story wall created by hewing the lower floor timbering.

HIP ROOF: A roof in which the four sides slope toward the center of the building from the plates to the peak.

JOISTS: Horizontal timbers to which flooring is nailed on top or laths of a ceiling are nailed to the bottom. The main framing structure of a floor.

LEDGER; Ledger board: A horizontal board nailed to the side of a heavier horizontal timber on which other framing members, such as joists, can bear.

LINTEL: Horizontal framing member that spans an opening such as a door or window and is used to take the load or weight of the structure above it. Early houses were Post-and-Lintel framed; this method is sometimes called Braced-Frame construction, or Post-and-Beam.

LIVE LOAD: The weight a floor will carry with furnishings and people on it, as opposed to Dead Load, which is the weight of the floor structure itself.

MORTISE: The area cut into a timber to receive a tenon in a mortise-and-tenon joint.

OVERHANG; Framed overhang; Hewn overhang: The projection of an upper story of a house beyond the wall of the floor below it.

PITCH: The slope of a roof from plate to ridge.

PLANK FRAME; Plank construction: House framing in which heavy planking is used instead of studs to form the exterior walls.

PLATE: Attic girt into which the rafter feet are pinned and which support the attic-floor joists. In a gable-roofed house there are both front and rear plates; in a hipped-roof house there would be four.

PRINCIPAL RAFTER: In a roof-rafter system that uses two sizes of rafters the principal rafters are the heaviest and carry the heaviest load. Between them lighter rafters fill in the space.

PURLIN: Horizontal timbers set part way up from an attic floor that are used to support the middle of the rafters. Also, narrow horizontal boards running across the tops of the rafters and rabbeted into them; the roof shingles are nailed into them.

RAFTER: The timber ribs to which the roof boards are nailed.

RAFTER FEET: The lower end of a rafter where it meets a plate at the attic floor.

RIDGE; Ridge pole; Hewn ridge: The horizontal hewn timber at the peak of a roof mortised to accept the top rafter tenons into which they are framed. Hewn ridges were introduced about 1800.

ROOFERS: Roof sheathing or boarding to which the shingles are nailed.

SETBACK: The distance from the road-line to the nearest wall of the house (see HEWN OVERHANG; FRAMED OVERHANG).

SHEATHING: The boards covering the timbers on the outside of a house under the roof shingles or under the clapboards. The roof sheathing boards are called ROOFERS.

SHED ROOF: A roof having a single slope; generally used on sheds and other small buildings and extensions.

SHORING: Temporary bracing.

SILL: The heavy horizontal timbers that rest on the foundation walls.

SLICK: A long, hand-pushed chisel used for chamfering the ends of clapboards.

SPAN: The open space between posts or walls.

STUD: The small vertical timbers that form an exterior wall. Studs run between sill and girt on the first floor and between girt and plate or upper girt on the second floor. The small studs that fill in the space under a window are called jack studs.

SUMMER; Summer beam: The largest timber of a house into which the joists are framed. Summers were used to break the span between walls by running at right angles to the joists.

TENON; Tusk-tenon: A tongue projecting from the end of a timber which, with the mortise into which it fits, constitutes a mortise-and-tenon joint.

TREE-NAIL; Trunnel: Tapered wood peg used to hold a mortise-and-tenon joint tight.

VALLEY: The internal angle formed by the meeting of two roofs at right angles to each other.

WHITE OAK: The hardest American oak. It is heavy and close grained and is used where strength and durability are required.

MASONRY, LATH, AND PLASTER

ANGLE BRICK; Corner brick: The front brick of a fireplace opening at the corner of the firebox. These bricks are shaped to form the angle of the fireplace cheek walls.

BAKE OVEN; Beehive oven: The brick or stone oven at the side or in the rear wall of a kitchen fireplace. The top of these ovens are domed and resemble a round beehive.

BAT: Half a brick.

BELT COURSE: A horizontal line or lines of brick that project from the face of a wall. Belt courses are used both as decorative features or to break the flow of water down a wall.

BOND: The method of laying stone or brick by overlapping to break the joints and tie the individual elements together for strength.

CHASE: A hollow or channel built into a chimney stack to accept electrical conduit, plumbing pipes, air-conditioning ducts, etc., so they will be concealed.

CHEEK STONE: The stones that form the sides of a firebox.

CHIMNEY STACK: The entire masonry structure of a chimney, including the chimney foundation, fireplaces, flues, and top above the ridge.

CORBEL: A horizontal projecting course of masonry that supports another course or courses above it.

CORBEL OUT: To build out one or more courses of brick or stone from the face of a wall to support a hearth, timber, or masonry.

CORNER BRICK or STONE; Angle brick or stone: The stones or bricks cut at an angle to shape the splay of the firebox of a fireplace. Corner bricks are the front (room-side) bricks of the firebox.

COURSE: Each horizontal layer of masonry.

DRAFT HOLE: The small hole in a chimney base connected to an air chamber and small flue leading to the back wall of a fireplace above and used to bring cellar oxygen up to aid combustion.

DRIP COURSE: A single corbel of brick or stone in the chimney stack as it emerges from the attic. The purpose of the drip course is to cast water running down the chimney top away from the peak of the roof.

DUTCH OVEN: A baking kettle or pot with a dish-top cover on which hot coals are placed. Not to be confused with a bake oven, brick oven, or beehive oven.

FIELD STONE: Stones of irregular shape and size found on the surface of the ground and used primarily to build foundations.

FIREBOX: The area of the fireplace where the fire is made.

FLASHING: Copper, tin, aluminum, or lead used around chimneys, over windows, in roof valleys, etc, to prevent water from entering.

GROUNDS: Strips of wood or plaster temporarily attached to walls to aid a plasterer in achieving a level and uniform thickness. In antique houses the trim of a room, that is the window and door casings, mop boards, chair rails, etc., act as grounds to which the plasterer can work.

HATCHING: The chopping with a hatchet of nailers in masonry walls or rough wall boards in a wood partition where lath will not be used. The rough surface caused by the hatchet will bond the plaster to the surface.

HEADER: A brick having its longest dimension at right angles to the face of the wall in which it rests.

HEARTH: The stone or brick on which a fire is made; fires were made both inside the firebox and on the hearth extending into the room.

LEVELING BLOCK: A timber placed in a masonry wall to distribute the weight above it evenly along the wall; also a board placed under the end of a stone fireplace lintel to level the lintel and provide a means of expansion and contraction so that the lintel doesn't crack from the heat.

LINTEL: A wood timber, stone, or piece of iron that spans the opening of the firebox and supports the masonry above the front of the fireplace opening.

LUG; Lug pole: A horizontal iron or wood bar set across the throat of a chimney above the firebox on which a trammel can be hung.

NAILER: A wood timber or board set into masonry so that wood can be nailed to it. For example, nailers let into the masonry above a fireplace will allow paneling to be hung on the masonry.

NEEDLING: The technique of making a series of holes in foundation walls through which steel beams can be inserted preparatory to moving a house in one piece.

RANDOM STONEWORK: Stone laid up in an irregular order, as a wall built of various-sized stones.

REVEAL: The side of an opening, such as a window or door frame; the jamb.

SCREED: To level wet plaster after it has been applied by running a board across it to scrape off the high spots.

SMOKE CHAMBER: A vital area in the throat of a fireplace above the lintel, the function of which is to lead the smoke up the flue but retain the heat. Also, a masonry chamber usually found in the attic connected to the chimney stack in which meats were smoked.

SOLDIER COURSE: A course where the bricks are laid on their ends so that their longest dimension is vertical and their narrow face shows.

SPLAY: The angle of the firebox walls.

STACK: See CHIMNEY STACK.

STRETCHER COURSE: A row of bricks set flat so that their long faces are parallel to the outside of the wall. A wall laid up of all stretchers is said to be laid in Common. If every seventh course is a header course the wall is laid in American Bond.

TRIMMER ARCH: A corbeling out from a chimney wall to create a ledge at ceiling height to support a hearthstone for a fireplace in the room above.

WEDGE AND FEATHER: A method used after 1800 to split stone by drilling a series of shallow holes and tapping wedges into them one after the other until the stone cracks along its grain.

DOORS, WINDOWS, AND GLASS

APRON; Window apron: The finish-trim board directly below a window sill.

BATTEN DOOR: A door made of matched vertical boards laid tight together and where the other side is made of horizontal boards. The two courses of boards are nailed together with wrought nails that are clinched on one side. If such as door has large-headed nails placed in a pattern, it is called a studded door.

BULL'S-EYE GLASS: A blown-glass pane of raised circular design and bearing the pintle left by the blowpipe. Bull's-eye lights were used in transoms but rarely in doors themselves.

CASEMENT: A window sash that opens outward on hinges attached to its vertical edge.

CASEMENT WINDOW: A window frame containing one or more movable casement sash sometimes combined with fixed sash. Casement windows were used in 17th-century and very early 18th-century houses.

DOOR FRAME: The surrounding framing in which a door swings. It consists of two upright pieces (jambs) and a head, generally fixed by mortise-and-tenon joints.

DOOR STOP: See STOP.

DOUBLE-HUNG WINDOW: A window consisting of an upper and lower sash of the guillotine type. In antique houses only the bottom sash moves.

EARS: The part of a window head or sill that extends beyond the jambs.

FANLIGHT: A semi-circular transom window with radiating sash bars often found above entrance doors in houses of the Federal period.

FENESTRATION: The arrangement of the windows in a house or wall.

FIXED SASH: An unmovable sash installed for light or to provide a view.

GUILLOTINE SASH: Sash that open vertically (as opposed to casement sash).

HANGING STILE: The stile of a door from which the door is hinged.

HEADLIGHTS: Horizontal line of window panes over a doorway.

JAMB: The side post of a door or window frame.

LEADED-GLASS WINDOWS: 17th- and very early 18th-century windows the sash of which have glass held in place by lead channels rather than wood muntins.

LIGHT: A window pane.

LOUVER: A frame with a series of horizontal slats that permit ventilation but exclude rain or snow.

MEETING RAIL: The lower rail of a top sash and the upper rail of a bottom sash that overlap when the window is closed.

MUNTIN; MUNNION: Small wood divisions that support the glass in a wood sash. In a leaded-glass window the dividers are called cames (see SASH BARS).

PALLADIAN WINDOW: A window found in Center-Hall houses that is composed of three pairs of sash; the two outside pair open, the middle pair is fixed and has an arched head.

RAIL: The horizontal window and door trim boards that hold panels.

SASH: The frame into which glass is set. It may be fixed or movable. Each sash consists of a top rail, bottom rail, side rails, muntins, glass, and putty.

SASH BARS: See MUNTINS.

SIDE LIGHTS: A vertical line of widows at either side of a doorway.

SILL; Window sill: The bottom of a window opening against which the lower sash closes.

SLIP STOP: In many 18th-century houses the left stop of the windows is removable, thus permitting the sash to be taken in for cleaning or painting.

STOP: A trim member that prevents a sash or door from moving beyond a certain point.

STUDDED DOOR: See BATTEN DOOR.

THRESHOLD: The sill of an entrance. Also, the timber under a door.

TRANSOM: A small fixed window above a doorway.

WINDOW HEAD: A cornice over the exterior head of a window frame. Also the top trim board or framing member of a window frame.

WINDOW LOCK: A wooden bar set diagonally above a bottom sash preventing movement of the sash.

WINDOW STOP: See STOP.

OUTSIDE TRIM AND ROOFING

BROKEN-ARCH PEDIMENT: See PEDIMENT.

CLAPBOARD: Thin overlapping finish boards, thicker at one edge than at the other, nailed to the exterior wall sheathing of a house as an outside covering.

CORNER BOARD: The vertical trim running from the water table to the cornice at the corners of a house to which the clapboards are butted.

CORNICE; Cornish: The horizontal projection just below the eaves and above the windows that conceals the rafter feet and plate. The cornice is composed of a minimum of two members—a fascia board and a soffit—but may be dressed with ornamental moldings, such as crown molding, dentil molding, etc.

CROWN MOLDING: See INTERIOR WOODWORK.

DENTIL; Dentil molding: A series of small evenly spaced blocks used as ornamentation in cornice moldings.

DROP: An inverted or hanging finial. Drops appear in the soffits of stairwells as a decoration or on the exterior soffits in framed overhangs of very early houses.

EXPOSURE: That part of a clapboard or shingle that is visible (exposed to the weather).

FASCIA; Fascia board: A flat horizontal trim board that is nailed to a plate concealing the rafter feet and plate; it is the front board of a cornice. In modern construction the gutter is attached to the fascia.

GRADUATED CLAPBOARDS: Clapboards that are not evenly exposed to the weather; they are less exposed at the bottom near the water table, and gradually the exposure is increased as they go up the wall.

PEDIMENT: A triangular space forming the gable of a two-slope roof, as that covering a front porch. Also, the decorative woodwork over a door or window of similar shape.

PILASTER: A column that is attached to and projects slightly from a wall.

PITCH: The degree of incline or angle of a roof or stairs.

QUOIN: Wood blocks projecting slightly at the corners of buildings that are usually made to imitate stone.

RAKE; Rake molding: See VERGE BOARD.

SIDING: The material used to cover the exterior walls of a frame building, such as clapboards, weatherboarding, or shingles.

SOFFIT: The underside or ceiling of a projection like the underside of a cornice where the thickness can be seen.

TRIM: Finished woodwork, such as verge boards, corner boards, crown moldings, exterior window casings, cornices, etc.

VERGE BOARD: The diagonally running finish boards at a gable end of a house that run from the ridge down to the plates and are nailed to the rafters. Verge boards are sometimes made decorative by adding a crown molding to their upper face.

WATER-TABLE: The lowest horizontal trim-siding board just above the foundation. The water table is wider than the clapboards.

WEATHERBOARDING: Wide horizontal boards used instead of clapboards on the rear and/or sides of a house. These boards are chamfered on their upper and lower edges so that they fit one to another on the same plane.

INTERIOR WOODWORK AND FLOORING

APPLIED MOLDING: Moldings that are nailed to another board rather than being carved out of that board.

BACK BAND: A small shaped molding nailed to the outside edges of door and window casings.

BASEBOARD: Mopboard; Base: The horizontal finish board that is nailed to a wall where the wall abuts the floor.

BATTEN: A piece of wood placed at right angles across the surface of boards to hold them together or to prevent them from warping (see BATTEN DOOR).

BEAD: A rounded molding used on most trim members in the 17th and 18th centuries wherever two trim boards meet on window and door casings, boarded walls and wainscoting, paneling rails and stiles.

BEADED BOARD: A board that has one or more beaded edges.

BEADING TOOL: A molding plane where the iron is formed to cut a bead.

BOARD AND BATTEN: See BATTEN DOOR.

BOLECTION MOLDING; Bolection; Roll molding: A molding that covers the seam at the joining of two boards. Bolection moldings are usually of high projection.

BUILT-UP MOLDING: Molding units formed by adding one molding on top of another.

BUTTERY SHELVES: Shelves in a buttery to hold provisions.

BUTT JOINT: The joining of the ends of two floorboards by butting them one against the other.

CASING: The boards covering construction members, such as posts, summer beams, girts, window, and door frames.

CHAMFER: A sloping or angular cut to round off the corner or edge of a board or timber.

CROWN MOLDING: A double-curved molding at the juncture of a wall and ceiling, or at the juncture of an exterior wall and soffit of a cornice, or applied to the upper face of a verge board where it meets the overhanging roof shingles.

DADO: Horizontal boarding running below window height around the walls of a room (see WAINSCOT).

DENTIL; Dentil molding: Decorative trim molding (interior or exterior) made up of blocks forming an ornamental row in a cornice (see EXTERIOR WOODWORK).

FEATHEREDGE; Featheredged boards: Panels or wall boarding in which the edges of the boards are chamfered to a thin edge for insertion into a groove in a rail, stile or another board (see BEAD).

FINISHED FLOOR: The final or top layer of floor boards.

FLAT PANEL; Sunken panel: A wood unfeathered panel between stiles and rails that is even in its surface plane with the rails and stiles that surround it. Also a panel between rails and stiles the surface of which is lower (sunken) than the plane of its stiles and rails. A panel other than a feathered panel (see DOORS).

GROUND; Plaster ground: Trim, such as door or window casings, to which a plasterer can screed (level) his plaster.

HALF-LAP: A joining of two floorboards by routing away half the thickness of an edge of each board so that they overlap with the thickness of a single board.

JAMB; Door jamb; Window jamb: The trim around the sides of a doorway or window opening.

LAMB'S TONGUE: An ovolo and fillet worked alternately along the edge of a board or timber as an ornamental termination of a chamfer.

MANTEL: The trim or paneling used to cover the masonry against a fireplace wall. The mantel can extend from floor to ceiling, thus manteling or concealing the masonry.

MANTEL SHELF: The trim surrounding the firebox, including a shelf. Modern mantel.

MITER: The joining of two pieces of wood at an angle without overlapping.

MOP BOARD: The horizontal molding on a wall closest to the floor boards (see BASE MOLDING).

NAILER: A board placed in masonry onto which another piece of wood, usually trim or stair stringers, can be nailed.

PANEL: The section of a door or wall framed by rails and stiles.

PLATE RACK: A shallow, horizontal groove cut in the top of shelves to prevent standing plates from slipping.

PULL: Wooden knob used on cupboard doors. If it was made of metal or ceramic, it would be called a knob.

RABBET: A groove or cut made in the edge of a board so that another, similarly cut, can be joined to it.

RAILS: Horizontal boards in a door, window sash, or paneling, which together with the stiles form a frame for panels or glass.

RAISED PANEL: A panel feathered on all four sides whose surface either protrudes beyond that of its rails and stiles or is at the same plane (see PANEL).

RETURN: See MASONRY.

ROLL MOLDING: See BOLECTION.

SCALLOP: Ornamental work on the open string of a staircase. Can be carved or applied (after 1800) (see STAIRS).

SCRIBING: Fitting woodwork to an irregular surface.

SHIPLAP: A method of joining floor boards (see HALF-LAP).

SINGLE-ARCH MOLDING: A molding with a single convex curve used primarily on door and paneling rails and stiles where they join feathered panels.

SIZING: Coating with shellac or glue (sizing) so that paint will adhere.

SLIP STOP: A window stop (usually the stop on the left jamb) that can be removed to release the sash so they can be taken in.

SLITWORK: Rough-sawn subflooring that is half the thickness of the finished flooring.

SPLINE: A strip of wood used to join two floorboards. The edge of each board is grooved to accept half the spline.

STILES: Vertical boards that make up a door or window sash or the vertical boards that retain panels in paneling.

STOP: See SLIP STOP or DOOR STOP.

TOMBSTONE PANEL: A panel on which the upper part is rounded like 18th-century tombstones.

TONGUE-AND-GROOVE: A method used to join adjacent floor boards along their long edges. One board has a groove rabbeted the full length of its edge and the other is tongued or beaded to fit into the groove.

TRIM: Finish woodwork such as moldings, door and window casings, paneling, wainscoting, etc. Trim does not include flooring or any structural work.

WAINSCOT: Finished wall boarding. When below window-sill height it is called a dado.

HARDWARE

BEAN LATCH: A door-latch handle, the back plates of which are in the shape of a lima bean; this is the commonest form of latch handle.

BUTTERFLY HINGE: A small hinge usually used on cupboard doors, the plates of which are in the form of a bow-tie.

BUTT HINGE: A hinge that attaches to the edge of a door and is mortised into the door and the hinge jamb.

CLINCH: To bend over the tip of a driven nail so that it cannot be pulled out easily.

CRANE; Swinging crane: An iron arm that swings horizontally, which is attached to the inside of a firebox and on which cooking utensils are hung.

CUT NAIL: Machine-made nails cut from an iron plate. The first nail-making machine was patented about 1796.

FOUR-STRUCK HEAD: The shape of the top of most 17th- and 18th-century forged nails formed by the blacksmith's hammer blows.

HARDWARE (Finish): All exposed metal in a house, such as door hinges, latches, locks, keepers, hooks, cranes, brass knobs, etc.

HARDWARE (Rough): All concealed hardware, such as nails, spikes, and iron fireplace lintels used in the construction of a house.

H HINGE; HL HINGE: Common shapes of 18th-century surface-mounted hinges. H hinges were used on narrow doors, corner-cupboard doors, and other doors where weight was not a problem. HL hinges of various sizes were used on interior-room doors. Exterior doors and 17th-century and early 18th-century interior doors used strap hinges. After 1800, butt hinges came into general use.

KEEPER: A small iron staple that retains the latch-bar on a door.

LATCH-BAR: The movable iron bar on a door latch that moves up and down when the thumb latch is pressed and released.

PINTLE: L-shaped pivot-pin that is driven into a door jamb and supports the strap hinge on a door. Pintles are also used to support fireplace cranes.

S-HOOK: An iron S-shaped hook hung on fireplace cranes from which kettles are suspended over the fire.

STRAP HINGE; Strap: A type of hinge in general use in the 17th century and the early 18th century for both interior and exterior doors. Although they continued to be used on exterior doors and some secondary interior doors, such as cellar and attic doors through the 18th century, they were replaced as the popular hinge by H and HL hinges during that period. Strap hinges are still used today on barn doors and gates.

STAPLE: The U-shaped retainer that holds a latch-bar in place. Also, the wood bar used on the inside of double doors as a lock is held in place with a staple on one side and a half staple on the other.

THUMB LATCH: That part of a door-latch assembly which when pressed down by the thumb raises the latch-bar.

TRAMMEL; Trammel bar; Adjustable tramel: A vertical iron bar with a hook at the bottom that is hung from the throat of a fireplace and from which iron utensils are hung over a fire (see S-HOOK).

STAIRS

BALUSTER: The small post that supports the handrail. There are usually two balusters to each step.

BALUSTRADE: A row of balusters together with their handrail.

BOX STAIRS: A staircase built between two walls; a closed staircase.

CIRCULAR STAIRWAY: A staircase in which all the treads are winders.

DOG-LEGGED STAIRS: A staircase that returns on itself. These staircases are found in Center-Chimney houses in the front passage where space is limited.

LEFT-HANDED STAIRCASE: A staircase with the handrail on the left as the stairs are ascended.

NEWEL; Newel post; Landing newel: Posts supporting the handrail. Newel posts can be located at the foot, the angles, and at the top landing of a staircase.

NEWEL CAP; Terminal: The top of a newel post used as an ornament.

NOSING: The part of a stair tread that projects beyond the riser on which it rests.

OPEN STAIRCASE: A staircase that has one side exposed in a room.

OPEN STRINGER; Face string: The inclined finish board located at the open side of the stairs. This piece of trim is often elaborately molded, sometimes with whale's tails or scalloping.

PITCH; Rise: The angle to the horizontal of a staircase; the slope.

PLATFORM: The landing between two flights of stairs.

RIGHT-HAND STAIRS: A staircase with the handrail on the right as the stairs are ascended.

RISER: The vertical member of a step.

SCALLOPING; Applied scalloping: The decorative ornamentation of the open string of a staircase. It can be either chiseled out of solid wood (early work) or made of applied moldings (after 1800).

STAIRCASE: A flight of stairs with the supporting framework, trim, balustrade, and newels.

STAIRWELL: The space through which a staircase runs.

STEP: Composed of two members—the tread and the riser.

STRAIGHT-RUN STAIRS: A flight of stairs with no turns.

STRINGER; String; String-piece: One of the inclined sides of a staircase that supports the treads and risers.

The word stringer is applicable to both the structural supporting members of a staircase and to the trim boards.

SWELL STEP: The lowest step of a staircase that has an outward curve.

TREAD: The horizontal part of a step on which the foot is placed.

VOLUTE; Ram's horn: The spiral section of a handrail that is attached to the first newel post.

WHALE'S TAIL: Ornamental molding either cut out of or applied to an open stringer in the shape of a whale's tail.

WINDER: A pie-shaped tread used on stairs. Staircases that are made up of winder treads are also called winders.